Essence

Mandi Lynn

Don't lose your Essence

Mandi Lynn

ESSENCE

To my mom and dad,
Thank you.
For everything.

Prologue

The first thing that the new mother notices about her baby is its silence. She knows something isn't right. It all happened fast, too fast. Unlike the shows she's been watching on TV, the doctors in this hospital don't hand her the child. They speak in quick, quiet words.

"Remove the umbilical cord from the neck."

"It's too tight. Cut it."

"Cole?" the mother asks, pulling her husband to her.

His sight shifts to her, but he only gives her a quiet glance before he looks to their child.

"Honey, is she all right?"

The father nods his head, but she can tell he's just trying to keep her calm.

The silence in the room is frightening. Newborns are supposed to scream out to the world to announce their birth.

The umbilical cord is cut away from the baby's neck. The mother still can't see her child. She leans forward to meet her daughter's eyes. The small infant's skin is blue; the skin around her neck is discolored from the cord's tight grip. Not a sound escapes from the tiny mouth. For a flash of a nightmare, the mother believes her child is dead, a stillborn, but then the baby moves. Her hands and feet feel around her, looking for something. Her mouth is open, seeking air, but nothing comes of the action.

"Cole?" the mother cries, seeing her daughter fighting for life. Her baby, her prefect little baby, was being strangled by the umbilical cord. It's been removed, but why can't she breathe?

"Shh... It's going to be all right, Jess." He hates himself for stating the words he doesn't believe. How long has it been? Seconds, minutes? How long can an infant go without air?

In the mother's mind the only thing she can picture is her tiny baby girl, cold and bloody, unable to breathe. This isn't how the infant should be greeted into the world. It's supposed to be glorious. A moment that neither the mother nor father would ever forget. The only thing certain is that it is a moment they won't forget, but they aren't sure if they want to remember if their daughter doesn't make it.

"Can she breathe?" Jess asks, gripping her husband's hand harsher than necessary.

At the end of the bed, the doctors and nurses mumble among themselves. In their sterile suits they look like aliens, working on the newborn so she can breathe. The parents can only watch as they wonder what is wrong with their child.

"Cole?" Jess's voice turns into a cry. She wants to ask the doctors what is wrong, but she fears, if she breaks their concentration, her baby girl won't make it. After nine long months of trying to keep this baby, the thought of never being able to hold her breaks Jess.

Cole looks over to the baby for a moment and spies an instrument that looks like a turkey baster but much smaller. He doesn't know what it's called, but he knows its use. One of the nurses takes it and uses it to clear the infant's throat.

"They're working on it," he says.

Jess's eyes are frantic, and he can see and feel her fear. Ever-so-slowly the room grows louder as orders are repeated, and a nurse is dismissed to grab something. One doctor stays, working over the newborn.

"Doctor," a nurse says, once she has arrived with a plastic bin that has a soft warm blanket on the bottom, curled around the edges.

Without a word the doctor scoops up the baby and places her into the transport incubator in one quick, fluid motion. The nurse rushes to another table and cleans the baby.

"Mr. and Mrs. Barton." The parents' heads turn away from their baby and to the doctor who now speaks to them. "Your daughter was born with the umbilical cord wrapped tightly around her neck. Although we weren't able to simply slip it off, we were able to cut it off to give her the air supply needed. Even after this was done, she still couldn't breathe, and we think she may have transient tachypnea."

"What is that?" Cole asks. Jess is quiet in her tears as the doctor speaks to them.

"It means she has fluid in her lungs. Recovery usually comes within the first twelve to twenty-four hours, but it can last up to seventy-two hours. There are a few methods of treatment, but we have to determine how much oxygen she has in her blood."

"Is she going to be all right?" Cole asks.

"We can't be sure. She's being admitted to the Neonatal Intensive Care Unit."

It's so bright. Even with her eyes closed, the light shines through her thin eyelids. But it's cold. Nothing like that warm enclosed place she's always been. It was weird, being there one moment and then not the next. It was like she was being forced out, no longer wanted. She wanted to fight it for some reason, to keep the warm comforts she'd always known, but she couldn't.

Out here it is cold. At first she only noticed it in her head and then...the strangest thing happened. Something touched her, and it was also warm. Alive and gentle, it coaxed her out of her home. Something went wrong though.

When her body enters this new cold world she wants to scream. Every fiber in her body tells her so. Fear envelopes her. What is this place? She wants to go back, but warm fingers keep poking at her and moving her limbs. Scream; it isn't safe. They'll take you home, if you scream.

But—no—she can't. That's when the panic came. She kicks and squirms, but no sound comes from her. Her arms contact something around her neck. It's a piece of her; she remembers it from home. It isn't supposed to be there, and the warm fingers—the things that took her from her home—keep fussing with it too. It's slippery like the rest of her body, but it hurts her. It pushes in around her neck; the warm piece of her is overtaking her being.

Something is missing from this new world she entered. She doesn't know what it is, but she needs it. Light-headed, her thoughts begin to fade. It's scary, but a breathtaking peace comes over her body at the same time. A bright light comes, but it's not like the one when she left her home. She can't look away from the light. It brings numbness and takes away the pain in her neck, so she follows it.

The slippery thing that was once around her is gone now, but it's not because of the light. The poking warm fingers had removed it. She grows agitated as the hands touch and move her, disturbing her peace—the light fades the slightest bit and so does the numbing, calming sensation. She is being wiped down with something soft. She feels so free with nothing around her neck, but her breathing is fast and rapid.

That's it! That's what's missing from this world. She needs to breathe, but something is still wrong. Inside she feels her heart work overtime to survive. In and out. In and out. It feels off and wrong, like something is blocking her from doing whatever task it is her heart needs so badly.

In the amount of time she's left without air, she can feel something leaving her. The light never disappears all the way, but it doesn't provide its peace. It stays, looking over her. She's torn in two.

No longer one entity, part of her leaves to follow the light. She knows this shouldn't happen and fights to stay as one being. She imagines her fingers reaching out, grasping the part of her soul as it floats away to the light, but whether she wills it or not, it goes.

She's tempted to follow it. The light radiates in front of her and begs her to follow. She's drawn to her soul that's left her. The decision is made, and she lets go of this foreign world. She misses the warm, closed-in home she had once known. The fingers pull her away and leave her here where things hurt. She can't breathe; her heart is always at a fast and labored pace. She again reaches out to her soul, leaving this body that grows colder as the seconds pass.

A loud noise is heard around her. A thump of blood passing through her body. As she fades away, its rhythm slows. *Thump. Thump. Thump.*

It's so close. The light grows brighter, inviting her. Peace increases around her, and she dreams she can fly; she can do it right now. Wings sprout from her back, taking her to the other half of her soul that has already left.

Thump.

The last heartbeat is loud, shaking her from where she flies in the sky.

"Please, stay with me," a voice cries. It's so familiar; it calls her home. She turns, but darkness surrounds her. All at once the light disappears and, with it, her wings. She doesn't fall but glides safely to the ground, as she is brought back to the world. Unknowingly she has made her decision. By turning to the voice, she let go of the light.

Thump. Thump.

She panics. Her heartbeat grows to a steady pace, and she can breathe again. Her lungs fill with sweet oxygen, and she exhales. But she knows something isn't right. The light is gone, but it took part of her with it. She was never able to grasp the other part of her soul, before the light disappeared.

A piece of her is gone forever.

The NICU is an unfamiliar place to most, but to some parents it has become a second home. They go in and out every day to visit their child who hangs on only by a simple thread. This is why any visitors have to be as sterile as possible, before they can step through the doors. For Cole this is only his first time visiting, but he hopes to not make a habit out of it.

A nurse leads him to a room. Inside are monitors and tubes, and, most of all, a large incubator that holds a baby girl. A document is attached to the side, and it reads Amelia Clarice Barton with all of her information and charts on it.

Inside the baby breathes fast, staggered breaths. Her body has a blue tint to it, but she's alive. Cole stares down at his daughter, completely amazed by her small size. Her lids are closed, but on the paper with her name, it says she has blue eyes.

"May I hold her?" he asks, viewing the IV that is attached to her foot, feeding her oxygen through a vein.

"Not yet. She isn't stable enough, but when she is, you can. You should be able to take her home shortly after that," the nurse tells him. He frowns but is thankful for the periodic beeping that comes from the machine, as it announces her heartbeat.

Jess and Cole take Amelia home a week after her delivery. Her vital signs are normal, and the fluids are cleared from her lungs. No permanent damage seems to have been done in the amount of time she was deprived of oxygen after birth.

Jess cradles her in a snug warm blanket just as the nurse taught her. It's supposed to resemble the feeling of being in the womb and bring comfort to the newborn. It helps, yet Amelia still cries at times. Cole and Jess thank God for that little scream, though, because it means she's alive.

Chapter 1

The Forest

Ring around the rosie.

I open my eyes quickly, and the forest surrounds me. Above, high in the trees, a canary displays itself, yellow feathers a bright spot in the otherwise green mass of leaves. His song stops abruptly, eyes wide to some immense fear he's not willing to tell. He's like a statue, listening. With a quick flap of the wings, he's gone. The forest grows eerily quiet—there's no longer a whisper of wind; the birds have stopped their songs—the silence is deafening.

Sitting on a fallen tree, I feel a shift in atmosphere. I tell myself it's nothing—just breathe. My fingers slip to the side and onto a log. Combing through the soft, moist moss, I close my eyes.

A pocket full of posies.

It's all just an overreaction. That's what moving does to you. It's new territory that hasn't yet been explored.

The only sound I can decipher comes from a waterfall, a few feet away from me. I can picture it now, even only having seen it once. The clear blue water starts its descent just inches from my feet, cascading into the pond below. I can hear it.

Ashes, ashes.

There is a sudden moment of realization. The song—I remember what it was about. The Black Plague. I had done a project on it once for school. The child's rhyme was really a song about death.

We all fall down!

A deep chill sweeps through my core but does not choose to leave. I don't falter; in fact I stay in place—not because I want to stay; I can't move. I am somehow bound. My vision blurs—just for a split second—long enough to send chills through my senses, as I lose control of part of my world, but short enough that I don't know whether or not it really happened.

My gaze darts around the forest, but nothing seems wrong. The trees sway; the water flows. I can't move! I will every muscle to fight, to run, to do anything; but I'm left in this forest, clueless as to what's happening. The more I struggle, the more my senses begin to fail me. My arms and torso are covered with a blanket of warmth that grows hot and uncomfortable.

Around me the forest is still, silent, unaware of the sensation that has chosen to overcome my body, keeping me rooted in place. Every muscle inside me is on the defensive, tense for some approaching danger that only the canary is aware of. There's a pressure on my limbs, sending the warmth to tingle in my body as if losing circulation of blood.

Opening my eyes, I see nothing is touching my arms. My fingers linger on the moss, and I concentrate on the feeling.

Panic deepens in my being, feeling the soft growth, hearing the flow of the waterfall. I look around me to see the bright forest I once considered safe—the green pine, the quiet creek, and the textured leaves that beckoned me to the forest in the first place.

There's a vibration in my back pocket, and a few seconds later, my phone begins to chirp out its generic tone. With the new sound my muscles go limp—as if being released from a trance—and I fall off the log and to the ground. On my hands and knees I slide the phone out of my pocket.

My mom.

Emma, get home before dark.

I rise to my feet and run in the direction of my house.

Racing through the trees, I jump over fallen branches and rocks embedded deep into the ground. I had never been scared for my life before, until now. I'd never known what it was like to run for your life. I don't concentrate on my breathing, or where I'm going—I just run.

Adrenaline pulses through me; I jump over fallen trees, rocks, and small streams. I can hear my heart pounding, and each breath I take becomes larger and more labored. For a second I wonder what I'm running from and look behind me. There's nothing, just the trees and plants of the forest.

I stop, catch my breath, but decide to keep going. I trip into a small stream that flows into a waterfall a few feet down. There's an objection of pain, as I drag myself up and out of the two-foot-wide stream. Tired, I struggle to turn myself on my back, looking at the sky as it models a striking blue canvas.

The longer I rest on the moist ground, the more I absorb what just happened. The scene replays itself in my head over and over. The sun hovering above beats down on me, and I cover my eyes. Lifting my right arm, I see my sweatshirt is completely soaked in the dirty water. My side is drenched.

With a sigh I lower my head to the forest floor, and the sun's rays fill and warm me. My body becomes heavy with sleep, and I can feel myself drifting, thoughts becoming less important and images blurring together.

Eventually instinct kicks in, and I sit up, to get back before dark and settle into the warm house. As my muscles cart me off the ground, I'm shocked by the jolt of pain in my side. I press my fingers into my ribs, feeling the throbbing grow more intense. Lying back down, I wait for the pain to go away.

Time passes fast when you're not in step. If you think for a moment that you can get it back, wake up—you can't. Some people think time is theory. Everything is a cycle of events happening over and over. If you think this is true, then be aware and learn from your mistakes.

Wake up!

When I open my eyes again, the sky is a burnt orange. It takes me a moment to locate myself. It's evening; the sun is going down. Despite what happened just hours ago, the forest is bright; there's a quiet rustle in the leaves from a small animal looking for food.

I pick myself off the ground, as my side protests with every move I make. My clothing sticks to my body, as if it's a second skin. Every move I make is greeted with a sharp pain, begging me to stay in place—don't move. The thoughts from hours ago flood my brain, gathering questions that need to be answered. Taking a deep breath, I slide out my phone and text my mom a message.

I'm on my way.

I run home, trying my best to navigate my way around the forest. I start a fast pace through the trees, ignoring the ache in my side.

My pocket vibrates again, and even though I know it must be my mom, I don't break stride. I don't let myself take a break to check it, knowing that, if I stop, I may not be able to start again. Whenever I stop, something comes over me, stalling my progress, keeping me here in the forest. So I press forward, seeing the woods thin out around me, as I approach my house.

With a burst through the final set of trees, I'm out of breath. I stop running and lean onto my knees with my hands, crouching as I feel my heart beat violently from within my ribs. The sky grows dim with the passing seconds, and my breathing slows back to normal. My vision comes to focus on my house. It's a modest home, small in stature but grand in appeal. The chimney is lonely, no smoke billowing from within. The lights inside my house are on, the walls flashing different colors as the TV changes channels, my dad trying to find entertainment after a day of work.

We are the only ones that live within a few miles—and for a good reason. I haven't always lived here. My family used to have a home in Florida where my mom researched animals. When a job offer with more income popped up in New Hampshire, we couldn't turn away. Strings were pulled to get a house built for us on the edge of the White Mountain National Forest. We're all here now, living next to a national park.

"What am I doing here?" I whisper, looking around at the scenery. It's beautiful, really. The top of the mountains are covered with a slight mist, making them appear eerie yet breathtakingly so. I remember how, just this morning, I had seen a moose pass through, while I was eating breakfast. This place is stunning, sharing habitats within nature, but it's not home.

I've lived here for almost a week, and I have yet to feel like this isn't just a long vacation. Part of me still feels as if we will pack up our bags and return back home where the beach welcomes us.

Still bent over, I lean over to run my fingers through the wet grass beneath me, remembering that it was raining yesterday—it rains a lot here. I thought it was just bad luck at first, but then my parents told me about the weather in New England—if it looks like a storm is coming, it is. Their words held true; rain comes and goes so fast here. Wind pushes hair into my face, and I pull back the brown strands. I'm content in my spot. I've caught my breath since all the running, but I'm not ready to move yet.

In my house the TV from the living room continues to light up, shining out the windows. It gives a glow to the otherwise darkening yard. I want to wait to see the stars come out but know I shouldn't let my mom worry. Straightening up, still aware of the fading pain in my side, I brush myself off before heading to the front of the house.

"Emma, you okay?" my mom asks, as I step through the door. Her long brown hair is tied back, like she always has it for work. She's still in her uniform of brown khakis and hiking boots. Right here—in the middle of nature—is where she's most at home. Sleeping under the stars is her haven.

"Yeah, I just got a little lost," I say. My mom scans me over, and I can feel her eyes rest on my sweatshirt. When I look down, half the cotton cloth is covered with mud, turning it from bright blue to a dusty brown. It's no longer soaked like it had been but is still in great need of washing.

"I slipped," I tell her, holding out my sweatshirt as evidence. It isn't a lie; I just wasn't telling her the full truth. The part of me that felt petrified begged to tell my mom what happened—it was as if a force possessed me. Whatever happened wasn't something as simple as falling and blacking out in the forest; it was something more.

She scans me again, not trusting everything I say but dismisses whatever I refuse to speak. "Do you want anything to eat? I left dinner out." She points to the table before turning to the sink to return to the chore of washing dishes.

I look where the food rests: meatballs and pasta still on their serving platter, ready to be eaten. It looks like it had been sitting for a while. I shake my head no.

"I'm actually a little tired. I'll just eat in the morning." I take off my shoes and throw them into the closet.

"You feeling all right?" my mom asks, appraising me for any cuts, scrapes, or other injuries.

"I'm fine," I assure her, watching her face calm. "I just did a lot of walking today." Out of the corner of my eye, I see my dad sitting in his chair watching TV, and listening to our conversation.

"Okay," my mom says, but studies me as I walk upstairs to head for my room.

Once I'm there, I shower, then change into sweatpants and a T-shirt that substitute for pajamas and sit at the bay window. Opening the shades all the way, I let the night shine in. The moon in the sky is only a sliver of light, leaving the stars to illuminate the dim night. After a few minutes of gazing, I find my iPod by the side table and slide into bed. Turning down the volume to a quiet background noise, I drift off.

Has there ever been a night where you didn't feel safe? Maybe you felt you were being watched? Or you couldn't close your eyes for fear of the unknown? If, for only a moment, you let your guard down and hear a sound—unidentified and quiet—maybe it was all in your head.

Never let your guard down.

I awake in the middle of the night. The bay window that lines the wall of my room leers at me. The moon is on the opposite end of the sky, and my family has gone to bed, leaving the house dark. I turn onto my side to have my back to the window, so there is less moonlight on my face. The earbuds of my iPod rest on my pillow. I put them back in my ears and skip through songs, until I find one that can soothe me back to sleep. Closing my eyes again, I drift, the music echoing within.

A soft breeze brushes my face.

I lift my head and turn back to the window and see it closed, just as I had left it. Pausing the music, I take out the earbuds to listen for the wind. I sit propped up with an elbow, leaving me in an uncomfortable position.

Nothing.

Lying down again, earbuds back in place, I turn up the volume of the music, telling myself to fall asleep. Don't think. The music swallows me, stealing my sense of hearing anything in my room.

A few minutes later another breeze pushes against the window, not coming from the outside, but wanting to go there— pushing the curtains even while the windows remain closed. I force myself to turn quickly, wanting to see what is there.

The curtains lick the floor, swaying back and forth ever-so-slightly. Transfixed by the movement, my eyes linger there, until a crash of wood calls more of my attention. My bay window hangs open, air cultivating from somewhere within the room escaping into the dark night.

Jerking away the earbuds, I jump from my bed, fear instilled in me, and my foot gets caught on something on my floor. There's a pulsing behind my ear, as I turn my head to look at my feet. My vision blurs, like it had in the forest, infiltrating the sense of being vulnerable. My sight is only gone for a moment, but it leaves me scattered and confused.

Maybe I hit my head when I fell.

Turning my attention to the bay window, the curtains rest parallel to the wall. The windows are shut, exactly as I had left them.

At that moment my breathing seems too loud. As much as I fight it, my lip quivers. The window had just been open—I was sure of it. Gathering myself in a fetal position, I curl into a ball on the floor. My eyes never close, but every now and then, they linger on the windows.

The digital clock reads 4:18, brightening a small corner of the room. I drag myself from the floor and hide myself within the confines of the bedsheets.

I'm engrossed by the window. I lay down facing the panes of glass, eyes open and music off, leaving me in the piercing silence of night. It seems like hours pass. I stare at the window, unchanging, challenging it to go against the laws of nature—to flash open or have a gust of wind rush through—but nothing ever comes of my watchful eye. I try to keep track of time with the moon, but I look at it so much, it's hard to tell if it has moved across the sky.

It's not until the stars begin to fade with the coming of dawn that I realize just how scared I am. For some reason it is the morning's rays of sun peeking through the bay window that finally allow the tears to stream down my face. The light rests over the seat made under the bay window, as if calling me with open arms to gather myself and cry, but I stay in place. I'm locked within my own world, never daring to leave the comforts of my sheets.

A question is lingering within my consciousness. It's filled with fear and anxiety and cowardice.

What's going on?

Fear instills me. It's fear of the unknown, the type of worry that ripples through your core whenever you're home alone—and suddenly there is a creak in the floorboards as the house settles. You always tell yourself it's nothing out of the ordinary, but it doesn't stop the fact that, for that moment in time, there was fear. This fear now, it's different. Unsettling.

All night I wanted to close the blinds of the window, but I never dared to step forward. Instead I curl in on myself like a coward, blankets forever enveloping me, like they can act as a shield. I'm flashed backward to when I was a kid, afraid the bogeyman will get me if I step foot on the floor during the night. Except this is bigger than the bogeyman.

Chapter 2

Unreal

I'm on the beach enjoying the sun. There are a lot of people on the sand just as any other day. The air is hot and muggy, leaving my forehead moist. The pier lines the right side of the beach, extending out over the water where the waves break. I abandon my beach chair and get up to go swimming in the ocean. When I step in the water, it feels ice-cold—not like the usual tropical water of Florida. I go to turn back, but the undertow catches me. Then I go numb. It isn't from the cold water though. This is a different kind of numb. I have no control over my body; I feel limp. Then I hear someone calling me...

"Amelia," says a whispered tone.

I step deeper into the water, following the voice that calls me by my birth name.

"Emma!" says a scared voice, a different voice. It sounds so familiar, although I'm sure I have never heard the voice before.

Maybe it just sounded familiar because the voice called me Emma—my mom and dad are the only ones who call me that.

I look around to see where the voice is coming from but find nothing, just the crowded beach full of people. Then I hear the whispering voice again.

"Amelia, come swim with me. I have something to show you."

I step farther into the water, until I'm up to my waist. The water feels so cold; it's like pins against my skin, but I can't stop walking forward. I look to the strangers swimming around me, but none of them even look in my general direction.

"Emma, don't move," screams the familiar voice from a distance. It is different this time, farther away.

I look back at the beach; everyone is gone, and so is the sun. The hot sand lays empty, no longer covered in the weekend beachgoers. There is no colorful sunset—just brightness...then darkness.

The whispering voice suddenly turns into many voices, each one sounding exactly the same, like a haunting echo reverberating off the walls of an asylum.

"Amelia, come join us." The voice sounds excited, happy.

"Yes, come, have fun," says another whisper.

"Come swimming with us, Amelia." The voices grow harsher.

My own will subsides. I follow the voices into the deep blue water, diving under a wave. When I come up for air, I'm not on the beach anymore. I'm in a forest pool. The water bites at my skin, clinging in droplets to my face and body, lingering like a lost ghost. Behind me there is a large rock wall, almost completely covered in a soft green moss. I look up only to see tall trees hanging over my head, blocking most of my view of the sky. Some sort of vague remembrance washes through me, and I'm frozen in place. I'm shocked when I realize the same thing is happening to me now as it had yesterday—this time stronger. The feeling in my core becomes more defined, and what had once been a loss of control grows to an unknown pull, calling me to deeper waters of the natural pool I now stand in.

"Emma, please, don't!" The familiar voice speaks, sounding as if it's crying.

I want so badly to obey the voice, but I can't. I tell myself to walk out of the water, but my limbs don't budge. It's as if I'm no longer in control of my own body. When my vision fades to a blur, my eyes respond, filling with tears that slide down my cheek. I'm brought to another world for a moment, the smell of sterile linen becoming prominent. Bleach and alcohol mix together, stinging my nose and throat. At first I thought that was what brought the ache in my throat, but there is separate pain, like a dark bruise now decorates my neck.

Coughing, tears blur my vision further, and when I blink them away, I'm back in the forest. Water soaks my pants, clinging to my thighs. I shiver in the cold, but the distinct smell of cleaners and the ache in my throat are gone as instantly as they had appeared.

"Amelia, do you see those rocks?" the whispering voice asks.

I look down into the pool and in it is something silver.

"Emma, don't! You have to fight! Don't do it!" The last part is a plea—crying, begging me to stop. This is my mental battle, no one else's, yet this unknown voice knows the struggle I endure.

"Yes, Amelia, pick one up and look into it," the whispering voice coaxes. It grows excited again, as my eyes linger over the rocks in the water. I'm mesmerized by their silver coating that is reflected through the pool. The voice that commands me is off and unnatural. The words are staggered and harsh, losing patience with me. *Look into it.* The words linger in my mind.

I start to walk forward again, the magnetic pull getting harder to fight. My muscles strain, trying to fight the force that controls me, but I still inch forward. I'm standing over the silver rocks, their glimmering surfaces inviting me to pick one up. I slowly start to bend down to choose one—it feels like, if I don't do what this magnetic pull wants, I will be split in half and topple over in pain.

"Emma?" It is a familiar voice again. This time a voice I know—my mom. She sounds scared.

"Emma? Emma, where are you? Honey? Where are you?" She sounds like she's getting farther away. I pull all my attention to her, instantly forgetting the silver stones and looking up to locate my mom.

Again, like in the forest, the thought of my mom is what stops me. But it's too late. My mom's voice is gone. I can't locate myself in the unknown forest.

Dreams are not lands of happiness. It is miscomprehended that bad dreams are nightmares. In truth, the only dreams we have are nightmares. When you are asleep, your brain wanders, bringing up thoughts of hopes and fears. During the night, thoughts of fear are what haunt you. Dreams are nightmares. Hopeful dreams are your wishes that will most likely never come true, which are their own form of nightmares.

The sky is bright when I wake up. I'm on my stomach with my pillow tucked over my head, blocking out any sound. I must have done this in my sleep, because I don't remember moving from the position facing the window. I rearrange myself and see my mom in the hallway, walking with boxes in her hands. I can hear her put them to the side, then she heads back down the stairs for another box.

"Emma?" she asks, peeking into my room when she passes by again. "Could you help me unpack these?"

I step out of bed and onto the hardwood floor of my room. Rubbing my eyes, the blue walls of my room come into focus. I look behind me to the window and see nothing out of the ordinary: curtains still parted open, window closed. I hear my mom coming by my room once more, so I put on a sweatshirt and head to the hallway to help.

"Could you just put away the things in the boxes? It's everything that needs to go in the bathroom, so there isn't much." She smiles at me, hair falling in waves just short of her shoulders. Even though it's still early in the morning, she's up and dressed, ready to take on the day.

The first few days of moving in were spent unpacking my room, so I could get settled, but the rest of the house is still living out of boxes. There have been days that I've just sat at my bay window. Mesmerized by the view, I was sure the thick forest was only an illusion put there to confuse me. The mountains never seeming to change but always holding just the same amount of awe and attention they had the first time I set my gaze on them.

Whenever my mom saw me looking out the window, she would comment, saying how beautiful the view was. I could see it—and I still do—I just don't know how to live here. We are secluded, surrounded by forest on every side.

Struggling to hold a heavy box that needs to be put away, my mom nods her head over to the three boxes on the floor and then keeps walking into her room to drop off another box. The first box I grab is marked Shampoo and Stuff. It's small but heavy. I put the shampoo, conditioner, and other soaps on the side of the tub, and anything else in a cupboard under the sink. The other two boxes are towels, toothbrushes, deodorant, and anything else you will find in a bathroom or linen closet. After finding a place for everything, I head out to the hallway again and see my mom standing at the top of a ladder.

"What are you doing?" I ask, watching her head reappear from a square hole in the ceiling. It's small, not much larger than the boxes my mom seems to shove through the opening.

"We have an attic," my mom says, laughing to herself as she walks back down the ladder.

"Can I see?" I ask, peering up at her.

She steps down and ushers me to go, as I step into the dark storage above us. Every time I lift my foot from the ladder, the wood creaks and shifts. My mom waits at the bottom of the ladder, holding the base steady. As soon as I'm at the top, I look into the dark, empty room. A musky smell greets me, the air filled with dust and loose insulation. "It's so hot," I comment, rolling up my sweatshirt sleeves to my elbows.

"Heat does rise, Emma," my mom tells me. Below me, she hovers over a box, trying to organize the contents inside, finding what needs to stay downstairs and what can be put away for storage.

I climb back down to the bottom, the rungs of the ladder shifting under my weight as I descend; my mom holds out another box to put away. "I know," I say, taking it.

"Put this up there." She points back to the attic and holds onto the ladder for support.

I look at the writing on the side of the box; it reads Baby Stuff. I go back up the ladder, holding the box above me and slide it into the room that's nothing more than unfinished emptiness. "At least there's a lot of storage space up here," I say, heading down again.

"Don't grow too fond of it. The only way to get up there is with this ladder, and I'm hoping it won't be sticking around in the hallway too long." She hands me another box and points to the spare room behind me that we're making into a home office.

I look over the box, reading aloud, "Work Stuff. You realize that almost every box here has the word 'stuff' on it?"

My mom smiles and sends me into the empty office room.

"I'm just saying," I tell her. "This is more than just 'stuff.'"

"You know what I mean," my mom says, taking her own box and following me into the office. We put things into place, and it slowly becomes more like home. The large grand desk my dad uses now has a computer with a printer not too far off. There's a small bookshelf with large, thick books filled with words and numbers about my dad's job that I will never understand. I take a mental picture of the room, realizing, as soon as my dad starts his work again, it will never be this organized.

"Have you finished your room yet?" my mom asks while she arranges books on a shelf. She piles those of the same height together and the smaller ones at another end of a shelf, stacking and assorting them to her liking.

"I don't know." I go through a box of papers that are for my dad's job and give up quickly, not wanting to lose anything important. "I don't think I will feel at home just by unpacking everything," I tell her, attempting to read a business chart, but putting it to the side when the numbers and words don't make sense.

"You just need to get used to things here."

My mom finishes the books and moves on to organizing the desk, arranging notepads, placing pens in a holder.

We continue to unpack, and eventually I realize I haven't eaten anything, so my mom dismisses me to go downstairs for breakfast while she continues without me.

"What can I make for ya?" my dad greets me as soon as he sees me step off the stairs. He's at the stove, already cooking his famous scrambled eggs, and I can smell bagels in the toaster, crisping to a perfect golden-brown. I stand at the entrance to the kitchen, taking in the scents. The stove is filled with pans. But only one has eggs nestled inside and ready to eat. I make my way to the breakfast bar, and when I sit down, I feel the sun on my back. Behind me the dining room opens, an entire wall consisting of windows to fill the house with light. In the center of the windows is a pair of French doors which open up to our small back porch to watch over the mountain range that is our backyard.

"Is any of that with jelly?" I ask, leaning over the counter. My dad smiles at me, his hair sticking out in all directions. He's not an early riser like my mom.

"Comin' right up!" He turns back to the stove, and flips and mixes the eggs to cook them evenly. I wait eagerly, seeing the eggs are cooked perfectly, the way I always like them—partially brown, but nowhere near burnt.

I turn myself slightly toward the sun that shines through the large deck window. The aroma of food from behind me smells rich, as I stare out through the window into the woods, the mountains peeking atop the trees. For a moment I feel homesick, missing our beach house, but I smile when my dad puts a plate of food in front of me.

"Ready for your first day of school tomorrow?" he asks, leaning on the chair next to me. I tried to beg my parents to hold off enrolling me in school because the year was almost over, but they insisted.

"Hmm...let me think," I say, taking a bite of food. "The house is a mess of boxes, and I have no idea what this school is going to be like."

My dad pulls out the chair to sit next me. He eyes me as I savor his freshly made scrambled eggs. "And I suppose you think these boxes will just magically unpack themselves?" My dad laughs, taking a bite of my bagel and getting up again to cook his own meal at the stove.

"It would be nice," I say, eyeing the pile of large boxes that sits next to our dining room table.

"Keep dreaming, kid." He cracks more eggs into the pan and begins to make himself an omelet.

The majority of the day is spent unpacking and cleaning. Even with the three of us, we don't get everything done that we want. After a while my parents tell me that I can stop, since I have school the next day and need to make sure nothing I need for tomorrow is lost in the world of unpacking.

I find my notebooks, and gather some pens and pencils from around the house. I don't know what else I will need, so I just put the things I have now in my school bag.

After a long, hot shower I spend the last hour of the day drawing. It's something I've done my entire life. Ever since I was little, I've drawn everything from plants and animals to more unexpected things, like raindrops and close-ups of leaves, revealing their true texture to the world. My parents were proud of me and even thought it would turn into something bigger.

They sent me to an art school when I was seven, but the teachers made us draw things the way they wanted. I failed out of the class. My parents were upset, because I was young for the class and only got in because they were friends with the owners. After I failed, the school put an age requirement on enrollment, because young students weren't talented enough to take the classes. That was eight years ago, and since then I've stopped publicly drawing. When the rules were changed because of me, I was humiliated and told my parents I didn't want to draw anymore. They didn't believe me at first, but when I stopped showcasing my art, they thought I had stopped altogether.

Now I just keep my work private and hide my drawings as soon as I finish them. It wasn't until recently I realized why I had failed out of the art class. My drawings have a very abstract quality. I take real-life items and draw them, but when I'm done, they look like a hidden picture within scribbles. My parents have always appreciated the drawings I made, but others have a hard time seeing the picture.

Taking out a blank piece of paper, I then lay down on my bed, using a freshly sharpened pencil to aimlessly doodle. I make strokes across the paper and let my mind wonder. The pencil makes light and dark marks against the page. Sometimes I let my hand rub against it to create smudges that leave black spots from the lead on my wrist.

I continue in the trance, until I feel I'm done. When I look down, I'm amazed by my own work. On the paper is a picture of a water hole, surrounded by a tall rock wall in the back. The water is crystal clear with small rocks reflecting through the liquid. I stare at the drawing, still amazed that I had just drawn it. What shocks me the most is the feeling that I know the place; it feels as if it's somewhere I've been multiple times, yet at the same time, it's somewhere unknown.

Never assume you are alone, because you never truly are. Only when your life has surely ended and your loved ones have forgotten you is when you are gone. Gone from this world and the next.

Sleep is when you are most vulnerable. It's a sanctuary and a curse; how you perceive it is up to you.

That night there's no whisper of the wind to frighten me awake. It's just me, sleeping, shifting, but never waking. The night passes on in a dreamless slumber. I'm on edge, muscles never relaxing, even when my mind drifts and finds its slumber.

Chapter 3

First Day

"Emma, time to get up for school!" my mom yells up the stairs.

My skin is moist with a thin layer of sweat. My comforter lies on the floor, having been kicked off during the night. Sheets are twisted around my body, fastening me to the bed. It reveals a night of restlessness I can't completely remember. Untangling myself, I get out of bed and drag myself down the stairs, already wanting the day to be over. My mom is at the landing of the stairs with a plate of warm waffles in her hands.

"Ready for school?" my mom asks, offering me the food.

"Ready as I'll ever be," I say, taking the waffles to the table to eat.

I take my time cutting the food into pieces, finding myself staring at the waffles like they have an answer to my problems. I eat slowly, and I feel the full weight of my restless sleep. Lifting my food to my mouth is an effort, my muscles weak with fatigue. My body begs for rest, but my consciousness is anything but tired. With each bite my mind searches for a reasonable explanation for everything.

"I have to leave early to get to work. Can you get on the bus by yourself, Emma?" my mom asks, gathering her things to leave.

My mom's voice pulls me out of my thoughts, and I'm brought back to reality for a moment. I look at her over my food; she seems concerned about my tired state. "I am fifteen," I assure my mom, pushing the plate of food away from me. I try to appear more awake.

"I know, it's just...it's your first day of school. It feels like I should be there." She shrugs, acting like a mother who drops off their child for the first day of kindergarten.

"Don't worry, Mom. It's high school." I try again to reassure her, grabbing the plate and dumping the small remains into the trash.

My mom hoists her large bag onto her shoulder and walks to the door, juggling different things in her hands like coffee, notes, and her cell phone. "Bye, Emma. Have a good day at school."

"Bye, Mom." I wave as she walks out the door, and I begin to ascend the stairs.

Not knowing when the bus is coming, I get ready as fast as I can and run outside in a hurry. I stand in the freezing cold for almost half an hour—longing for the Florida heat of my old home—before the bus finally comes.

When I step on the only form of transportation the school offers, I see it isn't very crowded. I can tell I'm one of the initial stops and have some waiting to do, so I sit in the first open seat. The entire way I feel as if I'm on a scenic tour. We drive through the mountainside as trees and greenery pass by the window. I can't help but stare in awe at the views. The rising mass of rocks loom over us, threatening to tumble down in a rockslide into our path. The sun peeks over a low-centered mountain, illuminating the sky with dullness; I'm disappointed, expecting colors. I look into the thick forest of trees that pass by my vision and imagine being able to see bears or moose pass through, unaware of the civilization just feet away.

The drive lasts about fifteen minutes, before the bus leaves the winding road that roams though the mountains and rides into town. Here the buildings are small; the majority are gift shops or restaurants that entertain the tourists. Eventually the bus stops in front of a small shack of a house that picks up a boy my age. He looks me over once before sitting down a few seats behind me.

Finally, an hour later, the bus arrives at my new school. Far away from any tourist attractions, the structure sits nestled between the mountains.

I step off the steep stairs and come face-to-face with the building I'll be in six hours a day, five days a week. It's just like any other school: red bricks, signs announcing events coming up. There aren't any trees near the school; in their place is a large parking lot students use to commute. My bus is the only one here. Everywhere else students sit in cars, visit friends, and talk among each other. However, no one waits at the entrance to the school. I find my way through the parking lot, and when the first bell rings, the other students finally gather their things and make their way to the doors in a slow, unconcerned manner.

"Hi, my name is Sadie. You must be Amelia," a girl says, matching her steps with mine as I pass a blue jeep with a dream catcher adorning the rearview mirror. Her blond hair falls in cascades over her shoulders, flowing over the books in her hands. Positive energy reverberates off her, and even though I don't know the girl, conversation seems to come easily to her.

I lose my bearings for a moment, not expecting to have another student talk to me so quickly. "Yes, and you can call me Emma," I tell her, hoping all she wants is to say hi to the new girl.

"Okay. Like I said, I'm Sadie, and today I'm your tour guide," she says, full of enthusiasm, adjusting the books in her hands to a more comfortable position.

She opens the door of the school for me, waving to another girl who passes by in the halls. "Tour guide?" I ask, taking in the halls. The lights give everything a yellow hue, and old posters from dances and fund-raisers coat the walls, even though the dates have passed. One bright sign announces that class dues need to be paid by February in order to go on the class field trip. It's May.

"Well...not officially. I like to help the new students," Sadie tells me.

As we walk through the halls, she tells me about all the clubs, events, and teachers at the school. She doesn't hold back on the good, bad, or boring. I show her my schedule, and Sadie gives me a map of the school and highlights the rooms I need to go to. She helps me find my classes, even when I don't need the guidance. At first I was hoping she would go away and leave me alone to venture through the school, but by third period, I find myself going out of my way to find her in the halls to ask for directions.

As expected, everyone comes up to say hello to the new girl. They all call me Amelia, and in return, I tell them to call me Emma.

It isn't as bad as I had thought—although the teachers do make me introduce myself to the class.

I used to be homeschooled until I moved to New Hampshire, so both my parents were worried I hadn't learned enough, but it turns out my mom was a really good teacher. I already knew what they were learning here, so I allow myself to daydream—which turns out to be a bad idea. Soon I begin to hack my brain for explanations for the dreams and the events in the forest—loss of vision, but filled with smells, many voices; none of it made sense or seemed to have a connection. My head begins to ache, and I quickly decide to pay attention in class—well, to the classroom.

Looking around, I see that the walls are an off-yellow hue, full of projects made by students—most of which looked like they only took minutes; I can guess those didn't get good grades. The walls must have been painted white at one time but have turned the yellow color. The classroom has a chalkboard that looks as if it has never been washed, and the floors are wooden and old. When someone gets out of a chair, it makes a screeching sound that brings my hands to my ears.

Then comes the last period before lunch: history. Like the other classes, I'm forced to introduce myself.

"Everyone, this is Amelia Barton," the teacher says, pointing to me. "She will be joining our class." Her glasses sit at the edge of her nose, just waiting to fall off. Graying hair puffs out in curls around her face, as she stands a small five feet tall.

"Um, Emma," I say with hesitation, fumbling with a stack of textbooks in my hands.

"Well, that's odd. On the paper I was given, your name is Amelia," she says, trying to find the specific one on her desk and then checking the drawers, after my document continues to remain out of sight.

"I know," I say, interjecting. "I meant call me Emma." I can already tell this is one of those clueless teachers—the only good thing about them is that you can easily get out of work. I look around at the other students, seeing them shake their heads and roll their eyes at their oblivious teacher. This must be a normal occurrence for them.

"Okay then, *Emma*." She enthuses on my name, showing me she knows. "Why don't you find a seat?" She gestures to an open chair in the back of the class that I take quickly.

When I walk by, a girl with dark red wavy hair looks at me with a scared face. It's odd, as if she knows me. Throughout class, she looks back at me with that same face. It's like I'm some relative that has been dead for years and is now standing in front of her. There is something familiar about her, but I can't find the connection. Everything about her is different; I'm sure if I had known her, I would remember.

When the bell finally rings, the girl gets up and stares at me again, as she passes—this time looking like she has a million questions. Her green eyes bore into me. Self-conscious, I look around me, hoping I may have mistaken her eye contact and she is really looking at someone else. When I look back, she's still there, her chin-length waves of hair obstructing her face. I begin to walk to her, but she dashes off, leaving her back to me, as she runs to her next class.

Sadie is in my history class, so we go to lunch together. There are tables that house ten students each. Everyone crowds around in clusters. The walls are decorated with nutritional facts, as if that will sway our eating habits. I follow Sadie to the lunch line. She smiles and hands me a tray.

"Here's a tip. If it looks like plastic, it probably tastes the same way."

I give an unsteady laugh and grab a sandwich that's in plastic wrap. A sticker on the package says it's turkey and cheese.

"Good choice," she says and selects a sandwich also.

She takes a seat at a table that has only two other girls. They engage in their own conversation, and I'm not even sure if they've noticed we've sat at their table. Sadie unwraps her sandwich and begins to tell me about everyone I will get to know. My mind is elsewhere, thinking about the girl that was staring at me in history class. My gaze darts around the cafeteria to see if she might be here also, but there's no sign of her. Finally I break down and ask.

"Who was that red-haired girl in history?" Sadie must have seen at least once how she stared at me.

"That was Eliza," she says, smoothing a long strand of her blond hair before returning to pick at her food. She takes one small bite of what is supposed to be blueberry pie and turns to me again. "Why was she looking at you weird?"

"I was hoping you would know," I say, looking at the fake wood patterns on the school lunch table. At least I know I wasn't the only one who had noticed.

"Eliza has always been real quiet," Sadie says, picking out tomatoes from her sandwich. "She keeps to herself. I invited her to a party once. She didn't come."

"Did she say she would come?" I ask, watching her put her sandwich back together, minus the tomatoes.

"She said her parents don't let her go out at night."

A few minutes later the bell rings, so we're forced to rush to class, everyone pushing to throw out their lunches at the same time.

The rest of the day is normal—Eliza isn't in any of my other classes. When I get to my locker to collect my homework before I get on the bus, she is standing there. Eliza has the narrow, tall locker next to mine. I keep my eyes occupied, entering the combination, gathering homework; all to make sure there is no eye contact.

I know she is watching me, because I can't hear her making any noise at all. I finish getting my books and leave for the bus, aware that Eliza is still soundlessly at her locker. I can feel her gaze on my back, as I leave the hallway, opening the double doors to the outside where a plethora of yellow school buses await.

I'm thankful for the fact that the bus isn't crowded and manage to sit alone again, taking out my iPod to pass the time. One by one more students file in and take their seats. Quiet conversations start, but most people tune out the world with music and headphones. The bus rolls into motion, and I watch as the school fades in the distance. Tonight's homework seems easy, so I take it out and start. I finish before my stop comes and spend the rest of the time looking out the window while listening to music.

My stop being one of the last, I step off the bus in silent motion. Crossing the threshold of the house, I see it's abandoned—my parents must still be at work. With the free time alone, I know exactly what I want to do.

I'm completely ready to go outside—cell phone, coat, some snacks—but there is a nagging thought bothering me. What if the voices or the magnetic pull came back? What if it's already starting, and that's why it feels like I need to go into the forest? Why do I want to return? I can't feel the pull, but for some reason, I do feel like I need to be there. No, I didn't need to be there; I just want to go. I was able to fight the pulling force before; so why not now? I want to explore, and that's all. Nothing more; so I go out into the forest.

I follow the same path I had just days before. Familiar trees and flowers pass by, and I know I'm going the right way. Birds chirp high above in the trees, but none of them are canaries. They are just plain brown birds. No stark yellow feathers in sight.

Moss lines rocks and the floor of the forest. Branches and foliage prevent sunlight from passing through, making the air cool. Here in the dense forest there's no breeze. The air is still. Waterfalls crash in the distance, giving off a constant singing chorus. I try to spot my footsteps on the ground, but it's all grass, leaves, and moss. There's no dirt path to give me direction.

Eventually I stumble upon the location I had found a few days ago.

Everything looks the same. The broken tree still sits on the ground of the forest. I notice that it has begun to rot. When I push against the edge, the bark falls to the ground in a soft rustle. I survey the area, spinning in a slow circle. A line of trees makes a sudden barrier. The branches intermingle and leave only a small space for movement. I can't see what's past the trees.

I stand in the middle of it all, waiting...but for what?

I gaze into the barrier of trees again, but nothing becomes clear. There's only thick vegetation. Turning around, I start walking farther into the forest. I can hear water flowing; not the usual quiet flow coming from the soft waterfall but more robust, loud—like that of an ocean.

I follow the sound, stepping over roots that stick out from the ground and find the source of the sound: a beautiful waterfall, taller than any I've ever seen, starting at the peak of a hill and cascading down. It isn't just one but many small waterfalls; each one leading to the next, working together to make the soothing sounds of the ocean. It is too beautiful to just walk away without enjoying. Nearby I sit down on a large rock and memorize this wonderful piece of nature.

There are probably hundreds of magnificent things like this hidden in the forest, all of them waiting to be discovered by wandering hikers. I step up, wiping dirt from my jeans, continuing in my search. It doesn't take much time to find more and more waterfalls, each one more beautiful than the next; all scattered and hidden within trees. I can't help but bask in their glory, wishing I can save this moment somehow.

That's when it happens: the eager need and pull to go into the forest. It begs me to turn around and follow its path. It's harder to fight this time. I try to lock my muscles, but I find myself wandering in the direction I came from. It seems as if, each time it comes, it's stronger, and I'm weaker. I gaze in the direction I'm being pulled and find the thick barrier of trees again. My feet follow unfamiliar commands, as the sounds of the waterfalls fade away. In front of me the trees act as a fence, stopping anyone with their dense and closely grown branches. The area I'm in is open and sunny, but in the trees—if you look between the branches—there is just darkness.

It starts to get dark, not just in the trees, but all around me. I look up to see where the sunlight has gone. Branches overhang, but farther up is an odd mist that is blocking out the last of the sun. It's purple and thick, high above the trees, descending toward me.

The closer the mist gets, the more powerful the pull becomes. It grows painful if I resist, and as I try to stay in one spot, it feels as if I'm being ripped apart in multiple directions; one part of my soul stretching me backward toward my house for survival, the other part pulling me up toward the mist and forward to the trees. What had once been a mental battle now feels very much like a physical conflict, as my muscles lock and eyes shut, tears rolling down my face. There is no stopping whatever is coming. I can only brace myself for this unknown danger.

I'm afraid, for what may lie ahead of me, for what may follow after I encounter this force. I don't know where I am, how I got here. Only that nothing is in my power anymore. It feels as if I'm counting down the last moments of my life.

I can imagine a lasso emerging from the trees, wrapping around me, as I'm drawn closer. It's a hopeless cause, but I pull my arms away from my body; they catch as if bound. With my eyes still closed, I feel my lips quiver, tears running streams down my cheeks. My neck grows heated, and for a moment, I can't breathe. It's as if my imaginary lasso has moved from my waist to my throat, as it suffocates me. Trying to gasp for breath, my body panics, until I have enough control over myself to dismiss the pull. I'm free for a moment, but the force of the pull comes back tenfold—but I can breathe.

Feeling exposed, I open my eyes and see another mist. Orange and more translucent, this one hovers above the ground, a distance away.

"Emma, don't go any closer to the trees." It's the familiar voice—the one from my dream. It sounds like it's coming from the direction of the orange mist, but I can't be sure.

The pull is getting worse; it feels like I'm going to collapse if I don't surrender. Whatever force that overcomes me now seems content on ripping me apart. I gasp for breath, and my heart races as the purple mist draws closer while the orange one fades, like food dye being dropped into a cup of clear water—dispersing until it's invisible to the naked eye.

"Emma, trust me, you can't go into those trees." I trust the voice, but I can't control my body anymore.

I inch forward.

The closer I move to the trees, the faster the purple mist descends, filling me with a more excruciating level of pain that is almost unbearable. My voice wants to cry out for help, but I can't. It's like going down a steep roller coaster—sometimes you can't scream. The purple mist is only a few inches above my head now, waiting for me to slip and lose this battle. Out of nowhere there is a slight breeze. I look over to the orange mist; it is no longer there, but the purple mist is still getting closer.

Without warning my phone rings in my pocket. A harsh wind pushes me to the ground, and I lose my breath. I panic, thinking it's over—that I lost. But relief washes through me when I look up to see that the mist disappeared. It left, just as quick as it came, leaving me awestruck on the forest floor.

My phone is still ringing. I let it continue to call out, my breath catching in my throat, allowing sobs to form and tears to spill. The phone sings out, tempting me to pick it up. I know it's my mom. I can barely breathe and know talking is not an option. I can't get my cell phone out of my pocket to text my mom either—my hands are shaking.

Slowly I get up and regain my balance, wanting to leave, before the pull comes back. I stand there for a minute, trying to relocate my feet. I start to walk away, but when panic kicks in, I run away from the forest. Clumsily navigating through the forest, I trip over rocks and fallen branches, scared the pull will find me again—I don't want to give the mist any chance to regain its control over me. Breaking through the last of the trees, I stumble into my yard and go into the house through the back door.

My heart screams inside my chest. I rush inside and lock the door behind me. It's probably a useless effort, but I do so anyway. I go window to window, closing every opening to the outside I can find. Then it occurs to me. My mom isn't home. Why did she call to check on me?

I take my phone. There is one missed call; the ID is my mom's phone number.

I scan all the rooms, waiting to find that maybe I glanced right over my mom in my rush to close all the windows. She's not here. When I glance at the clock, it's too early for her to be home anyway—she's still at work. I shut myself in the bathroom and take a shower, begging for the hot water to calm me. Nothing seems to help, as my hands continue to tremble, the hot steam running through my system like a sauna.

While in the shower, I put the radio on loud, daring my subconscious to make up feigned noises. I let the room swallow me, the beat of the music blocking out any sound, the steam disabling me from seeing anything farther than two feet away. I panic again, the steam seeming eerily similar to the mist in the forest. Turning the knob on the shower, the water turns ice-cold, until I finally just shut it off. Stepping out of the shower, I dry off, wrapping a towel around my vulnerable body. I sit on the floor for a long time, just trying to breathe normally again. Eventually my heart slows, and I'm able to close my eyes without fear of the mist causing me to open them in a panic.

Dressed, I go downstairs to the kitchen and make myself a bowl of cereal, not sure if my stomach can handle anything else. I eat quickly and drink a glass of hot milk, hoping that it will soothe me. While cleaning up the kitchen, my mom walks in, back from her work at a research station somewhere in the White Mountain National Forest. As soon as she reaches the kitchen counter, she dumps her handful of papers. With a sigh she attempts to organize it into a quick pile.

"How was your first day of school?" she asks, putting down her bag next to the papers.

"Um...fine," I mumble.

"Any potential friends?" She takes out her phone from her bag, checking the messages before plugging it in to be charged for the night.

"Well, there was a girl named Sadie who showed me around."

"That's good. Was she nice?" My mom goes to the refrigerator, taking out ingredients to make her own dinner, eyeing my empty bowl of cereal out of the corner of her eye.

"Yeah, she was nice." My mind flutters to today's earlier events. "Did you call me today after school?"

"No...why?" she asks, looking at me, closing the fridge door.

"Oh...I thought I heard my phone ring," I tell her shrugging.

I make my way to the hall, feeling my eyes grow heavy and thoughts becoming blurred and unfocused, sleep calling me. "I think I'm going to go to bed now. Night." I start toward my room.

"Good night, Emma!" my mom yells up the stairs. I can hear the microwave turn on as she makes a late dinner for herself.

I fall into my bed and pull the sheets over my head. I lay like that all night, curled in a ball. I don't dare think about the beach, afraid of another dream, so I grab my iPod to listen to music.

I concentrate on the lyrics, trying to find the meaning behind them. I do this until the battery dies. I don't feel like getting up to plug it into the charger, so instead I give in and fall asleep.

I'm still in my bed, when the orange mist comes through the window. I'm not scared like I was in the forest. I find comfort in the orange mist—there is never a pull that accompanies it. Lying dazed in my bed, I hear the voice.

"Emma, you must never go back into the forest." The familiar voice is stern.

"Why?" I ask, half asleep.

"I can't tell you. I hope I'll never have to."

Chapter 4

Papers

Do you feel it? The sense of being watched? I do.

I wake up shaking, not sure if it was a dream or real life. In the moment of the dream, I couldn't bring myself to be afraid of the orange mist, but now in the dawn, I find myself clutching the sheets of my bed. It had felt so real.

"Emma, get up. You're going to be late for school!" my mom calls me down to eat.

I get out of bed and go downstairs to find my mom getting ready to leave, bag in hand.

"Where are you going?" I ask, rubbing my eyes awake.

"I have to leave for work, and you have to get ready for school, or you'll be late. Your dad was going to give you a ride, if you woke up early, but he had to leave already."

"Late?" I ask confused.

"It's six thirty. Your bus will be here in fifteen minutes. Now go get ready!" My mom says, pointing toward my bedroom, as she walks out the door, so she also isn't late.

I run up the steps two at a time to get to my room. After getting dressed into the first thing I can find, I then make sure all my books are in my backpack, before I rush down the stairs. Once I reach the landing of the stairs, I look out the window, and see my mom's car pull out and round the corner to her work. Venturing through the kitchen, I find waffles in the freezer and pop them in the toaster. My hand fumbles through the cabinet for maple syrup, but there is none to be found. I rest my head against the wooden door of the cabinet, trying to think of a way to serve the waffles without syrup. Then, going back to the freezer, I remember how my grandma had put fruit on my French toast when I was younger—it should work with waffles too.

I take a bag of frozen raspberries, blackberries, and strawberries from the freezer, open the bag and put two cups of the combined fruit into the microwave to defrost. They finish in seconds, and I drizzle the heated fruit over the golden waffles. Perfect. I finish quickly, putting the plate in the sink, before I head out the door.

The bus comes to a stop when I reach the end of my driveway. And there she is. Eliza is on my bus, staring at me again with those scared green eyes. Her face turns from what looks like fear to relief, looking me over from head to toe. I walk past her seat and continue into the rear of the bus to put some distance between us. Eliza doesn't look back at me, so I pretend she isn't there. I stare out the window and memorize the landscape. The sky opens up to a blue glow as the sun begins to rise.

Once we get to school, I wait for Eliza to leave first, before I get off the bus myself. She's far ahead of me by the time Sadie greets me near the entrance of the school again. I'm able to guide myself to all my classes today, and when history comes along, Eliza is staring at me again but only for brief moments of time, as if she wants to be secretive about it, less obvious than the day before.

Lunch also seems to be just the same as the day before. Sadie and I sit together, as we talk and pick at our lunches, trying to decide if the food is edible or not—I make a mental note to pack my lunch in the future.

"My mom's in New York right now on a business trip, so it's just me and my dad," Sadie says, pushing the school's steamed vegetables to the side, as she takes out a small packaged cupcake. "He said it was all right if you wanted to come over or something." She splits the cupcake in two, offering me the other half.

I want to go over to her house—it would be nice to have someone from school I can talk to—but I can't go. There are so many things I can't explain that are happening. A pull that seems to haunt me, taking control of my body against my will; then there's the mist that accompanies it. I want to understand it, so I won't have to fear that it will come back, if it comes back.

"I don't think I can," I tell her, taking the cupcake half she offers. "We have a lot to unpack. My mom and dad still have a room filled with boxes."

"Okay, maybe another time," she says, not letting the information trouble her. We both smile as we bite down into the cupcake in unison, tasting the sweet frosting and chocolate-flavored cake. Sadie's eyes grow large as she stops chewing.

"What?" I ask, brushing off any cupcake remains from my hands.

She swallows before she speaks. "Eliza is coming over here," she whispers back.

I look behind me to where Sadie's eyes are focused. Eliza is heading toward our table, her dark red hair unmistakable in the sea of the student body. She stops just for a moment at our table, locking gazes with me before she smiles. Looking at Sadie quickly, she pushes a few sheets of paper in front of me before walking away from our table.

"Well, that was weird," Sadie comments, raising her eyebrows, as she looks at me. "What do the papers say?"

My gaze goes to the neon pink sticky note pasted on the front:

Please fill out and return to office.

Scanning the papers, I see multiple questions and a spot to fill in my student ID and other important information the office may need to identify me.

"I think it's forms that new students fill out," I tell Sadie, looking on the back of the sheets to see if there are more questions on the reverse side—there aren't.

"May I see?" she asks, glancing at the papers.

I hand them to her, and she looks at each for a minute, reading all the questions.

"Yeah, it's just new student info. I didn't know they still did that." Sadie returns the papers. She turns her attention back to her lunch, pushing the steamed vegetables around on the plastic tray, not willing to eat the food but content to play with it.

The rest of the day is normal. I get to my locker early, so there is no sign of Eliza. She's also missing when I get onto the bus to go home.

At home I find a snack for myself before starting the night's homework. After what seems like an eternal hour, I finish the last of my assignments, happily placing the books into my bag. The papers I have to fill out and give to the office still sit in my bag, so I resharpen my pencil and go to work with the questions. I print my full name, copy the number that is on the plastic ID card the school gave me, and move onto the questions.

Are you adjusting well?

Did you find your classes easily?

Are you having trouble in any subjects? If so, would you like a tutor?

I answer them all quickly by putting yes or no, even though there is enough blank space for multiple sentences.

Yes.

Yes.

No.

The next day when I go to hand in the forms, Eliza is standing near the office door. She sees the papers I'm holding and smiles, putting her hands forward to take them.

"Do I give these to you?" I ask, trying to look behind her into the office to see if the secretary is busy.

She nods in reply, but that's all. I give her the forms, and she walks away.

Arriving home that day, I get the feeling I've been waiting for since the first day of school: I want to draw. I've been anticipating this feeling for so long. I just haven't been myself since I came to New Hampshire.

I run up into my room, grabbing my journal. I need somewhere I can draw without risk of my parents seeing me. My dad is home early today, but my mom is still at work. I can draw in my room, but my dad might come upstairs. Even though this is a possibility, I decide on my room due to the fact that my dad is watching TV—I have a feeling that he will be there for a while.

From memory, I sketch the rocks around one of the waterfalls I had seen. There are roots coming up from trees around the edge and water flowing gracefully over huge masses of stone. Unlike other artists I don't erase my sketch marks. I leave them, because that's what I've always done, and it's a part of me. I like seeing the drawing slowly transform into something beautiful as darker strokes are added to the paper.

The best part about drawing things from nature is that they have so much texture. You can use one color, but by rubbing harder or lighter, it can look like many different shades. My drawings are mostly black-and-white with very little color, to get the right effect.

When I finish my drawing, I put away my journal, hiding it on a shelf in my closet where I store my old notebooks covered in sketches.

Chapter 5

Camping

It's summer now; not the hot muggy season Florida has but comfortable weather. I'm really starting to enjoy New Hampshire and its cool air, even with its sudden rainstorms and windy weather. I find myself asking my dad to drive me along the Kancamagus Highway just to see the view; the mountains' edge starting right next to the road, towering over our heads, until we can't see their peaks because of the clouds.

Today my dad and I do just that, taking a few hours to drive through the mountain peaks. He even convinces me that we need to stop sometime at the side of the road at one of the sightseeing stations to take photos. There are also trails made for hikers and tourists; you just have to pay a three-dollar fee that goes to funding the trails to keep them safe and cleared. My dad always tries to get me to stop at one, even though every time we drive by, I come up with an excuse like "my stomach hurts" or "I'm tired, maybe another time."

As me and my dad walk in the house after one of our famous drives along the highway, my mom greets us. "Guess what?" she asks. The news radiates off her, telling us immediately that something good is about to come.

"We won a million dollars?" my dad asks, laughing as he puts his coat on the rack next to my own.

She comes over to him, almost hopping with excitement, smacking him lightly in the back of the head, getting on with the news. "I got the week off! Do you know what that means?"

My dad and I look at each other dumbfounded.

"We can finally go on a family camping trip!" my mom says, the news seeming so obviously simple to her.

My smile turns into a frown. It's been so long since I've been in the forest. Looking back I can't even be sure if the pull I felt was real. As time passed, I told myself it was an outlandish dream. But now, going back into the forest, fear lingers at my feet with the possibility that the pull was real and could come back the moment I step into the expanse of trees.

"Where are we camping?" I ask, hoping the campsite is somewhere far away from the forest I've come to recognize behind my house.

"The White Mountains National Forest, of course. I found the perfect camping site! It's near a ranger station too, so we will have the bathrooms right there."

My mom goes into an endless rant, talking about the amazing sights we'll get to see when we go hiking; how there is a swimming hole open to the public that allows you to jump in off the tall rocks that surround it.

"How long will we be camping?" I ask.

"A week." My mom signals me to follow her into the kitchen where our calendar hangs on the fridge. Sure enough there it is; an entire week has the words CAMPING TRIP written across it in big bold letters, making it impossible for my parents to schedule anything else that week.

I look at the dates on the calendar. "This is tomorrow," I say, my finger resting on the box for July 27, the large letter *C* in "camping" taking up the entire box.

"We leave first thing in the morning, so we have to get all packed tonight!"

My mom looks around the kitchen, seeing the mess for the first time. Dishes are piled in the sink, the table still has lunch on it—my dad and I had been in a rush to leave the house and go for our drive, abandoning our lunch, half eaten, on the table.

"But first we have to clean," my mom says, already throwing out our unfinished sandwiches.

She wipes down the table and turns to the sink to get to work on the dishes. Panic bites at me from the inside, a small shiver starting at my fingers. No. I don't want to do this. I don't think I can.

"Do I have to go?" I ask.

"Yes, Emma," my mom says, scrubbing down pots, rinsing and placing them on a towel across the counter so they can be dried later. "You've been inside ever since we got here. You need to see the forest. It's beautiful."

I turn to the counter and grab another towel to help dry the dishes, feeling as if I've just been punished for something I haven't done. My mom smiles as I dry the pot and place it inside a cabinet. I smile back, but it feels forced.

~

By the next day we are fully packed for our camping trip and leave early in the morning. One thing my mom failed to say is that the campsite was only a few miles from our backyard. Paranoid, I become more alert of my surroundings, looking behind me several times and staying close to my mom, always looking for a way out in case it came to it.

The entire week I'm like this: always looking around, waiting for the mist to come out from hiding, expecting the pull to take over and the voices to be heard. They don't show up, but I never let my guard down. I go on hikes almost every day with my parents, and take pictures of the different waterfalls and rock formations, trying to keep up the act.

We decide to go swimming.

Standing on the highest ledge, I notice the lower rocks below to my right. My parents are already in the water, having jumped in using the lower rocks that require a five-foot jump at the most. Below me they tread water, waiting for me to follow them. I've already jumped in today off the lower rock like my parents, but my dad dared me to make the big plunge.

Still wet, fresh out of the water, my legs shake as I sling my arms around me, while the wind freezes my skin; the cold water drips off my body and through my thick brown hair.

"Come on, Emma!" my dad yells up to me. My mom begins to swim to the side in the shallow water and finds a rock to rest against while she waits for me to jump in again. I approach the edge, looking at the ten-foot drop and remember the feel of the ice-cold water. Up the stream there are waterfalls, but they all lead to this spot here; a deep pool—at least twelve feet—surrounded on both sides by the tall rocks that I now stand on. Widthwise the pool isn't very large, but it holds a lot of depth, leaving no possible way of encountering a rock when you hit the water.

"Jump off the lower rock if you want, Emma," my mom tells me. I can see her shiver as she clings to a rock sticking out in the shallow water that leads to the rocky shore.

"Amelia, Amelia." My dad shakes his head, as I back away from the high rock and make my way to the lower one. I hear his taunting laugh and stop. My arms and legs are covered in goose bumps, and my lips are starting to quiver without protection from the wind mixing with my wet body.

"Just jump in," I whisper to myself, taking three large steps back from the high ledge.

"Oh?" my dad says, seeing me brace for the jump.

I take the final stride, knees bending to propel me out and I leap, the ten-foot drop passing in a quick second. My feet slice into the water first, and then I'm in over my head. The cold water pierces my skin, reminding me that I'm not scared of the high jump but the water that awaits me below.

"You did it, kid!" my dad says as my head pops out of the water. My feet never touch bottom, and I thrust my legs and arms to keep my head above the frigid water.

"Your turn," I say in a quiver, rushing to the shore as I swim with a speed I didn't know I possessed—I didn't remember the water feeling this cold the first time I jumped in.

He laughs at me. "I'm crazy, not stupid," he says, swimming in front of me, joining my mom on shore.

After we dry off, we all go on a hike, hugging our warm sweatshirts around us. While my mom and dad look around at the trees and birds, I can't help but sneak a look over my shoulder every few seconds, expecting the mist to appear out of nowhere.

"You seem at little on edge," my dad says later that night, approaching me from behind as I stand facing the forest, my back to the glow of the campfire. His sudden occurrence causes me to flinch, and my dad laughs. "You okay?" he jokes, motioning me to join the campfire.

I turn around to face him and then sit by the fire, leaving my back exposed to the forest. "Yeah, I'm okay," I say, warming my hands near the flames. "I've just never seen anything like this before." I gesture to the mountains behind me that are illuminated by the sunset.

So that's how my week goes. Keeping up the facade so my parents don't see that I'm on the lookout for something that goes farther than what I can comprehend—something that scares me enough to keep me away from the beauty of the forest.

When the camping trip ends, I've never been so happy in my life to be home. I run upstairs and topple into my bed, falling asleep within seconds—fully dressed and exhausted from the week of worrying.

I think my mom must have seen me asleep in my room, because when I wake, I'm covered in a blanket. I look at the clock, and it's two in the morning. I take off my shoes and get changed into sweats; an instant comfort comes over me after a week of wearing jeans. My bed welcomes me as I fall back into the pillows, burying my face in the sheets. For the first time this week, I can finally let my guard down and relax.

Chapter 6

The Mist

It's one of those summer days where it's just too hot to do anything but lay down and sleep. The heat presses on me, and I'm too tired to do anything but become a victim to the humidity. Eventually I manage to drag myself out of bed to eat breakfast, but when I get down the stairs, there is no one in the house. Looking around, I find a note on the fridge from my mom:

> *Emma,*
>
> *Your father and I went into town to buy some groceries. We were going to tell you, but you were sound asleep. We will be back later today.*
>
> *Love you,*
>
> *Mom*

Setting aside the note, I eat breakfast and do all my chores. The heat makes all actions feel tortuous. Although today feels like any other summer day, something is off. It feels like I'm being watched, like something is lurking behind every corner. The sense is hard to ignore, but I continue with my chores, working up a sweat in the process. I've felt this way before, when I'm left home alone without warning. Like always, I double-check the locks on all the doors and windows—all of which are in their proper position, but paranoia still rises within me.

As I clean the living room, I close the window my parents enjoy leaving open because of the cooling wind we receive. Outside a brown bear roams near the edge of our yard. He's huge and probably weighs three, even four, times as much as I do. I lock the window, sliding the hinge into place as I see the bear prowl its way back into the forest. The hairs on the back of my neck rise as he crushes branches that have fallen on the ground.

The chores finish fast, leaving me to surrender to the TV. But nothing seems to occupy my interest; instead, I retreat to my room.

It's there, waiting for me. The purple mist floats around my bed, its cloudy essence forming mystical and hypnotizing patterns. I freeze at the wooden door frame, numbed by fear. The mist doesn't move from its position at first, but I become grasped in some sort of trance. Like a final puzzle piece snapping into place, the pull possesses my body, drawing me to the mist. It is as if all the time that I had spent free of the pull has built up and decides now to arrive, when I'm least expecting it. I grab the door frame for support, bracing myself for what is to come.

My sanity holds a scream within my being. I lose track of my surroundings.

I had no idea the pull could be this strong. The mist seems to call to me, the sensation of needing to be near it growing stronger as seconds pass. I'm steel being pulled to a magnet, no choice or decision. Just the simple fact that this is how it is. There is no escaping the mist and no winning any battle fighting the pull that comes along with it.

My muscles are tight, resisting the pull. My eyes are clenched, my lungs ready to scream at any moment, even though I know there is no one to come save me. The violet glow of the mist brightens as it starts to come closer, the mist moving away from my bed and toward where I stand, frozen at the door frame. Where is my mom? Why doesn't she call to save me? I feel my hope diminish as I realize my phone is downstairs being charged.

I'm losing. Allowing my body to inch closer, I give into the pain that absorbs me now. It surrounds every inch of me as I lose all feeling in my body, and it swallows me. The mist calms me like medicine, putting me into a trance. Although I have no sense of touch within my body anymore, I can see that the mist is swirling around me, blurring my vision.

A strong wind blows into me from every angle. My hopes lift for a moment, thinking the mist is gone, but when I try to move, it feels as if my limbs are disconnected from myself. I have no control over my body; the mist, now inside me, acts as the puppeteer— controlling my legs, forcing me to walk down the stairs.

I don't fight. The mist isn't hurting me. It feels almost like it is a welcome piece, a missing part. It feels right to have it enter my body. I let it lead me, refusing to withstand the pull anymore—I want this to end. I want the haunting to stop.

The mist leads me out the door and into the vast forest of the backyard. No longer inside the safety of my house, my breathing hitches, and my throat swells up. It feels as if I'm being constricted, blood circulation being cut off. I choke a sob, trying to gasp for breath, but a cooling feeling comes over me, leaving me able to breathe again, and I let the mist lead me farther without any restraint.

I advance through the forest on the only trail I've ever known. Entering the place where I had first seen the purple mist, I want to panic. This is where it all started; this is where I had my first encounter with the force that stopped my movement and turned into a pull. Lined in front of me are the trees that act as a fence, a barrier, from whatever lies within. I stop to regain control of myself, locating where my muscles are and trying to find their functions. I don't know what the trees are hiding, but I don't want to find out.

I'm only able to restrain movement for a moment, feeling something clink into place as I have control of my legs again, until the mist consumes my being again. I can feel the mist pushing me forward from the inside, and then suddenly the voice is back. It sounds like me.

"Move, Amelia, you have to go!" It's strained, panicked, and afraid.

I look around to see if someone is talking to me—no one is there. I'm alone in the forest as it glows with the summer's season. The voice. Whose is it? It sounds like me, but how am I hearing my own voice speak? I know it is mine; I'd heard it countless times in home videos, over a microphone—even once on the news after a tropical storm hit one of our favorite Florida beaches.

"Walk into the trees, now!" my voice yells.

My body jolts forward unwillingly, and when I try to protest, another cooling, numbing sensation fills me. I'm greeted by a calm influence, but most of all, I'm lethargic. Suddenly sleep fills me; I'm tired and nothing seems to be a better solution than to just listen to this voice.

Giving way to the sleep, my body walks forward, my mind stepping away momentarily—as if clocking out of a shift and allowing someone else to take its place. After letting go of control, I expect to feel soothed, but instead it feels like one of those dreams of falling. My mind is woken and snaps back into place.

"No!" I scream out loud. Fully aware of my losing battle, I step away, only to take two steps forward again after the pull controls me. For the first time I notice the tears that seem to flow over my face as I give into my burning need to cry, blurring my vision to what is going on.

"You will walk into the trees now!" my voice yells to me again, becoming frustrated.

This time I can't stop when the commands come; lurching ahead, I almost fall into the trees with the force of energy that expels from the mist. Hearing branches snap, my body bursts through the wall of trees and into an open area, a pool of water laid out in front of me.

It is beautiful; a perfect, clear pool. At first it's sand, but then there is water. In the water are small smooth rocks; they look almost silver. Behind them is a wall of rock. It's rough and coated in moss— I recognize it from my dream. It's all the same. The rock wall, the pool of water—I had been standing in it after the beach had disappeared from my dream. The voice—my voice—is also the same voice that told me to pick up the rock in my dream. I didn't recognize it in the haze of the dream at the time, but now it rings loud and clear. It's me.

"Go in the water now, Amelia!" my voice shouts with both fear and excitement lingering, waiting for me to follow the orders.

A stabbing pain erupts in my spine, and I jolt forward as if I have been electrocuted. I can't fight anymore; it's too hard. I've always known myself to never give up, but now I feel this is the end. The pull has won. I do what my voice says, standing in the water, waiting for the final commands. The cold water doesn't register in my brain; I can't even feel the wet clothing that presses against my skin in the natural pool.

"Do you see those rocks, Amelia?" my voice asks, sounding calmer now, but excitement still evident.

I nod. The stones are settled and untouched at the bottom of the pool, waiting for picking. They mirror me, and I see my reflection in the water.

"Do you want one?" my voice says kindly, coaxing me to pick one.

"No," I whisper aloud, my voice hoarse, feeling as if my throat may close in on itself. I look around at the area, surrounded by trees, with only this large open area and the natural pool of water.

"Yes, you do. Pick one out, Amelia."

I start to bend down but then stop. I suddenly feel scared of what might happen. I pray this is all just a dream; that I will wake up in the safety of my bed, maybe even crying, until my parents come in to make sure I'm okay. They will tell me this is all just a dream, and then they will make me some hot cocoa that will lull me back to sleep.

"Amelia, pick out a rock now and look into it!" the voice growls, growing impatient. Something feels as if it's bound around my throat, and I can't breathe. In that same instant my vision blurs once more, as it always seems to do when the pull is in control of me. My body is hot and bound; I can feel my heart beat inside my chest. I cough, gag, and soon I'm released. With full vision again I let the tears fall down my face more freely.

"Why?" I whisper, shivering in the water, even though all my sense has left me, wishing for nothing but home.

"Pick up a stone and look into it!"

My hand plunges into the water without my consent, and my fingers linger on a rock, curling around a stone. It's extremely smooth; it doesn't seem possible for a rock to be that smooth.

"Now, Amelia, look into the stone," my voice coaxes, as if it's making a deal with me.

I look down into my hand as my fingers open, revealing the small rock. It has a flawless silver surface—no, not silver; it's a mirror. I look into the rock and see myself looking back, eyes stunned.

"Finally." My voice sighs, sounding exactly like myself, and I'm not even sure if it was me who said the words.

Everything shifts. It seems like people are walking past me, looking at me, observing something near me. They stare at me like I'm a fish in a tank. I don't remember how I got here. I'm inside a pristine hospital, surrounded by a sort of plastic that acts as a magnifying glass to my eyes. Most distinct is the sound of beeping— a monitor. A man I don't know wearing navy blue scrubs stops in front of me, looks to my left, writes something down, and leaves again.

The sound of blood pulsing through my body grows louder. The forest comes into view again, but this time it arrives like a movie. I see myself standing in the water, stone in hand, as my body collapses into the natural pool, drowning.

Then everything disappears.

Chapter 7

Explaining

I hear voices around me—most of which I don't recognize. They are all talking about meaningless things: what they did today, what they are doing tomorrow. Then I hear someone talking about me.

"Emma's going to be fine. Don't blame yourself, Eliza. Once her soul found her, there was no stopping it." It's a female voice; one I don't recognize.

"I know. It just feels like Emma was my responsibility. How long until she wakes up?"

"We'll just have to wait and see."

I try to open my eyes to see who is talking about me, but I can't. I can't feel anything; I have a sensation of weightlessness. I try to move my fingers—nothing.

"I think she's waking up. Her hands are moving."

I'm moving my hands? I can't feel them. I try to open my eyes again and objects come into focus—a blue sky above me, the tops of trees, buds sprouting at the edges.

I look around, and there are at least forty people, ranging from seven to late sixties in age. I don't recognize anyone, but they are all staring at me. I look at who's standing closest to me. The girl from school—Eliza—is staring at me, but she looks upset about something.

"Are you okay, Emma? I'm so sorry. I should have kept a better eye on you," she says, letting the apology stream out in a single breath.

Why is she sorry? Nothing happened. The last thing I remember is holding the silver rock and passing out. The mist is gone now, leaving me in a peaceful state, where I finally feel free.

The familiarity of Eliza strikes again, like it had the first day I met her; she still looks exactly the same. It isn't the hair or eyes that are familiar; it's her voice.

Everyone is staring, waiting for me to say something. They all have the same type of tired face, like they never get enough sleep, but now their eyes are wide as they gaze upon me—I realize I'm laying down. I try to speak to them, but when I open my mouth my mind goes blank. Oddly, I don't feel scared but numb.

"Emma, I have to tell you something, well...more than something. It's a big thing," Eliza says, eyes pleading. For the first time I'm able to really look at her. Her face is small, her short ruby-red hair falling in curls. She's tucked her hair back, no longer obscuring her face from view.

"What happened?" I ask, moving my arms and legs to see if I have broken anything. When did I fall? All my clothes are wet, clinging to my skin, but they're drying fast in the sun. My only guess is that I've been in this position for a long time.

"It's complicated. Can you get up yet? I have to show you something," Eliza tells me, looking around at people to signal them to give me space to move.

I struggle to get off the ground, rolling my knees under my frame to scoop myself up. There is no point of contact between my knees to the ground—like when your feet fall asleep and they've gone numb, only aware of the sense of pricking needles, blood flow restricted—but I'm able to gain my footing and stand. Swaying a bit from side to side, I feel an unfamiliar sense of vertigo.

"Don't worry, you'll get used to it," Eliza says with a small smile, trying to comfort me, as I struggle with not being able to feel the contact of the ground beneath my feet.

Everything around me is beautiful. Like in my dream, there is the large rock wall surrounding the pool that holds the mirrored stones. Along the farthest side of the wall is a hole big enough for a person to walk into—a cave maybe—but it's covered by foliage. I'm encircled by the fence of trees and everything is green, covered by layers of moss and leaves, giving everything the same texture as a fairy tale.

Maybe it is just a dream. I take comfort in this possibility as Eliza takes my hand and guides me out of the water, a crunch of rock and gravel confirming that my feet are making contact with the ground. When we get onto land, Eliza looks at everyone standing around and nods. All of them understand at once and walk away.

Once they're out of sight, Eliza puts her hands on my shoulders and looks at me. There's great sincerity in her eyes as she speaks.

"Emma." She takes a deep breath, looking to the pool of water behind me before returning her gaze back to me. "You are no longer alive."

"What do you mean?" I ask.

"It's a long story...so I'll start from the beginning. After you were born, your body died, but your soul didn't. When your heart stopped beating...part of your soul had to leave the body. It was so you could live, in case the doctors were able to get your heart beating again—and they did. But by then, half of your soul had left you and came here—a safe haven for souls." Eliza motions toward the pool of water in front of us.

For a moment I remember a story my mom had told me. My umbilical cord had been wrapped around my neck, cutting off the oxygen supply my lungs needed. My frail body showed no signs of life, and even after they cut the cord from my throat, it was discovered that I had fluid in my lungs. My father showed me pictures from when I had first been born. My body had turned blue from the lack of oxygen—life exiting me—but I was kept alive by an incubator. In the Neonatal Intensive Care Unit my body was surrounded by tubes and wires while my parents anxiously awaited the news of whether or not I'd survive. Exactly a week later they were able to take me home from the hospital.

"Was it because I couldn't breathe?" I whisper the words, not even bothering to look up at Eliza, but instead staring at the gravel that coats the open area of the pool.

"Yes," Eliza said, seeming to understand that it's something I had no control over. "By the time you could breathe again, half your soul had already left because your body couldn't support it. Once a soul leaves its host, the results are irreversible."

"And the other half came here?" All my life I had lived with only half myself. I wanted to imagine all the limits I had faced, but I never knew.

"This is Phantom Lagoon," she answers. "When someone dies and only part of the soul leaves the body, it comes here where it can thrive and live apart from its other half. Your soul came here, unaware it was missing part of itself. When your family moved to New Hampshire, your soul craved to be whole, feeling the immediate organic connection you held with it. This is why, whenever you went into the forest, you felt a pull—a longing to be whole. You were being 'called' by your soul."

"That's what the magnetic pull was? My soul calling me?"

"Yes. Your soul was stuck here at Phantom Lagoon, so it tried to lure you here. Do you remember the purple mist?"

"There was an orange one too," I add.

"The orange mist was me. I was trying to protect you. But the purple mist was your soul. Souls that aren't whole can't go far from Phantom Lagoon and can only appear to their other half as a mist. That's why, when you were in the forest, the mist was going slow—it was fighting to move just as hard as you were."

"Why orange?" I ask, curious. "What I mean to say is, you have dark red hair. Wouldn't it be that color?"

Eliza laughs quietly to herself. "It's not my real hair color. Maybe I'll explain later," she says, stopping the discussion of this subject, as if some hidden emotion might appear that she doesn't want to reveal. "But the mist shows as your soul color...or 'aura,' as some call it."

"You said you were protecting me. What do you mean?"

"I was in your dreams, warning you not to go into the forest."

"Is that why you never talked to me in school? So I wouldn't recognize your voice?"

She smiles, seeming to appreciate the fact that I'm understanding what's happened. "Yes, I'm sorry about that. It must have seemed like I hated you."

"And the faces? Why would you look at me like that?"

"I didn't know how you would do overnight alone. I was surprised to see you acting so normal. I wasn't sure if your soul would find a way to get to you somehow. We have to come back to Phantom Lagoon at night. This place is what keeps us...alive, if that's how you want to put it."

"Why didn't the pull come when I was in the forest camping? Was it because I was with my mom the entire time?" I ask.

"The pull comes when you're least expecting it, but your mother has saved your life before. Well...it was me in your mother's body. You see, when you're under the influence of the pull, the only thing that can stop you is a loved one. So when you were being called by your soul, I would find your mom, take over her body, and call you. I would numb her, so she wouldn't know what had happened."

"Can everyone do that? Take over bodies?"

"Yes, it's called 'haunting.' It's not as bad as it sounds," she assures me, before I make any false assumptions.

"So why couldn't you just haunt me, so the pull would stop?"

"When you're born without part of your soul, only that soul can haunt the body," Eliza states, disappointed. She looks down at the ground, as if this is something she's tried to do—maybe she has; maybe it was me.

"Today? I thought you said my soul had to stay near Phantom Lagoon because it wasn't whole."

"There are always ways around that," she says with a simple shake of the head.

"So what did happen?" I feel like I still don't understand. There's something I'm missing, and I know it's probably something that will crack my brittle shell of emotion. Right now I don't know how to feel, but with one more piece of information, I feel as if I could burst.

"Like I said, there are always ways around it, and that's exactly what your soul did, so it could find you. Your soul haunted you and took you to the forest. It brought you to Phantom Lagoon and had you pick up a stone. The stones are what make Phantom Lagoon magical. When you look into one of them, it uses the mirror to capture your soul. That stone then becomes the color of your soul or aura. If you lose your stone—your soul—you're gone. We don't know what happens, whether we finally get to go to Heaven—we just don't know."

I look down into my hand. The stone is no longer silver but a deep purple—the kind that adorns flowers in the spring. One side is smooth like silk, while the other has small dents that can barely be felt when I run my fingers across it, but they're visible to the eye when compared to the flawless side.

"Protect that, Emma. It's your life now," Eliza tells me.

"How?"

Eliza holds out a necklace and at the end is an orange stone. Like mine, it's smooth with small dents speckled across the surface. Her stone is smaller than mine, but brighter, more brilliant in color.

"I found that this is the easiest way. It never leaves my side."

"What about my mom and dad? What will I tell them?" I ask, now occupied by memorizing the facets of my stone.

"You can't, Emma. They can't see you. You're not alive anymore."

I look up at Eliza to make sure what I heard was true. If I still had a beating heart, it would have stopped.

"I'll never see them again?" The idea seems so foreign. I've always known I'd move out someday, go to college, begin my own life; but never see my parents again?

"You can see them anytime. They just can't see you."

"So what now?" I say the words harshly, like I'm fighting with my mom, and end up using more venom than intended. "I'm a ghost, to haunt the Earth for all eternity?" I can feel a mass of emotions well up inside me—anger, pain, and devastation all at once—deciding now is its time to be expressed.

"No, not a ghost. We like to think of ourselves as an Essence," Eliza tells me, not even bothering to look me in the eyes. She stares at her own stone, caressing it.

"An Essence? What does that even mean?" I can hear my voice rising in volume the more I speak; a round of hysteria audible. My throat grows tight, like it always does when I cry—still, no tears.

"Something that exists spiritually, not physically," Eliza says quietly, eyes down, looking ashamed as she drops her stone, letting it fall to her neck once again.

We're in limbo; a cruel place between life and death. Life means living a normal day-to-day consistency with your family— whether it is a happy existence is up to you. Death means everything is over. All the hard times you've been through can be forgotten. But being an Essence means you're always here. It means seeing everyone die in front of your eyes. You can watch all you want, but can't interfere. It's a sadistic torture.

Chapter 8

Missing

I start my run through the forest, blindly falling again and again. A hope begins to grow in me, not sure what is real—whether my parents can see me, whether I'm still alive. For some reason none of this fazes me though. As I run, I forget: who I am, where I'm going, why it's so important to get there—what is it that matters? My pace slows, and I slump against a tree, sliding toward the ground, exhausted.

I clutch the stone in my hand and realize how ice-cold it has become. I clasp it in both hands and bring it close to my mouth, blowing my breath onto both the stone and my hands. It does not get warmer. Instead it grows colder, as it suddenly occurs to me.

Keep my soul safe. Phantom Lagoon is my home; my safe harbor. I no longer belong to a family; I am a loner. I feel no pain here, because it does not exist; nor will I let it exist. My soul is concealed in this stone; it is my life. I must let go, forget, and never look back. The blame shall be none but my own, for I was born of only half, to be reunited later in life. I am an Essence.

The words repeat. For hours maybe, until the thoughts become my own, and I believe the words. They are not mine, but they become brainwashed into my being, until I become them; and the panic, fear, and sadness leave the core of my soul.

I get off the forest floor and walk toward my house—how long ago had I started my run? I feel drained and dizzy but continue onward. No, this isn't important. I'm dead now; my parents can't see me. But I need to be sure they're okay.

When my house comes within view, I stop. I can hear my parents yelling inside, and I'm brought back into the real world.

I stay hidden within the trees that line my backyard. Through the largest window of our house—the one that lines the entire wall of our dining room—I can see my mom pacing, my dad sitting at the table, head in hands.

"Emma's going to be fine," I hear my dad say. It sounds more like he is trying to convince himself than my mom.

"There's no note. Where is she?" It sounds like my mom is crying. I move a bit closer to see better. A branch blocks my view, but as my mom makes her rounds, pacing back and forth across the dining room, I see her face, flushed and red. She holds her hair back and out of her face as she speaks into the phone.

"It's going to be fine. She must be out with friends or something." My dad sounds unsure of himself.

"Yes, thank you," my mom says into the phone, hanging up. "Sadie's parents said they haven't seen her." Her voice is frustrated, and you can hear the panic that lines the back of her throat.

"Try calling Emma again," my dad says. He doesn't look up and remains seated at the table.

"She left her phone here! Something's not right, and you know it!" My mom is screaming now, and my dad turns his face to reveal his tear-stained, red-rimmed, and irritated eyes. He rubs the wetness away, standing up to retrieve his own phone.

He leans against the counter. "Has it been twenty-four hours yet?" my dad asks, his voice quiet as he begins to dial the three numbers.

My mom can't even make herself say the words. Instead, she just nods her head as my dad punches in the numbers, slowly as if it's a trick of the mind. Nine. One. One.

I had no idea. I've been gone for an entire day? Trying to think back, I remember the mist coming to my room right before lunch, but it's dark now. My parents must have come home late when they realized I was missing and were forced to start their count of twenty-four hours. My parents are approaching the second night they will spend alone, not knowing where I am or if I'm okay.

"I need to file a missing child report," my dad speaks monotone into the phone. The word "child" makes me picture myself featured on an old-fashioned milk carton, how they used the packaging to advertise the missing and neglected.

He tells the police what I look like. Name: Amelia Clarice Barton—responds to Emma—young female, age fifteen, brown hair, blue eyes, last seen Saturday morning. I left no trace or clues as to where I had gone. I've never run away from home before and showed no signs of wanting to.

"She's my daughter," I hear my dad say. Hidden in the woods, I slump to the ground, feeling completely useless. Far away in the house I see my mom step out of her pace, going in the kitchen where my dad holds the phone. She takes it from him.

"Sir?" she speaks into the phone, her voice fleeting. "Please bring her home. We love her." She stops, taking a moment to gain a breath. "We're not going to stop until we find her." Her voice is stronger, more powerful and determined than the last time. "We're a family. I need her. Please, just bring my Emma home."

I'm missing and cannot be found.

I wish it were that simple. That all it will take is a small search party. But it's more than that. Even if I'm standing in front of them, I won't be seen. I want this to end, so they don't have to suffer while they wait for their daughter to come home.

"The police are on their way," my mom whispers, her voice just a quiver, as she returns to the dining room to sit in the chair. She looks up, out the window. I follow her gaze to the setting sun, colors of pink and orange fill the sky like a watercolor painting. She cries alone, staring at the beauty of nature.

Even as I stand feet from the window, I can clearly see the tears running down her face as my dad tries to comfort her while they wait for the police to arrive. I can't handle this. I want to walk through the door and give my mom a hug so much, but I can't—I'll never be able to give her a hug again. I'll never be able to finish my life. I'm stuck here forever in a land of spirits—a ghost, not an Essence.

The police arrive. They ask my parents countless questions: when they had last seen me, if I had been upset recently. They even call Sadie again, and ask if she had seen or heard from me lately.

"Were there any family problems going on that might have caused her to run away?" one of the policemen asks, writing down notes.

"No, we just came back from a camping trip, and she seemed so happy. She was at my side the entire time," my mom tells them, now wiping away tears with a tissue, as my dad sits with her at the table.

"She did seem to be a little on edge though," my dad adds quietly, almost afraid to say the words and admit there is something going on; something that he might've been able to give attention to and change. But there was nothing he could have done.

The entire time the police continue to take notes, carefully paying attention to what my parents say and how they react. The officers are automatons, showing no sign of emotion.

I stand near my house for a while, sometimes walking closer when it becomes hard to hear the whispers coming from my mother's mouth. Eventually I sit on the ground, leaning against the house, listening to the events going on inside. The sun sinks lower in the sky, the orange turning to a purple hue. My stone feels different as I run my hand over it. Looking closely, I see it's grown translucent. My soul is fading away. I can feel some sort of pain starting to form in my spine, spreading to other parts of my body, making it hard to think and figure out what is happening.

My breathing grows louder as I get up from the ground and start running to Phantom Lagoon, hoping that's what it will take to get my stone normal again. I want to look back at my house to where my parents are inside, being questioned about my life, but the sharp bite that starts in my spine tells me to continue forward until I reach the lagoon.

I near the fence of trees and break through them, hearing branches snap in my wake. The rock wall is the first thing I see, a horrific welcome into this world. Moss coats the rock like this lagoon has been here longer than anyone can possibly remember. Everyone who had been here earlier today is back and beginning to settle down for the night. All eyes look to me as I come to a stop, trying to gain my bearings. Eliza runs to my side and looks relieved to see that I'm okay.

"Are you all right?"

I nod to her, still gasping for breath from the run. With relief, I hold out my hand. In my palm is my stone, fully there— solid. The ache in my back is gone, as if it had never been there in the first place. "What was that?" I ask.

"If you don't come back to Phantom Lagoon nightly, your stone will start to fade. It was created here. That's where it craves to be," Eliza tells me as I follow her to the edge of the lagoon. Her eyes stare into the water. The silver-mirrored rocks lay inside, unclaimed by any Essence or human, waiting to be chosen.

"So we don't live forever?" I ask, running my fingers over the smooth side of my stone. "I thought we would, because we're not alive anymore." I can't help but feel a bit disappointed.

"We do live forever, but sometimes things happen." Eliza pauses for a minute—I can tell there is something she isn't comfortable saying—but she continues after looking toward the cave of the lagoon. "People forget to come back, or they lose their stone. Sometimes people just disappear, and that's it. Never to be seen again."

"They just disappear?" I ask.

"Yes, they were the ones that would come back to Phantom Lagoon every day. They'd never stray too far from it. Then, out of nowhere, they disappear."

I wake up lying across the bed of fern I had made the night before. I miss my real bed, my home, my parents—everything. Everyone else is still sound asleep on their own homemade beds— some better than others. I can tell who puts an effort into their living quarters. It's hard to live with so many people in one spot. We only have to deal with each other at night, but that's when people have the least patience.

I stretch out and see that my hand is still in a fist, clutching my stone. I uncurl my fingers and see the stone is the same: dark purple, dented in places, but remaining unchanged. I don't know why, but I expected it to look different. It's warm against my hand now, and I feel safe. I lay the stone on the sand near the lagoon, as I stare into the unending depth held in the simple piece of silvery stone. This is my soul, but it holds something more. When I went to my house, it turned ice-cold; then I had forgotten why I needed to see my parents. Here I pick up the stone again and feel it in my hands; rolling it over and over, memorizing it. It holds no secrets to be found—just a stone.

I look around me at the faces of strangers; some dating back centuries, to the time period they were born. Under a tree a few feet away, Eliza is asleep. I feel no belonging in this strange new world. These people hold no bonds, not like families do. Everyone keeps their distance from each other. There is at least three feet between everybody, even though space cannot be spared with such a large community. There is no love here; the feeling of friendship is distant and slight. I know it will stay this way, maybe even worsen as time moves along. I don't want to be here where there is no compassion.

I move along quietly, being sure I make no contact with anyone sprawled across the ground. I slide between the fence of trees and leave Phantom Lagoon.

It's early morning, and there's still dew on the ground to be dried by the sun's morning light. I close my eyes and take note of all the sounds: the singing of birds, the movement of the river, and most of all the quiet whisper of the wind. It reminds me of my mom: the cries she had made when she discovered that I was missing, the intake of breath she took before surrendering into my dad's arms.

I know I will hear her cries again soon, but I continue toward my house to be sure my parents are okay. Everything seems to go slowly today. No matter how hard I try to keep walking forward, I find myself stopping to look at the nature around me, my mind in a haze, easily distracted.

By the time I reach my house, the sun is in the middle of the sky; I spent the entire morning trying to get here. It never took me that long to get back to my house when I was human. Part of me wants to discover what's stopping me, but something in me just wants to push away the curiosity and move along—so that's what I do. At my house there are even more police cars. I go to the window and see posters all over the table that read Missing with my picture pasted underneath. There are people I know arriving to help search. Sadie and her parents are here too. She looks like she has been crying, as she clutches to her mom's side. Almost everyone from town is at my house to look for me and to put up posters. The sad part is that this is a common occurrence. Hikers go missing all the time in the forest—most of the time they are found alive, starving, but alive—others aren't as lucky.

My mom is at the table making calls, only to get the answer that I haven't been seen. My dad talks to the officers before they go out again to continue looking. Some search the woods while others go door-to-door. My parents are always at home waiting for the phone to ring—for me to call—but I can't. Maybe they are even waiting for me to walk straight through the door to welcome me with open arms.

The rest of the day feels unending. Things happen over and over like a movie is set on Replay as I watch. Friends comfort my parents, and police officers search. The cycle of pain that surrounds me now feels as if it will engulf me and take no pity. But of course it doesn't; that would mean dying, that would mean the end. There is no end; I'll go on forever so I can see my family suffer.

I wish there was a way to show them my body, so they know I'm no longer alive. That way they can stop searching and waiting for me. Is there even a body to show them? I set off to find Eliza as the sun begins to set in the sky, bringing with it nothing but cold for me and my family.

Everyone is gathered in Phantom Lagoon, walking around, finding a spot to sleep. Some lay on large boulders near the water, while others abandon the rocky beach for the soft sand that lines the trees. The water is still and silent as the sun glistens over the surface. Eliza is sitting on a large rock near the edge of the trees, while she stares up at the moon like it's a loved one.

"Eliza?" I ask.

"Yes?" she says, looking at me now, erasing any emotions that had been on her face a few seconds before.

"Can I ask you something?" I say, walking toward her, stepping over smaller rocks and tree roots sticking out of the ground.

"Of course." She motions me to sit next to her as she slides to the side, giving me room.

As I sit, I look into the large lagoon holding the mirror rocks that wait to claim another soul. "What happened to my body when I died?"

She tries to look at me, but I refuse to make eye contact. "Emma, if you were dead, you wouldn't be on Earth anymore," Eliza tells me. "Your body is here. It's in the cave. That's just where they end up. We don't put them there. They seem to send themselves," she says, pointing toward the mouth of the cave.

The entrance is still covered with leaves; nobody has disturbed its presence. It makes sense to have it covered—almost out of respect.

"Can I have it?" I ask quietly, looking at Eliza again. "My parents think I ran away, and they're waiting for me to come home. The police think I'm dead—or at least dying, lost in the forest somewhere—I don't want my parents to suffer anymore."

She thinks for a moment. "How will they find it?"

I didn't think of this. I can always make it look like an accident. Like I was in the woods hiking and fell. I'd be forced to take my body and throw it down a waterfall, but it will still need to be found somehow.

"What about haunting?" I suggest. "I could show them where to find my body, and put it in the woods or something."

Eliza thinks about it for a minute before answering. "That could work, but I think you should be the one to show them where your body is."

"How do I haunt someone?"

Eliza stays quiet for a while, thinking of the skill and technique involved. "It takes some concentration, but everyone can learn. I can show you, if you'd like."

"Thank you," I whisper, feeling lighter, knowing my parents won't have to keep searching for me much longer.

"We'll start tomorrow. We can use animals to train with, in case you mess up. No need to scare the humans," she says, hopping off the rock and back to the tree where she slept the night before.

Chapter 9

Lost Soul

I find a way to climb to the top of the cave in the lagoon that makes up the rock wall which overlooks the pool of water. It's higher than I thought but provides privacy. Looking down, I feel as though I can see everyone. Names still unknown, but some faces are familiar. Everyone has found slumber, curled into sleeping forms on the ground. As a human, sleeping this way would be painful. One man is sprawled across a boulder, but I know he won't wake up sore. The only physical pain we can experience now is when the sun sets, if we are outside of Phantom Lagoon.

Through the darkness I can barely make out the water that rests below. The moon glows on it, illuminating a small sliver of the water.

It's my second night here, and the new information Eliza has told me still buzzes around my head, waiting to be processed. I'm hoping, once my parents know about my death, it will be easier for everyone.

I want to cry—no, I need to cry. Everything I've ever known has been ripped away from me. I'm no longer part of my family. I can feel the emotions building up inside my being, begging to release, but something's holding them in check. Maybe I'm stronger now, but there's always this calm, serene state that I reach at points during the day that tell me to lie down and breathe. My stubborn side wants to argue with it and resist, but eventually, when I feel my emotions and memories of what I used to have pile inside me, I fall to the calm, dazed state of mind. It bothered me at first—I feel as if I'm being tranquilized—now I let it take me as need be.

When the sun went down, it took all the day's warmth with it, leaving me curled up on the ground, as if I'm a small child. Being an Essence means you don't have a sense of touch in the physical world—I can't feel the cold air, but out of habit I squeeze myself into a tight ball as the darkness approaches.

I hear the sounds of the forest all around me—right now just the quiet rustles of leaves here and there. There are hushed whispers below from others who are still awake, having quiet conversations. I close my eyes in an attempt to sleep.

Memories of my family filter through, reminding me of all the times my parents had tucked me in on the nights I claimed the monsters in my closet wouldn't leave. My dad always liked to humor me, opening the door and displaying the piles of clothes I had left on the floor, even though they had told me to clean it up. Sometimes my mom would even sing me to sleep, telling me to lie on my stomach while she rubbed my back. It always started the same: *Hush, little baby, don't say a word.* That was as far as I would hear; by the time she was on the next line, I was always fast asleep.

I feel my body tremble as a sobbing sound escapes my throat. I miss my parents—I miss home. I take a moment to breathe, knowing that, if I let myself slip into my emotions, it will be hard to stop. Somehow I manage to squeeze myself even tighter, until my muscles protest in pain. I feel a warm sensation from my hand and realize it's my stone. I hold it to my cheek while I concentrate on its warmth.

I drift but am never fully asleep. I stare straight in front of me; my eyes fixed open, looking incomprehensibly at the darkness that surrounds me. My stone feels warm as it comforts me. But not the comfort of a hug; no this feels forced—like a drug, pulling me into a sleep.

The warmth radiates through my being and that's when I realize something. We aren't supposed to feel anything—hot, warm; cold, cool—nothing. So how can I?

I take the stone away from my face but don't put it down— I'm scared it won't be there in the morning. Instead I put my arms around my stomach, clinging to my sides, trying to keep control of myself. I feel my eyes shut as I mumble, "It's going to be okay," in a faint whisper. I don't believe the words, but I continue to repeat them anyway.

At first everything is fuzzy, but once the blackness of the images clears to only the edges, I can see the rough outlines of what looks like my room. My parents are clearing everything out without giving it a second thought. They take all my belongings and put them in boxes before bringing them outside where there is a yard sale—mostly consisting of my things. I see strange, unfamiliar faces pick through everything I own before paying my parents and walking off. They smile as the cash is handed to them and soon all my things are gone forever.

My dad goes to the store to buy paint while my mom continues to clean out my room. She stumbles across my drawings and looks them over quickly before tossing them into a pile of trash. When my dad comes home, my room is completely cleared of anything that resembles my former life except the blue walls. My dad opens a can of paint and soon my room is consumed by the dark abyss of the walls, as they threaten to seal me off from the world I used to live in.

"They forgot about me," I whisper over and over to myself in the dead of night. "I thought you loved me." So badly I want to feel those tears fall down my face, but they never come. It occurs to me that an Essence cannot cry—feel emotion, yes—but no tears. This disturbs me and makes the reality of not being human even clearer. I lift myself from the ground, no longer wanting to stay in one place, and walk off into another part of Phantom Lagoon.

My chest is heaving as I trip over a root and fall to the ground with a slight thud. I try to stumble to my feet but continue tripping. It's hard to see where I am in the still dark night. Every time I fall to the ground, the only thing I can picture is my parents, offering their hand out to lift me up. When I do gain my feet again, I'm only filled with disappointment to learn I'm alone in the forest. Finally I collapse to the ground, my muscles tired, where I kneel, hugging my sides in an effort to try to keep myself together. I'm alone. It's what I wanted back in Phantom Lagoon, but now that I have it, it stings like a leather whip.

A ghost of a tear runs down my face as my sobs continue. I'm not supposed to cry—it's not possible for an Essence.

"What's wrong with me?" The aggravation I expect from myself is replaced by grief, and I grow more upset with myself as time passes. I want to scream, but when I open my eyes, I see it's raining. I wasn't crying—it's just the rain. My hands drop to my sides, and I slide to the ground. I again surrender into unconsciousness. My hands lock into fists, seeking my stone to act as a drug as it has before. With a tired mind, panic consumes me as I come up empty-handed, and paw through the leaves and grass of the forest floor. Frantically I think of the last time I remembered holding it. Definitely not while I thought I was crying.

I follow the instinct that tells me to retrace my steps. My gaze darts side to side, hoping to catch the purple hue of my stone out of the corner of my eye. Suddenly I trip and, out of some unknown miracle, there lays my stone—my soul that I must guard—unharmed and untouched by anyone. It sits, perched on top of a pile of leaves in the dim forest.

In one quick, fluid motion, I pick it up and run back to the lagoon. The trees no longer offer their protection from the rain, so everyone is awake and mumbling about not being able to sleep. We may not be able to *really* feel the rain, but in a way we can. It passes through our bodies, causing an odd sensation that feels like bugs are crawling across our skin. I hadn't noticed this before, because I had been distracted, but now I can't stop flinching, hoping to avoid the rain. Others are itching themselves, even though it doesn't help. I catch myself doing the same, but soon I'm able to block it all out. I'm back to where I had tried to sleep before, on top of the cave. Everyone else has gone into the trees, where there is a little more shelter. Not in the cave though—not where they have to look at their pale, lifeless bodies.

I take the alone time gratefully. I hope that no one noticed I had wandered off for a moment, but before Eliza goes into the trees, she looks at me like she's worried. I ignore her, sitting alone with my arms around my legs, while I look to the sky as it releases the rain.

Keep my soul safe. The unknown thought passes through my head as I finger my stone. *Phantom Lagoon is my home, my safe harbor. I no longer belong to a family; I am a loner. I feel no pain here, because it does not exist; nor will I let it exist. My soul is concealed into this stone; it is my life. I must let go, forget, and never look back. The blame shall be none but my own, for I was born of only half, to be reunited later in life. I am an Essence.*

I'm not dripping wet. I'm not cold. I'm truly dead.

...Not human.

Chapter 10

Training

To my dismay I don't wake up sore. I feel no need to stretch, like I did when I was human, so I just roll onto my back to look toward the sky. I can breathe easier now that I am no longer curled into a ball, so I take long, deep breaths as the birds sing their morning melody. The air is crisp, and the rivers are fierce from the water they received overnight. As the sun reaches its way across the horizon, I pull out my stone.

What had once been a deep purple now has a violet glow as I hold it to the sun. It's slightly transparent against the morning sky, letting me see through the depths of the soul that lies within. The violet surface looks like marble with different shades of purple swirled into the stone. I can see the flaws more clearly now. It is covered in small nicks, making it appear almost spotted. But on the back is a large dent and the color of the rock is different. It's a lighter purple—lavender. In the deepest section of the dent is a pale brown—it's small and hard to notice, but it is there. The flaws in my stone have grown in number and severity since I last looked at it.

This stone is my soul. The nicks on the surface, those are my flaws—visible to everyone. Of course there is the large dent. It's easy for everyone to see. What you can't see is the pale brown spot in the center—only if you look close enough. So, in a sense, this stone is just like me. If you look close enough, you can see my deepest flaws. They have grown in both size and number, but there is beauty in this. In the sun, it appears to be marble, reminding me that no matter how many flaws I have, there will always be beauty.

I am not perfect. I don't want to be. To know there is not one stone like my own is a blessing.

As the sun's rays stretch high, I think of my family, where they lie, still asleep. I'm so close to them, but they are forever out of my reach. Seeing the sun rise only makes me feel worse, because I can no longer share this moment with my family. I imagine it though; I try to conjure up the last things I said to my mom and dad, but to my shock I can't. I had never valued my life. I realize that now.

Eliza peeks to where I am stretched across the rock, still looking at the sky. She doesn't come over right away, and I don't look at her.

"Rough night?" she asks, climbing the rock to slide next to me. I sit up and look at her before looking down to where the edge of the cave ends with a drop. I can feel her gaze on me, but I just lock my arms around my knees. Out of the corner of my eye, I see her hand reach out to me, but she thinks better of it and lets it drop to her side again.

"I heard you last night," she says.

I look at her, expecting her to laugh at me, but instead it looks like she understands. Eliza doesn't pity me; she realizes what I'm going through.

I rest my chin on my knee, while we sit in silence. I hear Eliza adjust herself, but she doesn't leave. In fact, she sits there next to me, while I soak in my silence. I watch everyone leave Phantom Lagoon as they go about their daily activities. Eliza stays. Finally when we are alone, I turn to her, thinking she must have fallen asleep. She is looking at the lagoon with the most intense stare.

"You'll get used to it, you know. It's not that bad...as long as you have friends." She must feel my stare, because she looks over and smiles. "So do you still want to learn how to haunt?" she asks, jumping up and offering her hand.

I grip her outstretched fingers and can't help but smile as she leads me into another part of the forest.

We finally reach a large field full of wildflowers and animals feasting on the green grass that covers the area. Eliza runs to the middle of the open greens and turns in circles to get a full view of the area.

"Come on, Emma," she says, waving me over.

I walk past a herd of deer, calculating each step, and I'm surprised when they don't flinch when I come near—in fact, they come closer.

Eliza starts laughing as I approach her. "You should see your face. Have you already forgotten you are not human?"

I look at her, confused, until she finally answers.

"Animals have an extra sense, I guess you could say. They can see an Essence's spirit, but they aren't afraid of us, because they know we can't hurt them. They call us Fairies, I think. We appear to them as our soul color, but that's it—just a vague outline. They only know the general spot where we stand."

When I reach the middle of the field where Eliza stands, everything takes on a new mood. I forget about my problems and focus on this one event, which, as Eliza seems to be displaying, is going to be fun.

"First, I'll give you the basics," she says, turning to me, the field behind her. "We pass through the living—anything with a heartbeat. Flesh doesn't exist in our world. A human or animal can simply walk through us, completely unaware we occupy the same space as them. However, if you concentrate, you can become one with them—momentarily share the same body. Objects that aren't living are just as real to us as they are to humans...but there are exceptions. Like a ghost, you can walk through walls. It's not always the most enjoyable sensation. You can't merely walk through a wall. You have to force yourself and concentrate on where you want to go." Eliza looks over at the deer in the field.

"Today I will show you how to haunt. I'll show you how it's done," Eliza says, smiling.

She walks over to the largest deer and stands beside him. He looks at her for a moment before turning his attention back to the food in front of him. She holds out her hand, like she is going to pet him, but instead she vanishes.

The deer stops eating and looks up in all directions. It starts walking toward a small family of birds and jumps up in an unnatural way, its legs bucking out like an untamed horse kicking off its rider. The birds fly away from the deer, and Eliza shows up again next to the deer. At ease, the deer begins to turn around to eat in peace again.

"What did you think?" she asks, walking back to where I stand.

"You did that?" I say, pointing toward the deer, now completely immersed in eating again.

"Well, yeah. Have you ever seen a deer do that before?" Eliza starts laughing. The large deer lifts his head to us for a moment, as if he can hear our voices and then turns to the grass once more.

"I have now," I say, joining her in the thrill of laughter.

"Okay," Eliza says, hands on hips, standing beside me. "All you really have to do is think about the person or animal you are trying to haunt, then you just touch them. Once you're inside, you're back in the real world. You can't see another Essence or hear them. You become that entity."

"I thought you said animals could see us?"

"Vaguely. So when I haunted that deer, I knew you were here, because there was a purple spot in the field, but that's all."

I nod, encouraging her to continue.

"Anyway, if you want them to do something, all you have to do is think it. And when I say think it, I mean you really have to try hard and focus. Shout it in your head. When I wanted the deer to jump, I just shouted 'Jump!' almost as if I was saying it out loud."

I remember when my soul had haunted me and how it would command me to do its bidding. *Walk into the trees, now!* No matter how much I wanted to stop, I couldn't. Haunting is just as bad as it sounds, no matter how fun Eliza makes it appear. When I was being haunted, I had no control over my body, but I have to show my parents the truth. I have to release them. It will be cruel and heartbreaking for my parents to see my lifeless body, but it has to be done.

"That's it? That's all it takes?" I ask. It sounds too easy.

"It may sound simple, but it's not. If you don't have a good soul, you can't haunt people." Eliza bends down to pick some wildflowers and stands up again, still mesmerized by the simple piece of nature she holds.

"What do you mean, *good soul*?" I ask, looking at the small purple flower with a spot of yellow in the center, while she spins it between her fingers.

"Basically if you use your powers to hurt other people, you can't haunt. It's for the sake of the humans. Would you want some psycho haunting you?"

I shake my head, agreeing with her, while she tosses the flower to the side and waits, looking at me.

"I'm not sure how that works really. I've seen it happen before. Some group wanted to use human bodies to play a prank, but when they tried to haunt them, they couldn't do it. Try and try again, they just couldn't gain access to a body."

"So how do I start?" I ask, looking around at all the animals that scatter the field, all of them eating.

"Well, what animal do you want to haunt?" she asks, trying to find where my gaze is searching.

Around the field there are mostly deer eating and small birds hopping around. I decide on the deer, because the birds will be too hard to catch. I point toward the smallest doe, seeing if Eliza approves.

"Okay, now just walk up to it and think about it. You will know when it's working," she says, finding a spot to sit on the grass, crisscrossing her legs, preparing to watch me haunt for the first time.

At first I just stand there, a mere foot from the doe. I concentrate. I feel foolish thinking to myself, "I'm a deer." Then, slowly...I reach out my hand to touch the doe, like Eliza had said. There is an underlying caution in me as I expect the animal to run at my contact, but she doesn't.

All at once warmth goes through me. Suddenly I can feel the fast heartbeat of the young deer, the grass underneath its feet, the sun on its back. With each beat of the heart, I feel a jolt of blood racing through the body I now occupy. I'm alive again.

Must eat fast, must stay safe.

I hear the deer think inside my own mind. Her thoughts are frantic, never resting or taking comfort in the fact of having fresh greens in front of her to survive. The only thing she seems to concentrate on is staying alive.

I can't figure out why the deer is so nervous, but when I feel a stabbing pain in my back leg, I realize I'm injured.

"Walk," I order, trying to test the leg and assess what happened. When the small doe tries to obey me, I can only hear an eerie cry escape from its mouth as it follows my orders.

"Look at your leg," I tell the doe.

When the small back leg comes into view, I can see that it's bloody and mangled. The doe isn't putting any weight on it, balancing on just three legs, her mind still preoccupied with thoughts of eating and trying to stay alive.

"What happened?" I ask myself.

Bears. Bears everywhere. One big, others small; laughing at us. Wants to eat us. Momma's gone. Papa left us; he left a'runnin'. Don't care about us. Only his safety. Big black bear took Momma and gave her to little bears. Saw it meself—bloody. Big bear went after me, but I gots away. Leg hurts. Tummy hungry...always hungry.

I didn't even realize the doe had heard me ask the question, but I can play out the event in my head so clear now, as if she was replaying the entire thing before me.

Chepi—the small doe—was looking for food with her parents, when they encountered a family of bears; one large mother protecting her two cubs. The mother bear went after the nearest target for food—Chepi's mother. Her father fled the scene at first sign of distress, and Chepi sat by as she watched her mother eaten alive. Only after the mother bear began to target Chepi, did she leave.

She's lucky to leave with only a broken leg. They must have strayed from the herd at one point, but it seems Chepi has found her way back.

"Chepi," I say. "What does your name mean?"

I be named after Fairies. I sees them. Two were here today. One be purple—that one was nexts to me. Other be orange—that Fairy be overs there. Orange glow spot. Don't know where's purple gone. Here it was though. They comes to see me herd. Said to keep the monsters aways from us. Theys keeps us safe.

"What monsters?"

We 'uns have a legends about them monsters. We lived here first, then they comes to kill us. They be dark color, walk on two feet like bears. Wore our families on them—showing pride mes think. Theyed have big sticks and throw them through ours bodies. They eat as like the bears did with my momma. Then more did come. These monster different color. They said they weres 'American' and killed 'Natives'. Theys haves 'slaves.' They be brown, but theys calls them 'black.' They be whipping them. These monsters be worse. They have things that make big bang and kills us—'guns' they called it. They kills their own kin too. They kills many. They make lines— theys call it war. We gots in middle of alls it. Whiles monsters kills themselves, we gots killed too. Nows they have more things that make bang and biggest thing kills home. They calls it 'dozer.' They be taking our forest. They be laughing at us. But we gots Fairies.

They comes here, and they be nice. They knows monster, and they will stops them someday. Then we be safe.

I'm speechless. Everything in history that has happened, seen through the eyes of this small deer. The Native Americans with the dark-colored skin, killing her herd for food and skinning anything that could be used as clothing. Then when we began to settle in America, we brought our weapons with us. When Chepi speaks of the lines, she called it war, I think she has the name right. I remember learning in history class that, when they had battles, it was organized in lines. When someone died in the first line, someone else would step up and take their place. Chepi mentions whites using the blacks as slaves—whipping them even.

I can't help but agree with Chepi. We are monsters. We've killed so many. Not just humans, but innocent animals and their homes. I wish I could tell Chepi that Eliza and I are the Fairies she speaks of, but I know I can't break her last hope.

I know I have to do something for Chepi before I leave.

"Chepi, the purple Fairy will be watching you. She'll help your foot." Then I step away from Chepi's body and back into the world where I am known as an Essence—not a Fairy that will save the small doe.

After I release myself from the deer, I'm not warm anymore. I have the same weightless feeling that I felt when I first entered the world of Phantom Lagoon. Looking toward Chepi, I discover that she has found me, staring in my general direction—but not at me.

I bend down to pat Chepi on the head, for a moment thinking I may accidently haunt her. But I don't—I'm not thinking like her—so instead my hand slips through her body, like I'm invisible, which I am. There's nothing I can do for this injured orphan doe, but she stares into my essence with admiration. When I hear something moving behind me, I see Chepi look at Eliza, now coming toward the two of us.

"How was it?" she asks, sitting next to me to feed Chepi.

"They're so human. We don't realize it, but they're just like us. Better than us in some ways. They seem to have a higher sense of what's right."

"I guess that's one way to look at it," Eliza says, getting up and brushing off her hands. "Remember, they only know what they see. I would say their opinions are too black-and-white, yes or no. Humans take the maybes into consideration. They've also changed a lot over the years. Humans don't mindlessly kill, like they used to. They have considered the planet's safety, and they're working on taking care of it. Slowly, yes, but trying. Don't get too absorbed into their story, Emma. It's the circle of life. Things die."

"We don't," I whisper, mostly to myself. It seems like Eliza hears me, but she chooses to say nothing in response.

"Can I show my parents my body now?" I ask, taking a deep breath, preparing myself for what's next.

"If you think you're ready. But humans have stronger control, so they will be harder. And before you leave their body, if you want to numb them, just say 'Forget,' and that's what they will do."

I stand up and move away from Chepi—I will probably never see her again; for all I know, she might not even survive the night with that leg. I follow Eliza back to Phantom Lagoon to retrieve my lifeless body from the cave, feeling the weight of the next task on my shoulders: showing my parents I'm dead.

I miss them so much.

Chapter 11

The News

"Are you sure you want to do this?" Eliza asks, standing at the mouth of the cave in Phantom Lagoon.

"Yes." I take a deep breath, remembering this is all for my parents.

Eliza walks into the cave, and I follow her. The walls are magnificent. They look as if the rocks have crystal embedded in them. When the foliage that covers the mouth of the cave is moved, the light hits the crystal, making them appear—not sparkling—but glowing with a radiant aura, welcoming us inside. The beauty stops there. Eliza lets the moss and thick leaves close behind us, and in return, the crystals lose their glow. We see what is hidden in the deep cave. Inside there are bodies—they look like the many faces I have seen in Phantom Lagoon. Other bodies I didn't recognize—I guess they are from the souls that disappear. Each person is propped against the wall. Some are seated; others lie across the ground in a never-ending sleep.

Every detail of the uninhibited human body is maintained, like the person may just get up and walk away. There's no sign of decomposition. The bodies have a familiar glow of life as they rest near the crystal—a flush of cheek, the face at peace. There is a girl curled into a small ball, her hands wrapped around her torso. When I look closely I see tears, as if they're fresh, frozen in place on her check.

"Emma." Eliza tugs at me. I look to her and then the girl again—that's her body. I didn't recognize it at first in the dark light of the cave, but now I see it. The odd thing is how happy Eliza's human body looks. Even though there are tears, her lips are curled into a smile; joy as she left her human life.

"Please," Eliza says, gazing down at her own body and seeing how vulnerable she is at that moment. I follow Eliza as she leads me away from her body and toward my own.

"Eliza?" I ask, slowing my pace until we have both stopped in the middle of the cave. She looks back at me and then over my shoulder to where her body lies comatose, then to me again. "Will I be able to touch my body?"

She nods her head. "Yes. The flesh is no longer alive, so it exists in our world."

She stares at me for a moment, and I wonder what she sees in my face, why she has chosen to help me, when no one else did. No words are exchanged between us, so she turns around again and begins to walk. We travel farther into the cave, and the ceiling becomes low above our heads. The crystal that lines the wall can't be seen in the darkness, so I'm only left to pretend there is beauty in this place full of death.

Eliza stops in front of me and breaks the silence. "Your body is around this corner. Do you want to go alone?"

"You can come if you want," I tell her. A nervousness forms in the pit of my stomach, and I can feel my limbs quiver with slight motion.

Eliza looks at me for a moment. She looks backward to where the mouth of the cave is, walking away without a word.

I stand there for a moment—I'm not sure why; waiting for courage maybe? Making the final steps to my body, the crunch of gravel beneath my feet seems to grow louder and louder. Finally I see myself around the corner, exactly where Eliza said I would be. The sounds of my steps echo as I come within mere feet of myself.

I look just as I remember: brown hair that falls over my shoulders, tanned skin from years spent in the Florida sun, and blue eyes that can't be seen because my lids cover them in this inert state. I can't believe that I'm looking at myself. Not my reflection seen backward, but myself, seen as everyone else sees me. I look as if I'm in a deep sleep, in an endless peaceful dream that can never be broken. My knees are drawn to my chest, arms wrapped around them, as my entire body is nestled against the crystal walls of the cave.

It's like I'm looking at my own body as a sleeping child. I don't want to wake myself or disrupt the slumber that is displayed upon my face. Even though I know my body is no longer connected to me, I want to think that I'm dreaming. Though my eyes are closed, my mouth is turned up in the corners, as if I'm smiling in a dream. It doesn't seem real.

I have already planned what I intend to do. I will haunt one of the police officers and lead him to my body. He will tell my parents what the police found. My parents will think it was an accident, and that I'm in Heaven watching over them. They will think that I'm happy in some other place and won't worry anymore. It doesn't matter if what they think is true or not, as long as they are happy.

I kneel beside my body as my arms fold around myself, lifting the body. The walk out of the cave is longer as I pass all the faces of Phantom Lagoon, trying to imagine what an Essence carrying its own human body must look like. Walking through the draping of leaves, the sun hits my body, and in this new light, my body looks old and decomposed. The crystal of the cave, now out of reach for my body, no longer supplies the fountain of youth it once had.

My body quickly becomes pale with a bruised hue, as if making up for the time it had been preserved in the cave. In my Essence arms, my body now feels stiff and cold, any sign of life gone. My face is also rigid, my mouth now just a straight, emotionless line. The difference is astonishing and, most of all, frightening. The muscles in my body don't budge or bend when I twist limbs to adjust and position my body that I hold. With a deep breath I turn my face away from my uninhabited body, now exposed to the elements, and make plans to dispose of it.

I roam the forest looking for the location of my death, feeling numb as I refuse to look down into my arms. There are very few places the police and their search parties haven't checked yet, but

I find one. It's a large waterfall, and even though it's a beautiful piece of nature, I look at it in a new way—the cause of my death.

I stand at the edge and look down at the drop-off. The waterfall may be pretty, but there are large rocks jutting out at the bottom. Not giving myself time to think about the details, I throw my body over the edge, seeing my face flash by for a second: pale and emotionless. I don't look to see the impact, but I can hear it fall several times, bones breaking in the process. With my back to the sounds of the waterfall, I let a choking sound release from my throat. I try to repress it, but as hard as I may, I still find myself shaking. I don't let that stop me from racing to my house to reveal the news.

My run is fast, and I still expect the tears to come down my face when my quiet, barely audible sobs escape as I dread the news my parents are about to hear. I put my hands to my face, as if I can wipe away the invisible tears.

The only thing I can think of is how my face looked as my body dropped into the waterfall. I was drawn, no longer in this world—nothing like how my face had looked in the crystal cave: dreaming and alive.

But then I remember my mom on the phone with the police, telling them that she wouldn't stop until I was found. And I have no doubt in that. I know she'll continue to look for me until all hope is lost. The only thing I can do is diminish that last and final hope. Whether or not my parents are ready to hear the news, they are going to receive it, so they can move on without me.

As I walk forward, my lips are sealed tight, face rigid, trying to keep quiet. My hands are balled into fists as I approach one of the hardest things I've done in my life. In the backyard where the trees stop, the house is in full view.

Through the windows I see my parents still at the phone waiting, both sitting at the dining room table. My dad's face reveals exactly what he's thinking: I'm dead; there's no doubt about it. It's been three days, and even if I just got lost while hiking, there is a very small shred of hope that I'm still alive. And that's the piece of hope my mom clings to, as if it's her own life she is trying to save. Sitting at the table, she seems completely absorbed in memorizing the lines in the wood. Her unblinking eyes bore into the table, never looking up. Her lips seem to move as if she is whispering something; then I see they are trembling.

I move to the edge of my house to look through the window into the dining room. At first I stand there, studying my parents and their faces. I have never seen them like this; their personalities are almost completely diminished. I hide behind a tree close by, feeling exposed in the open expanse of my backyard. I watch for what feels like hours but is really just minutes.

Time passes slowly as they both wait for the phone to ring. Nothing happens. Police walk in and out of our house to gather new information before returning to the search. Sometimes friends come by to see if I have returned. "Not yet," my dad always tells them. He says it as if I'm on my way home, just stuck in traffic. But the words aren't genuine; I can tell he is trying to keep friends and family from worrying.

"Emma? Emma, you're home!" she yells out, looking at me through the window.

There is no way; my mom can see me? I look at her and we stare at each other. A smile displays across her face, and I can feel the corner of my own lips rise in return. I want so badly to be alive to stay with my family, but I can't let my mom think everything is okay.

I run out of sight, hiding behind many of the trees that line the sides of my yard. Inside I hear my mom's chair groan as the legs rub against the hardwood floor. The front yard has two police cruisers and one man steps out, heading into the house. I focus my concentration as fast as I can, running full speed to his body.

The pulse of blood hits me like a freight train. The haunting isn't pleasant like it had been for Chepi. All the senses come to me in one overwhelming burst. The blood pulsing through the body I occupy, his lungs inhaling and exhaling, the itchy material of his uniform rubbing against his skin. He walks into the house I used to live in, as I try to place myself in this new body. The feeling of living again settles in, and I welcome the steady pulses of blood passing through veins, the warm feeling of life never changing but always remains magnificent.

Opening the door, the first thing I see is my mom at the large window in the dining room. She's looking for me.

Everyone has their full attention on my mom as she points out the window, telling everyone she has seen me, that I'm okay and alive—that I came home. But as the minutes pass, she waits at that window, expecting me to show my face again—or better yet, walk through the front door. Her face falls as I disappear once again, out of her reach.

I think she has finally lost it. The police officer thinks to himself.

Everyone is silent for a moment, trying to figure out what is going on.

"What?" my dad asks, hoping what she said was true, but knowing it isn't.

"Nothing...never mind," my mom says. She sits again, crosses her arms on the table, and rests her head there; all hope gone.

"Search the forest, find Amelia," I tell the police, wanting to quickly dispel the news.

"I think we should check the forest again. She might be out there," the police officer says, obeying my orders. Part of me wants to scold him for saying the words. It makes it sound as if he wants to check again, because my mom saw me. I don't want to raise anyone's hopes just to knock it down again.

The officer steps out the door, and two others follow in line. I want to tell the police to have my mom and dad come, but I know they won't be able to handle seeing me like that. They can hear the polished version of the story, only needing to know that I've passed.

Why am I searching again? We never find anything.

"Keep going, she's out there," I encourage as the officer takes the passenger seat along with his deputy, as they drive away. The thud of blood going through the man's system alarms me, having already forgotten what it feels like to be alive. I take in everything. The trees pass in a blur out of my peripheral vision as the cruiser speeds down the byway. Every now and then voices come over the police scanner, but the men don't pay much attention. I sit in the back of the officer's mind, only speaking commands when the cruiser goes in the wrong direction. Finally the sign I've been waiting for comes up. Sabbaday Falls.

"Pull over," I command.

"Try here," the officer I possess says, pointing to the sightseeing checkpoint next to a hiking trail. We come to a stop, and I let the officer take over his own body, as he wanders aimlessly.

The two men talk between themselves, completely unaware of my presence. In my mind I know they are getting closer. As they follow the dirt trail that lingers near the river, I can hear the waterfall in the distance. It's the facade to my death.

Fallen tree branches are crushed under my haunted officer's feet, and he's well aware of his surroundings, looking left and right for any sign of a lost girl.

My world stops for a moment when I see the end of our trail has come. This is it. My last chance to stop all this and turn the police around, so they'll never find my body. But instead I press forward. Behind the cover of foliage is the waterfall that holds my decaying body. The sound of rushing water is loud and clear now, announcing its glorious presence.

"Follow the end of the path," I say. They step through the greens and are greeted with flowing icy water that crashed into rocks. Within those rocks is a broken girl.

The only thing I can see is my brown hair strewn about. I'm mangled and contorted. The rocks around me hold my body and the water that rushes from the waterfall takes no mercy as it pushes against me, threatening to carry me farther downstream.

I force him to look away from my body, as I tell him what happened.

"Amelia Clarice Barton was walking in the woods and tripped. She fell into the waterfall and drowned. A freak accident." Then I left his mind.

I watch as the police examine my body and investigate the scene. The man I had just haunted tells his deputy the story of my death. They take pictures, and whisper about causes and how recently I have passed. It seems like hours pass as people in stark uniforms come and go. They never move my body, treating it like a crime scene. I feel like I'm watching an episode of CSI as they take samples from my body. I sit in the sidelines of the trees, watching, but not listening to what they say.

The investigation concludes for now, and they move my body away from the cold and bitter waterfall. As they place my body in a bag, I see my ripped clothing clings to my skin, broken bones contort my body, blood drains from my lifeless figure.

An ambulance comes, and uniformed EMTs take away my body. One man talks to the police officers—I can't make out what they're saying. Following the flashing lights of the ambulance, I venture away from the thick of the forest and come to the side of the road. As I walk closer, I see a woman tending to my body. She unzips the bag, looking down at my bloody face. The woman frowns, her eyes sad, as she runs a gloved hand down my face. She whispers something before again zipping the body bag. The woman closes the double doors of the ambulance as they prepare to drive off.

The police emerge from the woods and drive in the direction of my house. I follow the cruisers, noting how the ambulance goes in the opposite direction with my body, where it will endure further tests to find my cause of death.

The three police officers enter my house and ask my parents to sit down. My mom looks like she's just been crying as she claims her usual seat at the table. Both my parents wait, knowing there is news coming.

"We found her..." The police start.

"You did? Where is she? Is she okay?" my mom asks, hope now in her heart. Instantly she looks younger; with a smile on her face, all the weight of worry is off her shoulders.

"We found her body." The other police officer finishes. Quick, like a Band-Aid. That's the best way to give bad news.

"No! No, Emma is okay. I see her!" My mom points at me watching her. I'm standing at the window. How can she see me? I start to panic. Can everyone see me? I lie on the ground beneath the window while they look where I had just been standing.

They all come closer to the window, staring out into the forest, for some reason expecting to see me. The officers stand there with hope, even though they had just seen my body, dead and lifeless, sent off to a hospital morgue. How is it possible that I can be seen? I'm just a spirit now.

I have to get away; I can't watch my mom go through this. I either have to leave, or haunt someone and face their thoughts. As I peek through the window again, I see that everyone is occupied in the kitchen discussing something. My mom sits alone at the table, her head down. There's no sign of my dad for the moment, so I take the only opportunity I have.

I try to walk through the glass window, but it doesn't give. For whatever reason, objects in the real world are solid to me, but the more I tamper with the glass it starts to feel like gel in my hands. I try again, concentrating on manipulating the material to pass through. It works. The glass is an unwelcomed, cold sense. It passes through me like a thick, slow nuisance. Once I'm inside, my actions are quick as I step into my mom, brushing my hand against her shoulder. Her pulse is uncomfortable as I adjust to her body. Her skin feels warm, and I can feel the wet tears run down her face as she hides herself in her arms on the table. I'm not prepared for her thoughts as her hot and upset mind continues in a fast and unnatural pace.

No! No, Emma's not dead! I can see her!

Where is she? I just saw her. She was there at the window!

No, Emma can't be gone! She can't!

I can't stand it. My mom is screaming in her head that I'm alive. I can feel her pain as she hears the news. She wants to run from the kitchen and go into my room, hoping to find me there, waiting for a hug. The only thing that stops her from doing that now is the fact that she isn't sure if she can run. Her muscles feel weak and shaky, even as she sits here at the table. Her head is down, because she honestly doesn't have the strength or will to raise it.

"Emma is gone. She's never coming back," I tell my mom in a fierce tone.

Yes, she is! She's alive!

She repeats this over and over. A sharp pain goes through where my heart had once been, and it feels like I'm dying. I know that my mom loves me, always has. I also know I wish I had let her know that I loved her too. So I do this in the only way I know how.

"Emma loved you and always will," I whisper to her, hoping—just begging—for her to free her grasp on me and let go, so we can both go on.

Emma, please come back! I need you!

I want to scream, "Yes, I will!" But I can't tell her this; it will never come true. I take a deep breath and ensure my mom everything is going to be okay. I let each word come out harsher than intended as I coax my mom into believing them.

"You will go on without her, and you will be okay," I say as forceful as I possibly can.

No! I need Emma!

Her crying escalates, and she runs out of the room, pushed by some sort of adrenaline high. She passes my dad in the hallway, and he starts to follow but decides that she just needs time alone. She trips multiple times once she is out of sight and up the stairs. My mom lets out heaving sobs and loses her breath as she sinks into a painful cry that hurts both of us as we share the same body. She

manages to reach my room where my things are on the floor—
exactly as I had left them.

Emma, come back. Please, I will do anything.

I finally see the full extent of things. My bed is still unmade
the way I had left it; my dirty clothes waiting on the floor to be
picked up. My mom believes I'm coming back. She never thought of
the possibility of my death.

Please...please, come back...

My mom is begging now. How can I let this happen?
Through the window the sky begins to turn dark, telling me my time
today is almost up. She needs to let go.

"Emma will always be here, watching. She is your guardian
angel now. Emma will always be here in spirit. Remember that."

I leave my mom like that, sobbing in my room.

Chapter 12

Powers & Secrets

I stumble around and find my way back to Phantom Lagoon. It feels like I'm crying, but my eyes are dry. I still find myself rubbing them, like there is a tear to wipe away. I wanted to give my mom a hug so bad. I left her there on the floor to cry. Her only daughter is dead, and there is nothing she can do.

I walk into the lagoon and almost don't notice when Eliza comes up.

"I'm so sorry," she whispers. She steps forward, as if to hug me, but I go in the opposite direction away from her.

I peer down at the water of Phantom Lagoon. It's white and glowing from the full moon. It's amazing how beautiful this place can look and at the same time ruin so many lives. Looking around the forest, I see that everything is glowing from the moon tonight.

Eliza follows my gaze to the moon. "Some say that the moon is the heart of Phantom Lagoon. They say the mirrored rocks are from the moon, but I don't think the moon can cause that much sadness."

Eliza is frowning now—remembering something I suppose. I look at the moon closer, wondering if it really can cause all this. It's beautiful, just as Phantom Lagoon is. It seems like the moon is the possible cause of our problems.

"What do you think, Emma?" Eliza asks, looking at me now. "Is the moon too beautiful to cause any trouble?"

"Look around you, Eliza!" I'm surprised by the volume my voice takes. "This entire place is beautiful! Just because something is beautiful doesn't make it innocent."

Eliza looks down.

"Look, Eliza, I'm sorry. I've had a long day," I say quickly, hoping to make her feel better, but I know she deserves more than this.

She doesn't respond, and I walk away from everyone at Phantom Lagoon and toward a boulder. I sit down, letting out a deep breath and stare at the night sky—the moon shining over us.

The moon looks so bright. It has different shades of white and silver. I remember hearing stories of the man on the moon; that when you look at the craters, you can see a face. I see him now, looking down at me and smiling—at least this still remains in my world. I lost so much when I entered Phantom Lagoon—it's nice to see an old memory. Maybe the moon didn't cause this trouble, but something had to.

I stay like this the rest of the night, looking at the moon and thinking about my parents. I know my dad can handle this, but my mom? She looked so...lifeless. It wasn't like I had died, more like a part of her had died.

Eliza walks over to see if I'm okay. She sits down next to me but doesn't say anything.

"Eliza, you said humans can't see us," I say, watching the moon's reflection in the water of Phantom Lagoon.

She looks at me. "There are always exceptions. You, for an example, could see our souls because your soul was calling you, so it wanted you to see us. Other than that, if you aren't being called by a soul, humans can't see us."

"My mom can see me," I say in a numb voice. "She looked right at me when I was at my house. Twice. She even said, out loud, that she could see me."

"Are you sure?"

"Yes, she told my dad and the police that she saw me at the window. I had to haunt her to get her to stop," I tell her.

"Maybe it's your..." Eliza starts to say, but trails off into her own mind.

"My what?" I look at her now, more curious than ever.

Eliza thinks for a minute, finding a way to word something correctly. "Well, some of us have powers. Simple things that let us interact with the human world. They don't differ much. It's very common to have people with the same powers. Sometimes we have an extra ability to use in the human world—to be seen, heard, or touched."

I can actually feel a smile forming on my face as I clutch my stone in my hand, waiting to hear more. "Does everyone have powers?"

"Mostly. Some don't or haven't found theirs yet," she says, matter-of-factly, looking forward.

"What's your power?" I ask, wanting, almost begging to hear more.

"I can appear to be human. I can be physically there while others can't. I go to school like everyone else. I love having this power because I don't have to be just an Essence," she says, smiling. "I can be partly human. It's rare to have that—to have all abilities, the only limit being Phantom Lagoon calling me back at night."

"So is my power to appear to other humans?"

"It seems so. You should test it. See if humans can hear you. Try to touch them too. You may have more than one power to interact with the human world like me."

The next morning I try to make a plan, some sort of goal for this day that can help my mom let me go, but things struggle to come into place. I think about showing myself to my mom and what may happen if she can see me. I don't know what to do. There is a whole list of options to test my powers, but the safest ones don't involve my mom. Pushing aside the idea of powers, I realize I can haunt my mom again and show her something; something that was never meant for her to see. My drawings.

Ever since I've turned into an Essence, I have no desire to draw anything. I have a feeling that I'll never have that urge again. But that doesn't mean I have to forget about it. Maybe this will be the one thing that will let my mom know who I really was—who I really am.

Later in the day I reach my house. It's comparably quiet since all the police cars and family and friends have left. I see my dad isn't home either. That can make things a lot easier if my mom can see me; my dad won't think my mom is crazy, like everyone seemed to believe yesterday.

Using the spare key under the mat, I enter the house, quiet and still. I decide to take the time alone to make a necklace to hold my soul. I go to my dad's desk where there are things like wire and string. I take the long silver wire and wind it around the stone over and over for safe measure. I shuffle through the desk looking for wire cutters and remember that my dad put them in the garage. Once I'm there, I hunt through the toolbox and find them easily, cutting the last of the wire and tucking the remainder in, so there are no sharp points. When I go back inside, I look through all the drawers to find some sort of string. I stumble across my mom's small sewing kit, and see a leather cord and other bits of fabric mixed in. I untangle the leather and tie it around the stone.

My necklace hangs against my collarbone as I walk up the stairs, listening carefully as I track my mom's location—whimpering in my room. When I walk in, I see she is asleep, but it's clear she's having a nightmare. She's sprawled across my bed, face embracing the covers. For a moment, I think that I might be able to solve this problem; that I can show my mom I'm okay, and she'll be able to move on. Maybe if she can see me and keep this whole thing a secret, everything can work out—but only as a last resort. I will have to try my best to make my mom unknown to this world.

I walk across the room and over to where my mom lays asleep. I can hear her mumbling to herself, and I'm tempted to shake her awake. Instead I stretch out my hand and step into her body.

"Wake up," I tell her.

When she stirs awake, she is confused until she remembers why she is in my room. The events of the day before wash into her mind as she begins to cry again.

Emma. Emma. Emma. She repeats my name over and over in her head.

"There's something Emma wants to show you," I tell her.

Emma wants to show me something?

"Yes, now go over to her closet."

Once she gains her bearings, she crawls out of bed and toward the closet door. She stretches out her hand and turns the knob with great care—it's like she thinks something is going to jump out at her. First she is confused and starts to look through my things. When she finally sees my drawings hidden in the back, her face is filled with awe.

She doesn't do anything at first. She just sits on the closet floor holding the drawings, but then a tear escapes her eyes. My mom opens my sketchpad and comes across drawings of our home in Florida, and her mind is flooded with memories of me when I was little.

The drawing she holds now is of our backyard tree house. It's not very high or big, but it was mine. When I was small, it was the only place I could be alone, because my parents couldn't fit through the door. When I had grown out of it, my parents wanted to tear it down, but I wouldn't let them. After that, I drew the little house in the tree, because I knew one day it would not be there. I wonder if it still stands.

Did my little Amelia draw these? my mom thinks, running her hand over the paper. She remembers all the days I had spent in that tree. How during the summer I refused to come out, because I was protecting my kingdom. How I had made her bring my lunch to me. How I sometimes slept there during those long summer days. She didn't mind though—she loved me and the imagination I possessed.

"Yes," I say.

Why didn't she tell me? They're beautiful.

"She was afraid. After the art classes when she was small, she feared her art being criticized. Emma kept them hidden, even if she thought they were wonderful."

Oh, Emma, I'm so sorry. You have a gift; share it with the world! She clutches onto the drawings as if they are her saving grace. A new set of tears comes as my mom starts to look through my drawings, each one different in their own way. The one she pauses the longest on is of our old house. In her head, there are the memories that come from that house; the one I grew up in.

I know that, if I'm going to show myself, this is the time to do it. I wonder if she will be able to keep a secret like this from everyone. "What would you do to see Emma again?"

Anything.

"Would you keep a secret from everyone, including your husband?" My voice drops as if I'm crying.

Yes. She's so sure, so fearless.

"You can't tell anyone where she is. You'll be the only one who will be able to know." My voice comes out ragged and breathless as I realize I'm about to be reunited with my mom. This act is selfish. My mom doesn't need to be reunited with me; I'm the one who needs this.

Her face is bright as she reassures me. *I won't tell anyone. I promise.*

I step out of my mom's body to reveal myself. The warmth of her body leaves me, and it's like peeling off a strip of tape as my being begs to remain in a body. It's something that didn't happen with the police officer or Chepi. Maybe because this is my mother, it's harder to leave her body. But I finally do, and the lack of all my senses that greets me is a cold, hard slap in the face into an unwelcoming world.

Her mouth drops open, and she runs at me for a hug, right through me, reminding me that she is alive and I am dead. But she can see me. It doesn't matter if I'm not there physically.

My mom turns around to look at me. I thought she would be scared of me—that she may want to run away from her ghost daughter—but she just looks at me. Then she smiles. That's when the crying starts. My mom falls to the floor, face in her hands.

I watch as her shoulders go up and down, her entire body shaking. I want to approach her, but I know that I physically can't.

"Emma," she whispers, wiping away tears, a smile forming on her face.

"You can't tell anyone," I tell her again. I'm ready to leave, that maybe she'll think it was a dream. But when I see her smile at the sound of my voice, I know I made the right choice.

"Emma, is that really you?" my mom asks, reaching out to me.

"Yes, but... I'm not alive anymore—or dead. I'm a ghost now, or an Essence," I say, struggling with the words.

"What does that mean?" she asks, getting back on her feet now, never taking her eyes off me.

"I'm never going to Heaven. I'm here on this Earth for the rest of my existence." I didn't want to tell her this. I want her to think that I'm in Heaven, but the words slip from my mouth.

"How did this happen?" she asks, traveling back to my bed, sitting down and patting next to her for me to sit.

"It doesn't happen to everyone, but it's long and hard to explain. I can guarantee you though, that when you die, you will go to Heaven. Just stay away from the forest," I say, sitting farther away from her than she likes.

"Emma, please, just tell me."

"No, promise me that you'll stay out of the forest."

We sit in silence as she thinks things over. "All right, Emma, I promise. But are you going to come back again?" my mom asks, the fear of me leaving again undisguised in her eyes.

"Of course, why do think I told you?" I say laughing.

My mom breaks down crying, this time with tears of joy. I hear the door open down the stairs. My dad is home, and I have to leave before he too knows the secret.

"Dad's home. Remember you can't tell anyone. Not even him," I tell her, for a moment wondering why my dad shouldn't know. But having my mom know is risky enough; I don't understand what the consequences of telling the secret are just yet.

As I leave, she looks at me one last time and smiles, finally relieved that I'm not gone forever.

Chapter 13

A Lost Father

"Emma?" Eliza comes from the thick trees that line the lagoon. She steps away and into the sunlight that shines through between the tall greens. "Could she see you?" She's apprehensive as she speaks, seeing something in my face but not knowing entirely what it is.

I smile. "Yeah, she could."

She's thoughtful for a few seconds, processing what this means. Then the question comes that I was waiting for. "Did you tell her to forget?"

"No," I say. "I can't do that to my mom. Not after everything she's been through. I'm not going to make her learn her only daughter is dead all over again."

Something ignites within Eliza, and it's as if I can see her eyes ablaze with a hidden passion, but she still manages to hide most of the anger as she speaks in a low tone. "What did you do?"

"I told her."

I expected her to lash out at me, but she's brought to utter silence. Eliza stares at me, completely bewildered, her jaw held open waiting to form words. "Emma!" she finally says. She speaks to me like a toddler who is picking up something that could hurt me.

"Eliza, you're not the one who has to watch their mom fall apart over their death." My voice sounds more like a whine when the words come, but it doesn't matter. What I said means something to Eliza, and it hit a nerve.

"Don't you dare say that," she says, her shock again to be replaced with anger. "You're lucky to have a mother that cares enough to show that emotion. She's not afraid to show that kind of weakness. You should be honored."

Eliza walks away, pulling her arms around her torso. She follows a path that leads away from the lagoon and toward a nearby waterfall that is within earshot.

"Eliza!" I shout out her name, demanding her to stop.

She turns to face me quickly, exposing her face that is contorted by the emotions of pain and fear. "Did you tell her that you're an Essence?" Her arms are still wrapped around her; she just seems so frail and vulnerable.

"She doesn't know what it means exactly," I say, mesmerized my Eliza's raw emotion.

She takes a deep breath, growing inpatient. "Does she know of Phantom Lagoon?"

"No." The word is a whisper, and from the distance between us, I wasn't sure if Eliza even heard, but she nods and continues to walk away.

"She won't tell anyone," I say, mostly to myself.

"That's not the point! She has free will, Emma. She's human!" Eliza shouts to me, but neither stops nor turns to look at me.

I approach at a slow pace, but the sound of my steps seems deafening. I know my cover has been blown once my foot catches on a tree root that shoots out from the ground. A few feet away Eliza sits on a boulder facing the waterfall that cascades down from a small cliff on the side of the mountain.

"I'm sorry." Her voice quivers as she says the words. I travel the last of the distance between us and join her on the large rock that is just shy of making contact with the water that streams around us.

I turn to Eliza, but she refuses to look at me. Instead she chooses to face forward, not really seeing anything but maintaining an unending gaze.

"What you did today...it's the same thing my father did," she finally says, a coy smile playing across her face, yet it manages to disappear just as quickly as it came.

"What do you mean?"

She takes a breath, her body shaking in the process. "How you told your mom, because you knew that she wasn't going to accept you as being gone. Well...that's the same thing my father had done." Her eyes light up for a moment. "My father died when I was fourteen. My mother and I came home one day, and he didn't. We waited and waited, but he never came back. We called the police, and they started searching. Nothing."

Eliza looks like she is struggling to speak, her hands fidgeting with her words, but she continues. "Soon everyone gave up hope and started to accept that my father was dead. My mother and I never stopped searching for him. Until later."

She stops and closes her eyes, like she's trying to find the strength to continue her story. She reflexively wipes her eyes before continuing. "The police came to our house with evidence. They had found a car on the side of the street. It was my father's. There was no sign that he had been there in days, but there was a trail near the road. My father hunts in forests all the time. He loved to hunt.

"The police followed the trail and found what they were looking for. They showed my mother the pictures of what they had found that day. By that time, my mother had already lost all hope, so it wasn't as hard for her. I wouldn't accept it though. I remember running up to my room that night, screaming to have my father back. I didn't eat. I didn't do anything. My mother called in doctors to come help me.

"My mother told me that she was going to send me to a 'camp.' Somewhere I could forget about what had happened and have fun. I told her that I wouldn't go, and that someday I would get better. She said that I had to, that it would be good for me. The next day before my mom came home from work, I ran away. I didn't want to live anymore. I found the spot where my father's car had been and followed the trail the police had traced, and found where my father's body had been." Eliza pauses again, taking a deep breath—remembering.

"At that moment I could sense something. I could feel my father. At first I thought it was because I was where he had died, but later I found out otherwise. It was my father. He was there watching me, protecting me. Then I heard him.

"'Go back home,' he had commanded. I felt myself jolt backward unintentionally. I know now that my father had been haunting me. I didn't want to leave, not when I could be with him.

"'Go back home, Eliza!' he had commanded again. That time I didn't move, but I knew it was my father talking.

"'Daddy?' I had asked aloud. Everything was silent after that. I couldn't feel my father's presence anymore, and it crushed me.

"It was getting dark, and I was tired, so I just lay on the ground—I was beyond caring. I woke up in the middle of the night in a police car. The next day my mother punished me and said I was leaving for camp in the morning. I went on strike by locking myself in my room. I didn't eat or drink anything. I knew it was useless. There was no solution. My mother was pounding on my door, trying to convince me to come out. I was in my room for hours, refusing to leave for anything. I kept my lights off and windows closed, there in my own darkness." Eliza looks to the sky, expecting to see something. She seems entranced in her world, seemingly trapped there in her own torture, as she stares into the night sky. After a few seconds she sighs and continues.

"Then it happened again. I could sense my father's presence." She smiles at the simple memory.

"'Go see your mother, Eliza. Go eat.'

"'Daddy?' I had asked again. I expected my father to disappear like the day before, but to my surprise he stayed, so I asked again.

"'Daddy, is that you?' I waited and finally he answered.

"'Yes.'

"I asked him where he had gone, and he said he couldn't answer. He said that it was a secret. That no one else could know about him, not even my mother. He told me to be brave and that everything was going to be okay.

"Things were different after that. My father came every day to make sure I was okay, which I was. I was okay—but that's all—not happy, but not sad either. I told myself I could survive this. But my family was torn after my father's death. My mother had eventually started dating again, and she was now working two jobs. I never got to see her much anymore. This is how it went for a few weeks, my father visiting me in secret and my mother working. Whenever my father wasn't around, I was alone. It felt like I was the only one in the world, and it scared me. I didn't know what to do with myself. My father always had to leave at night. He wouldn't tell me why.

"One night after my father left, I couldn't sit still. My mother was working her night shift, so I was home alone. I went outside to get fresh air and go for a walk. I didn't know where I was going, but I knew that I wasn't staying in the house. Eventually I came here. I don't know how, but I did. I was at Phantom Lagoon. It was so beautiful the way the moon lit the entire forest. I could sense a presence, not just one, but many. I knew that this should have scared me, but it didn't. One of the strongest senses was my father's. Then I saw the stones in the water. They were so beautiful, it didn't seem possible.

"I was drawn to them, not like you were, Emma—I could've stopped if I wanted, but I didn't. I had given up on life by then. So I picked one up, and when I woke up, I saw my father for the first time in months. I was so happy at the time, until I saw his face. He looked like he was in pain. I thought he would be happy that I was one of him now—an Essence! Then he told me what we were. It was my worst nightmare—to be here, never to die and move on. I had given up on life. I wanted it to end, but it was just the beginning. The beginning of an eternal life.

"My mother found out about my death. She took it the same way as she did for my father's—if not better. Out of everything that had happened to me, this is what set me off. I was mad at her for not crying for me. I wanted to haunt her and take revenge, but my dad told me that was wrong. When my mother was little, her father had abused her every time she showed weakness. My mother was hit every time she cried. Soon she showed no emotion; even if she wanted to. Now instead of crying, she just goes into solitude. She hides her pain from everyone including herself. I felt bad for ever being mad at her, but my father told me there was no way I could've known—my mother didn't want me to know; she thought it was another sign of weakness."

A twinge of guilt eats away at me as I realize what Eliza had been talking about when she said I was lucky to have my mother care so much about me. I can't even imagine what it would be like to pass and have my mom cruise through the event with ease. The feelings of abandon and neglect linger in my being just from thinking of what it must be like.

"Eliza, I'm so sorry. I had no idea about your mom..." But she stops me before I can continue.

"It's not something you should have known. It's okay to want to tell your mother. It's because you love her," she says, turning to face me for the first time since she started her story.

I nod, understanding but also wanting her to continue.

Her gaze rests on the space in front of her again. "After I became an Essence, everything was okay. My father and I could finally be together. It was like that for eight years. Then one day my mother went to the hospital, because she had been in a car accident. My father was gone the entire day, watching over her. I stayed here at Phantom Lagoon, because I couldn't stand to see my mother like that—dying, surrounded by her own blood, knowing there was nothing I could do to help.

"Later that day she passed away. I expected my father to come back, but he didn't. I had lost him again. I hated myself for not going with him. My father disappeared, just like so many of us do.

"After he disappeared, I wanted to forget everything and start over. But you never truly forget. I tried to disconnect myself. I dyed my hair red, because before I had dark brown hair, exactly like my father's. Whenever I looked in a mirror, I would remember him—and it hurt. So I dyed my hair. I regret it now. That was the only connection I had left. Sometimes I have a hard time remembering what he looks like. But whenever I do," Eliza says, fingering her necklace, warming it in her hand, "I just look to the Heavens and hope he's there with my mother—even if I can't join them. At least my true hair color made me feel a part of them, but I don't anymore. As an Essence we don't grow, so I can't get my hair back to its original color. I could dye it again, but it's not the same."

Eliza looks up at me, the pain written clearly across her face. Her greatest weakness is displayed in front of me, and she does nothing to hide it. In this state she appears as a completely different person.

"Sometimes I just wish I could disappear too. Ever since my father left, I've been wishing this. I've waited so long for it to come true." She puts her head into her hands and again starts to cry her tearless sobs.

"Do you think that disappearing is the only way out of here?" I finally ask, once she calms down.

"I don't know. Some think that, if you save a life, it's sort of a ticket out of here. That's why I tried so hard to save you. I guess I'll never know." She shrugs, having given up on finding a way out. "But it's not like when you disappear. When you disappear...you cease to exist." Her mouth trembles the slightest bit. She clears her throat, shaking away any fear that has built inside her. "But saving a life could mean passing on. It could mean Heaven. We just can't know."

"Has anyone ever saved a life and moved on?"

"Maybe. If they did save someone's life, they might have moved on, but none of us knows if it works."

Chapter 14

Testing Limits

Somewhere in the woods outside of Phantom Lagoon, I wander aimlessly. The summer air is moist, and my footsteps are quiet in the grass. The area is bright, lit by the sun, with thick greens hanging over like a natural canopy. The atmosphere is a personal sanctuary, but I can't stop my mind from reeling with worry. Finally I succumb and kneel to the ground.

The smell of moist dirt fills my nose, and I let it calm me.

When I was little, my mom brought me to the beach one day instead of doing our usual homeschool studies. She used it as a field trip to learn about the different ecosystems of the ocean. That was the first day I saw a starfish. It was small, orange, and at that time, it was about the size of my hand—which would probably be just my palm now. I remember my mom when she found the starfish in one of the tide pools in the rocks.

"Amelia, come look at this!" My chubby six-year-old legs carried me over in a rush, eager to see my mom's discovery.

Upon walking over, I saw the unidentified animal. To my eyes it was unreal. A star! An animal the shape of a star! It was a thing of dreams. "It's so pretty, Mommy!"

"It's a starfish," she told me, coaxing the little sea creature off the surface of a shell. "Here, hold out your hands."

I did so with the utmost care, laying my palms flat for the beautiful creature. My mom placed it in the center of my hand and kissed my forehead. "There's a lot of little creatures like this in the tide pool, Amelia. You just have to find them."

The living star moved slightly in my hand, and I swear it glowed, but maybe it was my child eyes playing tricks on me.

Then it dawned on me. "I need to put him in the water, Mommy, or he'll die." I rushed over to her, anxious not to hurt the creature that was more fairy tale than real. I held out my hands to my mom, offering her the starfish, so she could place him back in the water to live. "He's a fishy. Without water he'll die. Hurry!"

My mom bent down to take the starfish, but she didn't put him back. I remember this aggravating me. She was going to let the magical fish die.

"No, it's not that kind of fish. He can't swim, but he does live in the water," she told me.

"But how does he move?"

She smiled, pointing to one of the five points of the starfish. "Those. On the bottom there are little things that act like feet. There are hundreds of them that help to carry the starfish where he needs to go. He's slow, so if you watch him, it won't seem like he's moving."

"Oh." That's all I could come up with. How could a thing that small have hundreds of feet? I was bigger than the starfish, and I only had two feet. "How does he find his family if he's slow?"

My mom smiled at me and returned the starfish to the water. "Sometimes the world just brings us together when we can't do it ourselves."

Looking around the forest, I see how alone I am—more alone than I have ever been. There are no lost souls, no animals, no humans; nothing. Inside me I'm falling apart, coming unhinged. Everything that's happened to me is out of the ordinary. I try to think of what a strong person might do, but I can't. The thing is, this is something that very few people go through, and those who do are an Essence. They can't share their stories of how they got through the rough times and came out on top. The truth is that I don't think there's a top. As an Essence, we're just here. There's no real meaning to our existence.

That's when I hear the laughing.

The laughing from a child, so innocent and small, nothing more to worry about in life than getting that one toy.

I follow the sound, looking for the little piece of joy. The closer I come, the more I can hear. The parents, also laughing, are calling out to someone named Kenzie.

Coming across an opening in the trees, I make sure I'm hidden. I look around and see several campers and RVs. There's a little girl with blond ringlets; she is so small and fragile, but looks like she can take on the world. She's running around in circles, tripping multiple times, while her parents chase her. The girl looks to be around the age of three.

I come in closer but remain unseen in front of a bush. It feels as if I'm watching a lost home video. Something ignites in me, and I instantly feel warmer as I watch this young family.

"I'm gonna get you!" yells the mom as she lunges toward Kenzie.

The dad is standing behind a bush, waiting to pounce at the right moment, like a cat hunting prey. The mom forces Kenzie to run in front of that bush, and the dad attacks. He springs at her, holding her down, and she giggles as the mom starts to tickle her. Kenzie's giggling gets so loud it turns into screaming.

"Stop! Stop! I gotta go pee!" she says in between her laughing. The dad releases his hold and starts laughing even harder as the mom runs Kenzie to the bathroom before it's too late.

After a few minutes of waiting, the mom returns with Kenzie. They are laughing and having fun.

I can picture myself joining them, a big sister playing with Kenzie. I want to be a part of their family, but there is no room for me. Jealousy consumes me as they laugh in their carefree world. How easily humans can forget how lucky they are. Their world could be stripped away at any moment, but here they are running wild.

The mother leaves after a while to make food in their RV. About twenty minutes later she announces that their meal is ready.

Kenzie and her dad go into the RV for dinner. Only then do I notice that it is getting dark; the sky is orange and purple, pink shades in between. I decide to stay, not as an attempt at suicide—I can't do that to my mom—but as an experiment. No one knows what happens when you disappear or how far you can push your boundaries before your soul leaves the Earth for what can only be thought of as forever.

As the family eats at the picnic table, I watch the sun go down through the trees, the last of the rays licking at the branches, leaving the forest to glow with an orange hue. I find myself monitoring my breathing more. I have to concentrate in order to inhale normally. As it gets darker, my breathing turns into gasping. The cord around my neck grows heavy, and the stone hangs like the weight of the world. It becomes hard to stay hidden in the trees as my breathing becomes louder, so I have to back away a few paces, the rustle of brush only a slight mask to my struggles for air.

"Campfire! Campfire!" Kenzie starts to run in circles again while her dad makes the fire. In the dark, from my distance I can see him lighting matches, and putting paper and dry pine in the fire pit. From inside the RV, I can see the mom tending to the dishes at the sink near the window, while she watches her husband and daughter.

I back up more, as I begin to feel as if I'm being crushed. Without knowing it, I begin to lower to the ground until my back is to a tree. The familiar scent of the moist, mossy bark does little as my mind is losing its hold on the world. The small contact as my torso touches the ground makes me lose control, and I let out a scream. It's quick, but full of enough fear and pain to attract attention.

Kenzie locks gazes with me as I fall to the ground, clamping my mouth shut. Her dad also hears the scream but can't locate its origin. I know Kenzie can see me as I sit, my entire body bracing for oncoming danger, but I also know that Kenzie's family heard the scream.

It feels like someone is holding me down, hanging a knife above me as a threat of what is to come. My scream is muffled by my hand covering my mouth, but it can be heard if someone listens. Kenzie's expression tells me that she can hear me. She gazes at me from between the trees. In my throat my voice is strong, but the only sound that comes is a quiet whine. Closing my eyes, I lose my breath. The cord around my neck grows heavier, until I can't receive any air. My vision blurs, just as it had when I was human and my other half had been calling me to Phantom Lagoon. It's happening all over again. Just like in the NICU, it's as if the umbilical cord is tight around my neck. The only thing left for me to do is wait for the doctors. But there are none here for me. Instead I lay in the forest, a victim of my own decision.

I know that I should be running to the safety of Phantom Lagoon, but I can't break the hold of Kenzie's eyes. She looks at me, not with fear, but worry. She turns to her parents for a moment, seeing their attention is occupied somewhere else, and sets her pace as she comes toward me. I force myself to remain quiet, as I dig my fingers into the ground.

I have no desire to leave for safety, feeling the pain consume me. At some point I tell myself that this is okay; maybe it's for the best. But my mom's face enters my mind. I see her on our last camping trip together. It was when we were a whole family. My soul was threatening to take me away to the forest, but even with the danger looming behind my back, I could enjoy that time with my family. I remember the cold water that I had jumped into—it felt like needles going into my skin, but it's nothing compared to what I feel now.

My fingers go to my neck looking for my stone, following the choking sensation that lingers on my throat. Panic sets in when I realize my stone has disappeared. My soul is gone, and I'm next. My neck is unadorned except for the pressure bringing me closer to the ground as I lose my bearings.

Kenzie is still walking toward me when I break into a run. There's a quick glimpse of her face, fear from my sudden movement as I jump up. She stops at the edge of the forest, right before the trees grow dense. I stumble over roots and rocks, make mistakes, wrong turns, and fall into small rivers and streams. The water soaks my clothing, making it heavier as my run slows to a walk full of wasted energy.

Still I run even faster, forgetting the hurt, the pain; only that I need to survive. Not for myself but for my mom. My life matters very little, but I can't leave thinking that my mom will slip into a world of sorrow over my death. The closer I come to Phantom Lagoon, the easier it is to breathe. Although the crushing weight around my throat never lets up, I find the strength to go on, to find a reason.

I'm surprised at how fast I'm able to get back. Familiar trees and landmarks begin to appear, showing me the way to safety. I run even faster, faster than I could've imagined.

With the new adrenaline, I start a hysterical laughter. It could've been a near-death experience, but here I am, laughing like it's nothing more than a race home with friends. I feel so free, like nothing matters; that running can solve all the problems in the world.

I plow through the fence of trees that are around Phantom Lagoon and fall to the ground. My senses pound around me, and the world spins in a sense of vertigo. Everyone stares as I lay in the dirt, still partially laughing. Eliza is the first to approach me.

"Emma! Are you okay?" she screams, almost, as she scans me for any sign of injury.

With a cough, only a single word forms with my voice. "Wow."

Chapter 15

The Truth

"You're so stupid! I can't believe you almost got yourself killed! Do you know how close you came to being dead for good today?"

Eliza has been going on ever since I got back, and she shows no signs of letting up.

"Emma! Look at me! Do you want to die? You went out of your way to make sure your mom knew you were alive, and now you go out and almost get yourself killed!"

I sigh, knowing it's useless to explain; she won't listen anyway. "Eliza, I wasn't trying to get myself killed. I was just trying to...change things," I mumble under my breath, hoping she doesn't hear the last part.

"What are you talking about?" Eliza asks, looking directly at me.

"I just needed to get away and understand things, okay? That's it. I went too far, and when the sun went down, I started to run back."

She lowers her voice, but stays stern. "Emma, tell me the truth. What were you doing out there?" The question is simple, but her eyes tell me a different story.

"I'm sorry," I say. "I didn't mean for anything to happen. I just wanted to see how far I could go."

"And then what?"

Die? Maybe I would have been lucky enough to move on.

She looks at me, waiting for an answer I won't give—not with everyone in the lagoon watching us. I avoid Eliza's gaze and stare at everyone else instead. When I make eye contact with them, they look away, but only temporarily, until they turn back to watch.

"Emma, come with me." She doesn't give me a chance to respond. She takes me by the arm, moving toward the cave behind the pool of rocks.

"Why are you taking me here?" I ask, trailing behind. I try to drag my feet, but she just tugs my arm harder.

"Because nobody goes here."

I start to pull in the opposite direction. "Eliza, please. I can't look at what's in there. Can't we go somewhere else?"

"Not if you want to be alone," she says with one final step into the cave. I continue to try to escape, but Eliza has a good grip on me.

The crystal lining the walls shimmers at the momentary sunlight and distracts from the bodies within, but when the ferns fall over the entrance, they close us off. Inside the cave it's dark; but everywhere I look, there are faces of the dead. Having lived in Phantom Lagoon for a while, I can recognize some of the faces, sharing the same unchanged qualities, forever preserved in this cave. My breathing echoes and travels down the expanse of rock and crystal. Eliza guides me deeper into the cave. We make a different turn in the path, away from where Eliza's body is hidden in an endless sleep. In front of us there is a small trickle of water as we round a corner and come to a small pool where the cave stops. It's a dead end, but water flows from cracks in the walls into a pocket of water only a few feet wide. Eliza lets go of me, and I stay where I am.

"I come here sometimes when I really need to be alone. Nobody else likes to make the trip—not if they have to walk past their own pale faces." Eliza sits down, and I see the ground has changed to a soft white powder at the edge of the water. She dips her hands in the pool, making ripples with her fingers.

I lean on the wall closest to her and sit down, but I stay away from the water. It looks like liquid crystal and is thicker than water as Eliza runs her hand through it.

"It's not a liquid. Nobody knows what it is. It's just one of Phantom Lagoon's wonders."

It's amazing how she looks at Phantom Lagoon. It's caused her so much pain, but she still thinks it's beautiful.

"You can tell me what happened today, Emma. I'm not going to judge you. The first days here are the hardest. You try your best to do what's right, but everyone still gives you a hard time about it. It's like high school."

"I guess that's one way to put it," I mumble. But she's right; it is just like high school.

"Emma, I don't want you to kill yourself."

I sigh, hearing the words I knew Eliza was trying to express earlier. "I'm not trying to kill myself."

"If that's what you want to tell yourself, then go ahead, but I know you better than you think, Emma. I can see the pain in your eyes. I know what it's like. I've been in same position before."

"Really?"

"Not anymore, but after my father disappeared from Phantom Lagoon...it was hard. After that I knew he was truly gone, and when I found out my mother had died the same day—it was unbearable. I was alone, and it felt like I was falling apart. I didn't want to live anymore. Unlike you, I didn't test my limits. I knew that my father wouldn't want that. I did come close once. I was pretending to be human and went to the nearest city. It was stupid, really. I tried to get myself killed by walking in traffic, almost causing accidents. Then I realized that, in trying to kill myself, I might also kill others at the same time. I didn't want that—to know that it was my fault that somebody else died because of me."

"Did you try other ways?" I ask. "Would it even work if we killed ourselves as if we were humans?"

"I doubt it will work. I don't even know why I tried," Eliza whispers. She dries off her hands in the sand and folds her arms across her chest like she is cold.

"So what did you do?" I ask.

"I came back."

Eliza looks like she is losing control over her emotions. You can tell she still misses her family. Eliza is able to gain composure again and stares me straight in the eyes to make sure I'm listening.

"Emma, everyone goes through this here. They might not want to admit it, but they do. When you arrive, your first instinct is to get out. You take the road of suicide. Nobody wants to live forever apart from those we love. Witnessing your family's and friends' reactions when they realize you're dead, watching as they try to cope with the pain and loss, seeing your family and friends die years later, then knowing that you will never see them again, because you're still stuck here on Earth.... It's excruciating."

"Why do they all hate me so much, if they've done the same thing?"

"They know the consequences of telling the secret. Some have done the same as you, just as my dad. Eventually they'll follow you here and become part of this." Eliza pauses and looks at the bodies that line the cave walls behind our backs. "It's considered murder. There's no stopping it once a human's here. They will pick up a rock from the lagoon." Eliza turns to face me, making sure she has my attention. "Emma, they'll get over it eventually—the watching eyes will stop—but if your mom ever follows you here, it will get worse."

"Did they think of your father as a murderer when you followed him here?"

"Yes," Eliza whispers, almost too quiet to hear. "They wouldn't even let me near him when I first came here. It wasn't his fault. It was mine."

Eliza starts to walk away into a small tunnel that breaks off before the end of the cave. I follow, wanting to make sure she is okay. She crawls inside and kneels down next to a stone the size of her torso that looks like it has something carved into it.

David Wingsett

1935–1993

A beloved father who never let go.

"It's not his real grave stone, just something I put here in memory of him. The date is when he disappeared from Phantom Lagoon."

I crawl in beside her; it's tight but I see the grave that's nothing more than carved stone. "I'm sorry, Eliza. I'll make sure that my mom doesn't follow me."

I sit next to her outside the tunnel where there is more room; we stay like that until neither of us can keep our eyes open any longer. Oddly I feel safe.

Chapter 16

Pink

Eliza and I awaken to someone yelling and shaking us by the shoulders. "Get outside now! A human's in Phantom Lagoon!" Opening my eyes, I see our messenger is a dark-haired boy, younger than me in his physical appearance but acting as if he had the higher authority. As Eliza stirs awake, the boy leaves the cave, running back outside.

It takes me a moment to place what's going on. Beside me Eliza struggles to her feet, still groggy from sleep. She runs out after the boy. Then the information sinks in. A human—in Phantom Lagoon. It could be anyone, but after Eliza's story, I'm nearly convinced it's my mom who maybe followed me into the forest, even after my warnings.

I jump to my feet, stumbling most of the way over jutting rocks and loose sand. At the end of the cave I stop. Here in Phantom Lagoon lays a girl, golden ringlets saturated in water as she lies limp in the sand. Someone I don't know drags her body from the lagoon and lifts her to position her small frame against a rock. The stranger walks away silently, letting others look at the small girl to see if anyone can make connections as to who she is. People shake their heads; the face is unfamiliar. But I know her. Her name is Kenzie.

I step forward, lifting her head off the rock. Her face is perfectly unharmed, but it lies in a trance of sleep. "Kenzie, please, no, this can't be happening." This little girl, no more than a stranger to me, feels lifeless in my arms.

Trying to remember anything I learned about first aid, I check her vital signs, trying to find a pulse. It's there. A small, faint pulse of blood going through her body, but it's there. I put my head near her face and feel her cool breath. She's okay. Kenzie is still alive; her body is dead weight in my arms, but her vital signs are there.

"You know her?" asks a voice. I turn, placing Kenzie back against the rock. It's the boy that had woken me and Eliza. He looks ten, wearing old blue-jean overalls with a tan and dirty long-sleeved shirt underneath.

"I was watching her family yesterday," I say, looking back at Kenzie, seeing her chest rise and fall. She's human, but it's like I can see the life draining out of her. Kenzie's pink. Flush cheeks fade away to a pale sick face, and she frowns even though she is in a sleep. It's as if her spirit is aware that something is happening.

"Did they see you?" he continues to question.

I turn back to the boy. I'm not sure if it was the simple fact that I'm not a morning person or if it's that the boy just doesn't rub off on me well, but I can feel the anger build up inside me as he continues to speak.

"Does it matter? She's here now," I say, trying to get him to either go away or help me keep Kenzie alive, as a human.

I take her hand, being careful as I pry her fingers loose, checking her hands. They are empty. A smile crosses my face, the relief is overwhelming. I push her curls out of her face as they cling together in ringlets, because she had been in the lagoon's water.

"You'll be okay," I say, looking to the pool of water with the mirrored stones that chose to spare Kenzie.

The boy steps into my line of view. "It's too late. She already found one. It's already turning her soul that color." He says the blasé information so obvious to him, because he now holds the stone. I take it from him as he displays it, as if it's some treasured prize. Whether I want to believe him or not, it was true; the mirror stone now held a pink hue.

My heart drops.

Kenzie. She's so small and new to this world. She doesn't deserve to take the form of an Essence. I hold the stone within my fingers like it's my own, keeping it safe while the small stranger of a girl lies asleep, as she leaves her human life and enters this new forbidden world.

I turn the stone around in my hand. "How do you determine soul color?" I ask, watching the color of Kenzie's soul shine through the stone.

"Don't you know anything?" He starts laughing. In a way he reminds me of my little cousin. He's ten, and this boy looks to be the same age—maybe younger. I can tell he won't be helping me in any way—like my cousin, he is only concerned about himself.

"Eliza?" I ask, turning to her, hoping I can gain helpful information.

She steps forward, also looking at the floral pink the stone now seems to take. "The color of your soul depends on your personality. Your color, for example, is purple—which stands for things like nobility, transformation, enlightenment, and mourning. Things like that."

"What's pink?" I ask, seeing the color glow with prominence before my eyes.

"That's a mix between red and white. Red is energy, desire, and violence; all things that are intense. White is the opposite; meaning forgiveness, cleanliness, birth, innocence, and peace. So that means pink is things like excitement, love, and joy. Basically what every little girl is like," she says, smiling.

"How long before she wakes up?"

"Everyone's different. Hours, days. We don't know," Eliza informs me, looking at Kenzie as her body lies limp and helpless, transforming and changing, as her human body is left abandoned without a soul to occupy it. All we can do is wait.

"How did she get past everyone?" I ask, looking around at half-asleep faces—some still dozing even with all the commotion. Most are gathered around us, looking at the scene unfolding before them.

The boy starts to yell in my face, stepping closer to me, and I find myself reaching my limit of tolerance. "We were all asleep! We didn't think you were going to have a friend follow you home!"

"Who are you to yell at me?" I say, standing up to show I am not only taller than him but obviously older by many years. "I didn't do anything. It's not my fault she followed me here." I don't want to fight with him, but I need to defend myself. If this is someone I will live with for eternity, then I'm not going to be the underdog in the situation.

"That would be Tyler." A woman starts to walk toward me, pushing Tyler to the side. "The number one cause of fights here at Phantom Lagoon. You can only guess why."

My eyes must have been full of questions because she laughs. "My name is Aida de Luna; but you may call me Luna."

She looks in her twenties and from a different century. She wears a dress that is old and exhausted—it's magnificent though. A ballroom gown. The colors that had once been bright greens and oranges are now musty browns. The dress has a deep square neckline and is wilting, worn down by use. She has long golden-blond hair that is tied up away from her face. It's composed of curls and ringlets that had once looked ready for a special occasion but now fall to the side. Her face is glowingly clear and pale—luminescent in the sunlight. She's beautiful. Out of everyone here at Phantom Lagoon, she looks like she's been here the longest.

But the most stunning thing is her eye color—white. Her iris isn't the natural blue, green, or brown, but a very pale gray, almost gleaming. I find myself mesmerized by the simple color opposed to the different stripes and patterns seen in a normal iris.

"We may be waiting for Miss Mackenzie longer then you think. Can you tell me what happened?" She has a strange mixed

169

accent. It's subtle though—French maybe—but I'm guessing she can speak more than one language. Luna carries a presence with her that makes you listen and cooperate, but her smile is of someone loving and gentle.

"I was watching her family yesterday. They were camping." I say almost to myself. It feels like I'm looking at someone straight from the history books.

"Your power is to appear to humans, correct?" Luna asks. Her smile is welcoming. I know she is just trying to sort things out, but I can't help but search her features. She looks so young, but she's dressed as if she was very high in society—maybe not now, but when she was born. I remember what I had learned in history class, trying to place her time frame. When settlers first came to America, we were poverty-stricken, trying hard to stay alive. Later on when we gained independence, we had also gained riches, but not the kind she wears. Luna's clothes are very detailed with stitching and different lace around her bodice. Even the highest in society didn't have clothing this extravagant. The one place I had seen someone dress this way in history was somewhere in Europe. That's where the greatest artists and composers were always found—during the Renaissance; of course they would have only the best clothing during that period of time.

"Is that your power?" she asks again, trying to gain my attention.

"Yes, I can be seen by humans, but they can't touch me," I say.

"Did you make sure you were out of their sight?" she asks kindly, though I could hear the seriousness of the situation in her voice.

"I hid behind a bush, so they wouldn't see me. Once it was dark, it got hard to breathe, and it felt like I was being crushed. When that happened, I screamed, and Kenzie looked at me. Her parents heard me, but they didn't see me."

"You were able to get back in time?"

Luna sounds amazed, not angry. I braced myself for a scolding, feeling the immediate authority she held, but it never came.

"Are you kidding me?" Tyler yells out, his voice booming over our hushed conversation, as more people woke up groggy and ignorant as to what is going on. Everyone's gaze is on Tyler, confused as to the reasoning behind the yelling. He points to me and shouts, "She came barging through those trees laughing!"

"I don't know why I was laughing," I whimper. "It felt like a rush..." I shiver, remembering the pounding of my heart; not sure if I could make it back in time and also the feeling of absolute freedom, nothing holding me back.

"Well, Emma, I suggest you stay here until she wakes up." Luna walks toward the cave, as if she is about to enter, but instead skims her hand along it, turning into the forest where she disappears out of sight.

"Why haven't I seen her before?" I ask Eliza.

"Luna doesn't come out much. She acts as our support system. She's been here the longest. Not much surprises her. When you told her what you did yesterday, she seemed pretty amazed. I guess that's never happened before."

I turn my attention back to Kenzie; she looks like she is sleeping, but her stone is turning a more pronounced pink as time passes.

"What are we going to do now?" I ask, staring at Kenzie, hoping she would magically wake up and be alive. No—more than alive; I wish her all the happiness in the world, but I'm the one who has taken it away from her.

"What do you mean *we*?" Tyler says, crossing his arms in front of him. "You caused the mess. You fix it."

Everyone has left the scene by now, returning to their normal day-to-day lives, no longer caring about gathering around until Kenzie opens her eyes—all except for Eliza.

"We wait," she says, shrugging and sitting on the ground next to Kenzie.

"And her parents?"

"Probably looking for her. They will think she got lost and call the police. We can do the same as we did for you—show them the body. They will think she tripped or something. It will be hard for them, but life goes on for humans."

I start to picture Kenzie's family from yesterday. "They were so perfect, their little family, so happy and carefree. Then I ruined it all."

"It doesn't help anyone when you think like that," Eliza says. "Right now everybody's hate for you hasn't seemed to increase even though Kenzie followed you here—so call yourself lucky." There is some hidden malice in her voice that she isn't willing to display fully. I feel a wall between the two of us as some unknown anger brims inside her.

"I'm sorry, Eliza. I was stupid for letting Kenzie see me, for letting her get this far into Phantom Lagoon. I'm truly sorry—for everything." The words seem fake—a usual form of apology— nothing sincere about it. But I mean every word I say, needing to have Eliza in this journey I'm forced to call my life.

"It's okay, Emma," she says, letting out a big sigh. "It's just...I wish they had been this accepting for my father. Although they're probably only letting you stay near Kenzie because they don't want to deal with her parents. This is the youngest person to come here. Nobody wants to see the parents' reaction when they realize their child is dead."

Chapter 17

Angels

Kenzie wakes up and starts to scream. Her face turns a fiery red with the effort it takes to expel all that noise. Her call is piercing and loud. I'm afraid that her parents might hear and come looking for her; that they will come to Phantom Lagoon and fall under the spell too. Kenzie turns to me and a look that can only be identified as anger crosses her face.

With one last scream she runs at me with a vengeance.

I bolt up off the ground, bracing for impact. Nothing comes. I look down and see Kenzie still in her state of coma; her face revealing no sign of emotion as she lies across the rock. It was just a dream. I didn't even know I had fallen asleep.

Eliza looks at me, confused. "What's wrong?" she asks.

"Nothing."

Eliza turns her attention back to Kenzie. She must have been awake the entire time, always watching to make sure she is there when Kenzie opens her eyes for the first time to see this new world into which she was brought.

A small smile starts to slip through Eliza's lips.

"What?" I ask.

She points to Kenzie as she whispers, so as not to startle her. "I've always wanted a little sister."

Kenzie's big brown eyes open to look at the new world around her; first confusion, then happiness as she sees me—a familiar face. I can't help but smile back, as Kenzie gets up to hug me. As she stands, her body is left behind. I thought I was seeing double—that maybe I might be sick—but then I see Kenzie's former body slowly fade away as the Essence is left behind in its wake.

"Don't worry," Eliza whispers to me, seeing the shock on my face as Kenzie continues to embrace me. "That's normal. The Essence has to leave the body. The owner of the body can't see it. It doesn't want to identify the body as itself."

It doesn't want to. I can name off thousands of reasons why. Her body disappears to its temporary residence of the cave. Soon it will be moved again to a location where Kenzie's parents can find it to stop the search, just like I had done for my family.

"Hi!" Kenzie says with bright greeting eyes, wrapping her arms around my waist. I hug her back lightly, but I struggle to find words, to explain.

Eliza steps in for me. "Hi, Kenzie. I'm Eliza, and this is Emma," she says with a light laugh, pointing toward me. "We are going to take care of you now, okay?"

"What about Mommy and Daddy?" she asks, pulling away from me and directing her attention to Eliza.

Eliza takes a moment to think about the question before answering Kenzie. She looks around for help herself, but everyone is either gone or watching us emotionlessly.

"How about I tell you a story?" Eliza opts.

Kenzie's eyes lit up at the word. "Okay!"

Eliza holds out her hand, and Kenzie takes it quickly, following her to the same large rock that Eliza and I had been sitting on the night she had told me about her father. Eliza picks up Kenzie and puts her on the highest point of the rock. I sit next to her, watching her face carefully, while Eliza stands in front of us, so she can make direct eye contact.

"Do you know that you are very special, Kenzie?" Eliza asks.

Kenzie gets excited and starts clapping her hands. "Mommy says that all the time. She says I'm very, *very* special. I'm Mommy's little girl, but I'm a big girl!"

I put my arm around Kenzie and try to say something to her—she is special; she is still Mommy's little girl; what she is about to find out is my fault. But with a dry throat I can't get the words to form.

Eliza smiles and tucks some of Kenzie's blond curls behind her ear. "You are very special, Kenzie. You get to do things others don't." She is a good actor; she makes this seem like a good thing. "Your Mommy and Daddy were very nice. They gave you to us. It was their choice. This is good for you. You get to live with us now."

Kenzie's face falls the slightest bit, but she's still full of enthusiasm. "What about Mommy and Daddy? Do they get to live here too?" she asks, looking around for them. Her little hand pushes me away the slightest bit to improve her line of sight as she gazes past me.

"No, Kenzie. Mommy and Daddy can't see you anymore. Do you want to know why?" Eliza asks, making sure she understands.

Kenzie keeps watching the lagoon, but when she finds nothing, she looks down at her hands, now placed limp in her lap. Eliza waits for her to answer, but when she doesn't, she continues.

"You're an angel now. You get to live forever. You don't have wings yet, but you will. One day you get to fly up to Heaven, and be with your Mommy and Daddy again."

"I want Mommy and Daddy now!" Kenzie starts to cry tearless sobs, her face full of agony. She looks down toward the ground, seeing how far of a jump it may be, wanting to run back to her parents. To a regular person this looks like a normal fit a three-year-old would have, but her cries hold true emotion—too young to understand the full extent of being an Essence, but she knows enough that it means good-bye to her parents.

I hug her, whispering in her ear. "I know, Kenzie. We all do. You know what? When you get to see them, you'll feel so happy that nothing will matter." I take a deep breath, dealing with my own loss that comes with leaving my human life behind. "Nothing will matter..." I linger on the words.

Eliza joins in our group hug, as we let Kenzie cry herself into her new life. I caused the cries that erupt from the little girl next to me, and I wish I had been more careful that day I had seen her parents in the campground. After a few minutes Kenzie looks up at the two of us with sad eyes. "Are you my guardian angel?" she asks. "Mommy said there is always a guardian angel looking over everyone." Kenzie looks at me with glossy eyes.

I release a small laugh as I pull a strand of hair out of my face. "I'm more of a big sister. I look after you, but I make mistakes."

"You too? Are you my big sister too?" Kenzie asks, looking toward Eliza.

She just nods, not trusting her voice, but a smile crosses her face. She wants this. Eliza has always been an only child, and when Kenzie came into Phantom Lagoon, I could spot that small sort of happiness in Eliza as the idea of having a little sister posed in her mind.

"I want Mommy," Kenzie says, clutching her hands around Eliza's neck. She buries her face in Eliza's shoulder, and I watch as her small body heaves with cries. Kenzie wants her family, and I would do anything to bring them to her, fully alive, but it's an impossible task.

Chapter 18

Reality

"Emma, where have you been? I've haven't seen you in days!" my mom says as I step into the house. She approaches like she's going to hug me but, remembering what happened last time, stops. She looks me over like she hasn't talked to me in years. "Oh, honey, it's been so hard. Your father is so upset, and your grandparents are trying to make sense of it. Your funeral is this Sunday. Are you planning on coming?"

I think of what it may be like to see everyone I know mourn my death. People lined up in a church somewhere, looking to each other for support.

"I'm not sure." I stumble around, thinking about it. "They might see me." We walk through our house—no, my parents' house—I don't live here anymore.

My mom sees my hesitance. "It's okay, Emma. You don't have to go. I was just making sure that you knew, so you could if you wanted to."

Attending your own funeral is almost like an unspoken dream. People always imagine it, even though it's something that's supposed to be impossible; and here I am, turning it down.

I stare at the floral wallpaper in our vintage-style dining room while I weigh what I'm about to ask. "Can you make sure of one thing?"

"Of course, anything," my mom agrees.

I look down at the floor for a second before looking straight into my mom's eyes, to show how important this is to me. "I don't want people to act like I'm gone forever. I'm here, and I'm staying. They don't need to know the truth. Just make it known that, even if I'm not alive, I'm not gone. This isn't going to be some sob story about a teenager who died in the forest. It's going to be a story about a girl who lived her life to the fullest.

"But things happen. Everything went wrong, and I fell. But life goes on, and we learn to live with what we have, not what we wish we had. That's how I want people to remember me. I also want you to display my drawings, because they are a part of me that nobody got to experience—a part of me that people should have seen, but I didn't let them."

My mom's silent for a moment, her eyes glossing over with the slightest bit of tears. "Oh, Emma, yes. I'll do exactly that." She walks toward me again—wanting to hug—but sits down at a nearby chair.

Oddly this is important to me: how I'm remembered. I don't want my family to be treated differently, because they lost a daughter. I want them to be able to forget about the bad times and remember the good. I don't want people to come up to them every day saying they are sorry for their loss. Because it isn't a loss; just a little piece of their haven had broken off. People can patch things; it still may hurt, but that's life.

Reality is knowing that you will get hurt. That there's no stopping it, but you still try. Even after you're hurt, you first want to suffer through it, for some reason thinking the afflictions will help. You find out later that the remedy is time. Time supposedly heals everything. How can you know though? Is it when you forget or when it doesn't hurt to think about it anymore?

My mom went through this, and I could tell time wasn't going to be a factor of healing for her. She wasn't willing to let go, so I had to save her. I told her my secret, and in doing that, it brought on the reality of what really happened. It also brought the sense of joy that my mom could still see me. Not nearly as much as she would like, but I'm still here. I can keep her safe.

I wish I could suffer this alone, but my family also has to. My mom, knowing there is no afterlife for me. The rest of my family and friends, thinking that I'm dead and that maybe I have found Heaven. Kenzie, I brought her into this life; if it weren't for me, she would still be alive. Kenzie's parents, they only had her for three years. Three short years; years I'm sure they will never forget. Soon they will find the body of their only daughter, and their world will be torn. Then there's Eliza; she stuck with me through all of this. Already she has suffered so much with the loss of her own family.

I spend the rest of the day with my mom. We do chores around the house for fun—though I would have never said that before my life ended. It feels so good to spend time together. She washes, I dry. We work alongside each other to dust the small nooks and crannies that never get enough attention, and unpack boxes—the ones that I thought would never find a place. We sort through the remaining moving boxes, getting caught up in memories. One of the boxes is filled with my mom's china from her wedding—she tells me all about it, even goes to get some pictures to show me.

Another box is filled with small infant clothing, old and worn. I see a tear running down my mom's face. She excuses herself quickly to go to the bathroom. Approaching the box, I see exactly what my mom had collected. The contents are baby pictures, toys, and more clothes. They were mine. Little booties and onesies.

There is a photo of the day I was born, surrounded by wires and gauze taped to my small body in the NICU. Machines are around me, keeping my tiny beating heart alive and feeding me oxygen.

There's another photo; this one shot in the front yard of our old Florida home. My entire family stands around me; I'm only a few weeks old—this must have been when they took me home from the hospital.

I'm in my mom's arms, but she isn't looking at the camera. She holds me with the gentlest arms, looking down into my bright blue eyes. A little tuft of hair is on my head, and my grandma is standing to my mom's right side with a little pink hat, about to place it on my head—she doesn't know the picture is being taken.

My dad—the only one in the photo conscious of the camera—smiles as he holds up one of my small hands with his finger, triumphant. My grandpa has his hand on my grandma's shoulder, as he looks down at me with the same expression as my mom.

My small face is looking toward my dad while he holds my hand, and my face is almost comical. My eyes are half closed, and my mouth is wide open—it's hard to tell whether I was crying or yawning.

My mom walks back in, and I hold out the picture to her. "Do you miss when I was little?"

My mom sits beside me and takes the photo. She stares at it for a while before answering me. "Of course I do, but everybody grows up. I knew you would leave someday, just not so soon. Parents don't want to think of the day their kids move out. I wasn't ready for your death."

She puts her hand out to me, and it passes through my shoulder. I try not to notice the wince, as she backs away from me. How is it that I can hold physical things—like this photo—but not come into contact with living things? It's not fair.

Beside me I hear my mom sigh, realizing we are on separate realms now. "But I want you to know I can take care of myself, Emma. I don't regret you telling me what happened, but you need to let go too. Someday I'm going to be gone, and so is your father. You need to keep yourself safe, not us. I love you, Emma, but you need to prepare yourself for that day.

"You'll be alive for the rest of eternity. Time will fly for you. I don't know which breath is my last, so make sure you're ready." She brushes a tear from her eye and continues. "I couldn't handle the thought of you being gone, but you're going to have to be stronger than me, Emma."

Now I'm the one who needs to let go. And she's right; she'll be gone someday. I told my mom my secret, because I thought she needed me, but it was the other way around—I needed her.

"You need to savor your time, Emma. Forever is just a fraction of infinity. Don't waste it." She hands me back the photo. "Keep it. Always remember us."

Why does it sound like she's saying good-bye?

"I'll never forget you, Mom." When the words form from my mouth, it sounds like I'm crying. I take a deep breath so my mom can understand me. "No matter what. I'll always be watching you— even if you forget. I'm not going to leave you until I have to," I say, clutching the picture; the one of my family that will remain in the physical world even after they've passed.

"Oh, Emma."

In her eyes I can see her ache to embrace me, but her body doesn't make the forward movement, like she's done so many times before forgetting I'm just an Essence.

"You don't have to leave, if you don't want to. I just want you to know it will happen someday. Until then you can visit as much as you want."

We just look at each other for the longest moment. It is the first time I have ever really looked at life. I know, from this point on, I will never overlook a sunset. Never hate the rain. For I know that life is too precious to be looked at with a mere glance. It's meant to be treasured and remembered.

My life has been torn, but I can appreciate this small moment. Even if we can't touch each other, we can be together. My mom can see me, and I can still talk to her. I'm not alone—I have Eliza. I will need her even more someday. I only hope I will be ready then. That I can take on the death of my parents and appreciate all the moments we had together. I know it will be hard, and it won't be easy, but my mom is right—forever is a long time; it should not be wasted.

Someday this will all be forgotten. My mom will become old and will forget, but I won't. I'll always be watching my parents. Even when they leave, I'll remember them, even when the rest of the world doesn't.

I look over to the small bookshelf and see that there are new books with their bindings creased from reading. My mom notices me looking.

"I like the way they make the impossible happen. How you can escape to a whole other world. It makes you think."

I smile at her before we go back to cleaning.

When we finish the last of the household chores, my mom finds a movie and puts it in. It's some musical, but even though neither of us like the movie, we both enjoy talking about it and making jokes.

It's a fun day—one I haven't had in a long time.

Mackenzie

Kenzie adjusts as much as she can without parents. She loves everyone in Phantom Lagoon. They seem happy to have her here too. She lights up the area with a new glow that keeps everyone awake and alert—mostly because if they don't, Kenzie will find a way to get into trouble.

You can tell though, in her eyes, something isn't right. Sometimes I'll catch her just watching, staring out into oblivion waiting for her parents. The way she rubs her eyes, waiting for the tears that don't come. Her body will quake, but she never falls from her sorrow. She's the little stranger that followed me to Phantom Lagoon because she thought I was hurt. She's a strong soul.

That doesn't change the fact she's in pain. She misses her family and friends. We try our best to make her feel more at home. Luna comes out and sets up the area so it looks like a classroom and tells stories. Some are so original and detailed that you can't believe she's making them up as she goes along. Her stories are about mythical creatures whose hands are webbed. They have wings arching from their backs—not for flying but for swimming. They don't hunt animals though. They act as fertilizers; eating the sand and spitting it out, as it is filled with minerals. They are called Defenders. In Luna's story they protect a pond, much like Phantom Lagoon, from anyone who strays into the area.

Today Luna lets Kenzie choose what the story will be about—the Defenders, monsters, and Fairies.

"Angels! Like what I am!" Kenzie says in the happiest voice you can imagine.

Luna looks up at Eliza and smiles. She begins to tell the story just as Eliza had but with more detail and magic. At the same time she also makes it seem so real, as if it is true.

While Kenzie is enticed by the story, Eliza takes me to the side so nobody can hear.

"Kenzie's parents are looking for her. They need to find the body so they can know the truth." I take a deep breath. I knew this was coming, but I was hoping it could be avoided somehow.

"Okay, I guess there's no way around it." I start to walk toward the cave where the bodies are kept. Eliza follows and helps me find Kenzie's body. Hers is deep in the crystal cave, a few feet away from where my body had been. Her abandoned human body is curled into a ball, thumb in mouth. If it weren't for the fact that I know that Kenzie is outside with Luna, I would have thought this was her right before my eyes. I cradle the body in my arms, the small child feeling light. Eliza walks in front of me as we head out of the cave, keeping watch to make sure Kenzie won't see us.

Just as my human body had, once we leave the safe quarters of the cave, Kenzie's body begins to decompose. Her limbs stiffen and an odor emits from her skin. Her body grows heavy in my arms, as if weighed down by death in its truest forms.

Eliza and I walk, our gazes forward and away from the body of the girl that we think of as a sister.

"What's the plan?" Eliza asks once we are out of sight of the lagoon. We had been walking in silence for a long time, waiting to be sure Kenzie had no way of finding her body.

"You're helping me?" I ask, stunned. It's not that I don't expect her to help; more that I thought this wasn't something that was her obligation, like it was for me.

"Of course, she's my little sister too. Her parents have the police scanning the area around the campsite." Eliza stops for a second, imagining Kenzie's body as her family discovers the death. "A broken leg...and we put her at the end of a pond. So it looks like she fell and tried to swim out."

We search the forest for a pond that has a small cliff and large rocks at the bottom. A mile away from the campsite we stop and make our plan.

There's an area nearby that has a drop-off that leads to water. It isn't deep but has large jutting rocks in it. Once the police find the body, they can put the pieces together.

They will think Kenzie had wondered off during the night and got lost. It was dark, so she couldn't see her way. She walked off a ledge and fell into the cold water. The drop was short, but Kenzie's frail bones couldn't withstand the impact, and she broke her leg. She tried to swim to the shore, but the pain in her broken leg slowed her down. Kenzie was able to get to dry land but suffered from a broken leg and hypothermia. She died later that night in her sleep, her heart slowing with each beat.

I'm frozen in place staring at Kenzie's deathbed. I feel Eliza take the body from my hands and walk toward the edge. I robotically step backward toward the safety of the trees.

What we are doing is crazy: staging a death. We have to give the appearance of an end to this little girl's human life and break any connections with her family. This is the only way to do it. It feels cruel but somehow human. But most of all it's quick, effortless. It is the easiest way to give bad news—blunt, harsh, and to the point.

"You might want to cover your eyes," Eliza says in a monotone.

She kisses the forehead of Kenzie's body and hugs her. "I'm so sorry," she whispers, and there's a catch in her voice as she prepares to give Kenzie's body away. I close my eyes and turn around, so I won't see. I still hear the sound though—the loud thud and then the snap of the leg. It echoes in my head over and over, getting louder and more distinct with each repetition, leaving the memory to haunt me.

I open my eyes to see Eliza, face pale, walking down toward the pond. She drags Kenzie's mangled and bloody body from the pond and lays it on the sand, still half in the water, facing down. Just seconds ago she had been in my arms sucking her thumb—the picture of peace.

"Now they just have to find it." Eliza looks at me, seeing if she should also be the one to haunt the police.

"I can do it," I tell her.

We walk through the trees and toward the campsite. As we come closer, we hear police talking, still looking for Kenzie. From the short distance between us and the police officers, I can see they are examining the area for any clues as to which direction Kenzie might have gone. Her parents aren't there. The only humans there are a few stray policemen talking to each other, writing notes.

Eliza hides near a tree, while I approach one of the men from behind, stepping inside. I imagine being alive, the rise and fall of a human chest, the brisk wind that lingers in the air. The next thing I know, I don't have to imagine it; it's there.

She has to be here somewhere. Poor parents...

The feeling of haunting is...something I can't describe. I'm alive again, the blood pumping through my veins, the heat from the sun warming. I can feel everything again. It' so easy to become distracted in the sea of life, but I have something I need to do.

"Turn around," I tell him, fiercely. The human emotions surprise me. I take on the man's essence, his agitation of another case of a missing person. "Now."

He gives way quickly, following my orders.

"Let me control your feet," I command.

I feel his feet go limp as I take control. With his influence gone, I feel my agitation subside as the police officer's mind fades into the background. It's almost too easy to gain control, but then I realize it's because he's eager to close this case and end the long day. He relinquishes all his body unto me, and I almost fall to the ground with the surprise of the weight. Soon I'm able to control every muscle in his legs, becoming comfortable with the feeling of being alive.

Unaware I'm in their presence, the police continue their search, while I watch from the eyes of one of the officers. The body is nearby—a few feet to the left—and the pond is right there behind the trees. There's a hesitance in me as the police wander the area. Even though I know the body is just feet away, I don't want them to find Kenzie; I don't want her parents to have to hear the news.

The man I haunt begins to walk in the opposite direction I need him to go. A spike of anger grows in me, and I grow aggravated with human emotion—why is this man so upset? I fill his lungs with air and stop walking. Thinking of Kenzie's human body, waiting at the edge of the pond, I feel tears run down my face.

It's an amazing thing to have someone cry for you. In this man's body, I occupy him for just a moment, but it's a moment that allows me to feel human. As an Essence I cannot cry, but here, here I am normal.

I pivot the man's body to the pond, allowing his eyes to close. I struggle for a moment to leave this body where my emotions are expressed truly, but I pull myself away, as if peeling off a Band-Aid in slow agony. I don't let myself think about what will happen after I say the words, "Look there."

I leave, feeling the emptiness that accompanies me when I regain the form of an Essence. My world goes blind to the human sense of touch and other automatic functions of the living. The ground beneath me can't be felt even though my feet are clearly making contact. The wind blows my hair, but my skin doesn't feel its cold kiss.

Running to the tree that Eliza is hiding behind, I'm too far away to hear what the police officers are saying. I can see them talking into their walkie-talkies, and soon more police show up. They come prepared with a gurney, and more sirens scream out in help from the far distance.

Eliza and I both stand frozen as they remove the body. The police walk away to where the road must have been to meet with the coming ambulance—it all happens so fast. After a few minutes Eliza steps out from behind the tree.

"Do you want to see her parents?" she asks, wrapping her arms around her body, as if to shield herself from the winds that no longer buffet us.

I look in the direction the police went. "No, but I think I should."

"Do you want me to come with you?"

I can tell she doesn't want to by the way her arms cling to her sides in what can only be described as fear. The police are something she can only associate with her father's absence. They were there when he disappeared, and they were there when her mother got into a car accident that later took her life.

"No, I caused this," I say, trying to dismiss her to go back to Phantom Lagoon.

"You didn't do anything, Emma," she replies almost instantly, but in a quiet voice like she's tired of trying.

I look away from her, avoiding eye contact. "I've gotten off pretty easy so far. I think I can deal with this one thing." I walk away from Eliza and follow the trail the police had left behind. Eliza stands there for a while staring, not sure if she should follow or not. In the end she must have gone back to Phantom Lagoon, because there is no sign of her as I look behind me, making my way to the road.

As the trees disappear, the open line of asphalt lies before me. I can hear cars in the distance and sirens whine as they fly back into town with Kenzie's body on its way to the hospital morgue to be studied and evaluated to find her cause of death.

I shrink backward into the woods to keep a constant cover in the trees. The siren of police cars guides me to Kenzie's home. They drive fast, but another passes, giving me a direction to follow. After walking a short distance, I stumble across a small yellow house with a large backyard. People stand outside talking quietly, and others are just arriving to try to console. Some are on the phone, looking shocked as they tell someone the tragic story. A woman walks toward the door to comfort Kenzie's parents, but then she walks back to the front yard.

It's obvious I arrived after the police. The news has already been told, and the worst of it is over. I can still hear the crying, the pain in the voice of Kenzie's mother, with her father offering comfort. It is all concealed in that small house.

I creep through the forest going around to the back of the house. Through the window I view the scene like it is a movie, numb and oblivious to the reality. Her mother's head is buried in her husband's shoulder. He is patting her back while she cries—it is hard to tell, but he too is crying. You can see the silent tears slipping down his face. The mother's pain is very clearly displayed on her face; she is still sobbing.

I realize that I have no idea why I came here. There is no way I can offer comfort. I can only tell them that their daughter's death was my fault. I can do nothing.

Helpless I head back to Phantom Lagoon for two reasons. First, I'm running from what I caused—something I should have never done. I was stupid, and there is nothing I can do about it now. Second, I realize the sun is coming down. There is no way I can survive nightfall outside of the lagoon again. The memory of not being able to breathe and being crushed are still too strong.

Kenzie is the first to greet me and gives me a hug. "Where were you? You missed Una's stories!" A small laugh emerges from me as she pronounces Luna's name wrong. I'm happy she has no idea what her parents are going through.

Kenzie goes into great detail about the story. This particular story is about us—or what Kenzie thinks we are: angels with wings, acting as a normal person, but having great powers that you can't even imagine.

I sit down as Kenzie proceeds to retell the story to me. She slowly drifts toward sleep and starts to slur her words. Within a few minutes she is in a deep slumber, smiling as she thinks about angels.

Chapter 20

Sunday

It's today. I have to decide if I'm attending my own funeral. Until now my days passed with obscured edges, never allowing me to make out what is today and what is tomorrow. The physical world is a universe away, yet it presides to go on in its slow pace. The arrangements for my memorial were all made without my attention, and people gather to remember my life. Eliza is going because she had known me in school. It's all part of her act—being human. My family will be going as well. I'm not being forced to go. I'm not being forced to stay here in Phantom Lagoon either. But there is a smaller part of me that wants to know. I tell myself it will be too hard; that seeing everyone will make me feel worse than I already am. Then there is that little tingle in my stomach that itches at me until I tell myself I will go.

On and off—I can't decide.

Finally I come to a conclusion. I will go; I will have to hide, but I want to know who will be there, who will be crying, who cares about me?

I'm surprised when I arrive. There are so many people. I'm able to recognize all the faces, but I can only put names on very few. The principal is there, and so are some teachers. Sadie is there with her parents. There are fresh tears in her eyes as she clings to her mom, while her dad stands a foot away looking at his daughter.

Eliza walks up to Sadie as if they have been friends for a long time and gives her a hug. Sadie is surprised at first but welcomes it anyway. They go inside the church to find a seat together.

My parents are at the door of the church talking to everyone entering. My mom has tears in her eyes, but she is controlled. My dad is standing tall, showing he is the head of the family and strong.

The teachers all have tears but not the same as the others. They are crying over the death of a teenager, not one of their students who they'd known well.

There are students at my funeral that I had no names for. Some looked uncomfortable being around so many crying people. A small group of girls are huddled together, silently weeping.

As I scan the entire parking lot, each person is either crying or looks like they were about to. I only hope my mom can follow up on her promise.

One by one everyone goes inside to find a seat. I quickly run across the open parking lot and to a window with a bush that can camouflage me. I hide in it while looking through the stained glass window of the church.

My drawings are being displayed, as I had asked. Each pew has one hung at the end of the aisle. I feel pride as everyone marvels at my work. They are beautiful, and I can be proud of them—at least a little piece of me has been left in my place.

In front of all the aisles is the casket that holds my body. It's wooden and stained a natural, warm brown. There are flowers covering the top. Alongside there are some of my smaller drawings, making the scene appear beautiful—almost like a collage.

The mass passes slowly, but everyone stays at full attention. When it comes to the part where people say things about me, my mom is first to come forward. She walks to the altar faster than I had thought she would.

With a long breath she gathers herself, looking toward the crowd of people mourning my death. "Emma's death was a sudden and tragic end to her life. I know for sure, though, that she will never leave us. Emma is here in spirit every day, even when you can't sense her. I know that if she were here now, she wouldn't want us crying but remembering her. Displayed around are some of her drawings. Emma made them but never showed anyone. I understand now how much talent she had. I only wish that I could've known this when she was alive."

She looks at my casket for a moment, staring at the displayed picture of me. A fleeting second passes, and I think she's done. A tear runs down her cheek, and she looks up, toward me where I hide outside the church, peeking through the stained glass window. My mom wipes away her tear and smiles at me before she continues.

"Emma was always cooperative. She moved here, even though she wanted to stay back in Florida. She did this because of me. We'll never really know what happened to Emma to cause her to leave us, but we just have to remember that she's watching now."

My mom looks on, past me and out the window to something else, which holds her gaze. She's not broken or lost, like I thought she would have been without me. My mom is strong, and I'm glad to have her. She releases the tension in her body and steps off the altar, wiping another tear from her eye and goes back to sit with my dad.

Sadie steps up to the altar next with red-rimmed eyes. I can see her body sway a bit as she stands in front of the crowd, but she carries on to remember me anyway.

"I only met Emma this year, and I may not know her as well as the rest of her family," she says, looking at my parents who hold each other's hands. "But I know I'll never forget her. If Emma is in Heaven today, listening to us, then I need to say this. I miss you, and I'll treasure the time we did have together." Sadie's voice clips at the end of her sentence, and I don't know if she had planned to say more, but she steps off crying and goes to sit with her mom, dad, and Eliza, who hugs her while others go to make a speech.

Other family members that I haven't seen in months tell stories of our fond memories at the beach or parties. The funny stories about me when I was little are what cheer up the crowd. In fact, in the end, everyone is happier than when they arrived.

Now my friends and family drive from the church to the cemetery. My parents are the first to get out of their car and go to my new grave. Soon everyone follows behind them in a quiet procession. The marker is a beautiful black stone, shaped as a heart; on it the most important words are carved.

Amelia Clarice Barton

1994–2009

An angel was torn from Earth one day to be taken back home but will always be in our hearts.

She can't be forgotten, and she can't forget us.

God rest your soul, Emma.

The casket is lowered into the ground and everyone puts flowers on the grave. What had once been a brown mound of earth is now a colorful pile of flowers ranging from yellow to blue and every color in-between. Eliza told me that items had been placed inside the casket during the wake. I chose not to go to that because I can't handle seeing my body again—it's something that is hard to comprehend, not only emotionally, but mentally. It's hard to make sense of it, as in why I am looking at myself until, again, I realize I am dead.

Saying their final good-byes, everyone leaves the grave and sends their prayers to my parents before making for home. I wish there is some way I can show them that I'm watching. If I had been a real angel like in Luna's stories, I would make a shadow shaped like a heart to show that I loved them; but I can't. Instead I hang in the far distance, just close enough to wait, but far enough to not be seen.

Chapter 21

ER

The next day I visit my mom to thank her for arranging everything, but when I get to my house, something is wrong. It's quiet—normally I will hear the TV on inside or someone talking. But today...nothing. I run inside using the back door that my mom always keeps unlocked for me. I search each room; nobody is home. The floorboards creak beneath my feet; the silence of the house scares me. Something is wrong, but I don't know what.

I stay there for three hours, waiting for someone to come home. The sun moves across the sky, reminding me I only have a limited amount of time in this place I used to call my home. I'm pacing inside the dining room, switching my view from the phone to the driveway. More time passes, and no one comes. It starts to get late as the sun kisses the tops of the trees, moving closer and closer to the horizon. The sky turns orange, creating a beautiful scene as the clouds look like a watercolor painting.

Staring out the back window, I look to the trees that call me to leave to the safety of the lagoon. I walk toward the back door, but the sound of an engine stops me—it's my mom. She walks out of the car looking worried. I sprint to the door and out to her.

"What happened? Are you okay?" I ask, looking her over. Nothing seemed to be wrong, but where is my dad?

When I look into her eyes, I see nothing but pain. Never before have I wanted to give her a hug so much. My mom wears no makeup, revealing dark circles under her eyes that tell me it's been too long since she's last slept.

"Your father. He's in the hospital," she says in a quiet voice, looking through her purse for something. When she doesn't find whatever she's looking for, she lets out a deep, heavy sigh.

"What do you mean? I saw him yesterday," I say.

She mumbles, looking through me. "We missed the symptoms. He's been complaining about headaches and dizziness. I didn't think much of it. Then he was vomiting, so I thought it was just the flu going around. We went for a walk to get fresh air, hoping that would help, but he kept tripping. He told me not to worry about it. He said he just needed some sleep. But he's been sleeping a lot for weeks. When he woke up this morning, I couldn't understand what he was saying. I called the doctor—I didn't know what else to do. They told me to bring him in immediately. They said he had all the symptoms of a stroke." My mom's eyes start to get glossy as tears came down her face.

"The ambulance took him to the ER. Emma, he had a seizure," my mom whispers, finally making direct eye contact.

It takes me a minute to process what is happening, before I can put all the pieces together. My dad had a seizure. "What? Mom, is he going to be okay?"

"We don't know yet. They have to do tests." She starts to shake her head, obviously overwhelmed by the day's events.

My mom's phone rings, and she holds it up to her ear. She stays quiet, just listening, while her face is blank.

"Okay, thank you. I'll be right over first thing in the morning." She hangs up the phone and looks at me. "They just performed an MRI, and they think he might have a brain tumor. That's what caused the seizure. They have to do more tests to see if it's benign or cancerous." Her voice breaks as she tries to tell me this. My mom begins to sob into her hands, and her entire body starts to shake.

"What?" That's all I can say.

"They can't know for sure yet," my mom tells me, the frame of her body quivering.

"But that's what they think?" I ask.

My mom just nods in reply, walking back toward the house for shelter. She will be alone tonight. My dad isn't there, and I can't be there. I watch her as she struggles to open the door and stumbles inside with shaky footing. She doesn't look at me as she closes the door behind her. No good-bye.

This is second time I had to leave her at night while she cried herself to sleep.

In the hospital my dad lays lifeless on the white linen. There are tubes hooked up to his arms and nose. The heart monitor on the side of his bed tells me that he is alive and well—for now...is all I can think.

"He must have had a stroke within the last few days," a doctor tells my mom.

"How is that possible?" she asks in return, watching my dad's still form.

"It's not uncommon. He probably didn't even know it had happened. You're lucky you brought him in on time. The situation looks bad, but it would have been worse if he had had the seizure while he was alone."

My mom nods and follows the doctor out of the room. I'm alone with my dad.

His heart beat goes up rapidly, and I view the machine and see the loosely patterned up-and-down movement on the monitor. Looking back to my dad, I see his limbs flail and shudder, and I can't help but scream. I rush over to him, afraid out of my mind that I may lose him.

"Help! Someone, my dad is having a seizure!" I drop to my knees at his bedside, while I begin the tearless sobs of an Essence.

Nobody comes to my aid as a nurse walks past the room without a glance in my direction. The machine beeps and wavers to warn of my dad's failing health, but no one stops to notice.

I try to help my dad and put my arms out to restrain him from hitting the furniture. The next thing I know, I'm passing through the human world, both my dad and his bed—then the floor.

Headfirst, arms out, I fall, screaming the entire way down, waiting for the world to catch me. As I do, all I can remember is my dad's face as his body flung itself wildly out of control.

I jolt forward off the ground. Back in Phantom Lagoon I realize it was a dream. I spend the rest of the night praying, hoping—screaming to myself, the Heavens, and everyone within the area—that it is something else besides cancer; something that my dad can be strong enough to overcome.

The next day brought with it numbness. I operate as if I'm a robot, programmed to do one thing. There are no cries that escape. As hard as I try, I cannot find emotion. It had been drained out of me during the night. I had not gotten sleep or found peace of mind. Somehow I'm able to get through the day but not without a thought of death, bad luck, or karma—what had we done?

People murder. People steal. People destroy everything. My family had done nothing. We didn't deserve this. But who does? Who deserves to have their heart torn straight out of their chest, where it's left raw to slowly rot until the pieces are picked up from birds of prey?

"What goes around comes around," my mom would always say. People who murder, their families don't get hurt by karma. Even if they did, the murderer doesn't care enough to be hurt by it. The truth is, those who kill, there's nothing out there they care about. Only themselves. So it makes sense for us to be the only ones affected by karma. The ones who make common mistakes and aren't perfect—people like me—we're the ones hurt; we're the ones who suffer.

Caring is our curse. If we don't care, we can't get hurt. But if we didn't care, the world would be a dark place to live. We have to deal with it and realize life isn't fair. People are taken out of our lives, and others live who don't deserve to continue.

I still find myself asking why. Why me? Why my family? But then I ask why not me? If it weren't me, it would be someone else—maybe someone who already has a bad lot. I know I can get through this. My dad won't live forever, and I know that my mom won't either. I have to learn to stay strong. I have other people in my life now. Eliza has gone through loss just as I have. Kenzie isn't old enough to fully understand what has happened—she may never. But they will act as my family when my mom and dad pass away. They'll be my support system, and I'll be theirs.

That's all I could think of last night—why?

But I'm able to function. I get up to make sure Kenzie is okay and find a way to entertain her. Eliza keeps asking what happened with my dad, but I can't get myself to say the words. The emotion is drained from my face, and when I try to smile, it feels unnatural and forced.

I become restless and return to my house to see if my mom is still there, or if she's left for the hospital to be with my dad already. Her car is gone when I walk into the backyard; there's no sign of her. Stepping inside, I go straight to the phone and dial her cell phone number. It rings five times before she picks up.

"Hello?" She sounds drained.

"Mom? How is he?" I ask into the phone.

"He has brain cancer, and it's already far along. They're going to treat it with chemotherapy and radiation. If they need to, they're also going to perform surgery." Her voice is monotone. The information isn't new to her anymore, and all her emotion is gone along with her energy.

"When will he be able to come home?" I ask.

"We don't know yet. They said they can't let him out of the hospital until they know he will be okay."

The only way he would be released early would be for a hospice. Or the doctors will say there is nothing they can do and send him home to die in comfort. If he's in the hospital, that means there's hope.

My dad could die very quickly. If he wasn't in the hospital right now, he'd most likely be dead. When he does die, I won't be able to see him in the afterlife. I know his life is limited, now more than ever. He won't grow old like I thought, but he's alive at present.

I hear him quietly grunt in the background of the phone. I wish I could be there to hold his hand with my mom. Then there are other voices—doctors and nurses—talking about different treatments and how they might help or affect him. Others rush to my dad's aid and coax him into taking medicine—not that it matters with an IV— and I hear him try to say he's fine.

I know he's not. If he was fine, he wouldn't have to depend on machines to keep him alive. One wrong move and his thin lifeline is cut. No way to repair it—the heart monitor would just read flat.

Another noise comes from my dad. Whatever treatment they are doing is painful. I gasp as I hear him yell out.

"I know it hurts. This should help..."

The phone line goes dead before I can say good-bye to my mom, and I'm left wondering what happened.

Chapter 22

The Promise

I was only four when my dad made me a promise. My mom had been called into work, and he had been assigned to watch me for the day. Before lunch I spent my time playing with my favorite stuffed animal, Barry. I thought I was brilliant for coming up with the name because it sounded like Beary, but spelled differently. My mom had taught me how to write out his name in my messy script. He was a big brown bear of course—about as big as I had been at the time. Whenever I hugged him, I would end up on top of him on the floor, so he doubled as a giant pillow. His fur was a mess, because I dragged him everywhere.

On that particular day my dad was trying to wash him. "Emma, don't you want Barry to be nice and clean?"

"No!" I said, clutching onto his dirty fur like it was my own life. "I don't like baths and neither does Barry!"

I ran outside into our backyard, taking Barry with me, aiming for the shelter of the tree house. My small legs could only take me so far, but I was ahead of my dad until I tripped. Barry's legs had been dangling, and instead of dragging him by the arm, like I usually did, I was gripping him around the neck. My foot caught on one of his paws, and the next thing I knew, my face made contact with the green grass.

I don't think my dad had ever heard me scream so loud.

He rushed to pick me up, but it was too late for Barry. When I had stepped on his leg, the seams gave out, and Barry was officially missing a leg. I didn't see it at first, because my eyes were closed, too busy wailing over the cuts and bruises I had collected when I fell. It wasn't until my dad picked up Barry that I saw my lifelong companion had lost a limb.

My dad didn't know what to do with me, so he took me and Barry inside to clean up. He rested me on the kitchen counter, running a wet cloth over my cuts. By then I had stopped screaming, but it was only because my throat hurt too much to continue. I just looked at my poor little Barry.

"Listen, kiddo. It's gonna be all right," my dad said, opening a box of colorful Band-Aids.

"But, Barry!" I said, though all that came out was mumbles and crying.

My dad placed a bandage over my scrapes. When he finished, he smiled up at me, but I met him with a frown.

"Barry," I said in a sad voice.

My dad sighed and kissed my forehead, before he picked me up and placed me back on the ground. Once my feet made contact with the floor, I ran to my bear, which had been resting on top of the dinner table.

"Barry." I grabbed him by the ear and hugged him tightly. As I did this, stuffing fell out of the hole where his foot had been detached. "Daddy!"

He came over and took the bear from my hands. "Fix him!" I shoved the bear toward my dad, who took it carefully from my grasp. He looked the stuffed animal up and down, examining the dirt-stained fur. I know part of him wanted to throw out the old toy, but I always refused to give it up.

"Tell you what," he started to say, kneeling down in front of me. "You let me clean up Barry, and I'll make him good as new."

I looked at my poor old bear that'd been through the world and back with me and tried to picture him clean. His fur would be a lighter color, maybe even softer.

"You'll keep him safe?" my voice whispered, quiet and low. A tear had started to fall down my face, but I didn't notice until my dad brushed it away with his thumb.

"I'll treat his life like my own."

I nodded my head and gave Barry a kiss. Touching his face, I saw how his fur had crusted together from when I had dropped him in the mud.

That night, without Barry, my room felt empty. The door was closed, so I couldn't see into the hallway, but I could hear my parents talking down the stairs with the television playing softly.

I curled myself into a ball, using the sheets as a shield against any monsters, but it didn't help. Within seconds a tap, tap, tap came from the other side of the room. I closed my eyes, begging the monsters to go, but they didn't.

"Mommy!" I yelled out, burying my face into the pillow. After what seemed like an eternity, I heard my mom slip through my door and come to my bedside.

"Emma, what's wrong?" She took the blankets off my body enough so they didn't cover my head. I rolled to my side to face her, tears welling up in my eyes.

"There's a monster tapping," I cried out. Within the next two breaths, I leaped from my bed and into her arms. She didn't expect it but allowed me to take comfort in her embrace.

"Shh... It's okay," she murmured.

"Daddy took Barry," I mumbled. "Barry scares the monsters away, but tonight he can't because Daddy took him."

When I opened my eyes again, I saw my dad standing at the doorway. With blurry vision I could barely make out my mom nodding her head and my dad walking out of the room. We were alone, just me and my mom, so she sat on my bed as I clutched her neck.

"Emma, what's wrong?"

"They're tapping," I told her in a scared voice, pointing to the far side of the room. Before I could even finish my breath they began again. Tap. Tap. Tap. "There!"

My mom listened for a second and began to rub my back. "It's okay, Emma. That's just the radiator. When it heats up, it makes noise." She pointed to where the noise was coming from, showing me the long piece of metal that made the length of my room.

I leaned into her, still too scared to feel safe in my room alone. That's when my dad walked in with Barry. Not some stuffed animal he bought to replace my friend, but Barry himself. He was clean, but most of all, he had all his limbs attached.

"Barry!" I called out to him, opening my arms to my friend. My dad walked over and placed the bear in my arms, and I hugged Barry tightly. My cheeks pressed into his fur, and it was soft beyond my imagination. I looked up to my dad and something in his eyes was sad.

"I'm sorry, Emma, I forgot to give him back before you went to bed." He sat on my bed also, next to my mom. I slid off her lap and onto my pillow. With the four of us here—Barry included—my bed felt impossibly small.

"Why did you take him?" I said with sad eyes.

"I needed to make him like new again. That meant he had to go way for a while—sorta like a retreat. See his leg? Now it's all better." My dad gave Barry's leg a little tug, and I was about to yell at him, but I saw Barry was still in one piece; in fact he was in the best condition I had ever remembered seeing him.

"But I had no one when he was gone," I told my dad.

"Emma, you have me and your mother. We're always going to be here for you. If you ever need someone to fight off the monsters in Barry's place, I'm your man." My dad smiled at me, and I loosened my grip on Barry.

"Always," my mom added, curling her arm around me to place me in her lap again.

"Really?"

"Pinkie promise."

My dad held out his pinkie for me, and I offered my own. My finger was so small in comparison, but it was a sealed promise just the same. As our fingers entwined, my mom leaned forward to kiss the crown of my head.

That night I slept at ease. My parents tucked me into bed again, this time with Barry at my side; but even if he hadn't been there, I wouldn't have felt alone. I slept knowing my dad gave me a promise. Like the princesses in the movies, he was my knight in shining armor. When the monsters or dragons came, I could always count on him to fend them away.

But now he couldn't do that anymore. My dad's armor has begun to rust and with it sickness came. He made me a promise, and I have no doubt he will always to try to keep it, but some things aren't possible.

My daddy won't always be here, that much is clear.

Chapter 23

Fear & Loss

It becomes treatment after treatment, and nothing seems to help. There are some side effects, like hair loss and vomiting. I watch through the window of his hospital room, as nurses hold a bucket to his face. My mom stays curled up in the corner.

His room is on the bottom floor, and when it's nice out, the nurse leaves the window open. After surgery, another surgery, while my dad is still under the spell of medicine, I climb through a window. At first I just stand there staring, waiting and watching. It's silent aside from the monitor beeping, telling me my dad is alive. I watch as his chest struggles to move up and down. His face, now worn with treatments, no longer looks the same. He's pale, and his skin is paper-thin. All his hair is gone, and he vomits after eating. Everywhere I look, there is some sort of wire keeping him alive.

I sit at one of chairs next to his bed. People are walking out in the hall, and I can make out some of what they are saying. One man is on the phone. "It's going to be okay. She can make it—she's a fighter."

I wish I could say the same for my dad, but his time is coming. I can see it; in the dark circles under his eyes, in his brittle skin, in every part of his bandaged body. Momentarily I wonder who this girl is they are talking about. I hope she is okay for the sake of her family. I know how one lost life can damage someone.

Out in the hall someone shouts orders, and a wheelchair goes by that holds a mother with a swollen belly, pregnant. Her face is red, and she's clutching her husband's hand, as he pushes her wheelchair down the hall to deliver the baby. Life comes and goes out of this world.

I'm startled when I hear a gasping sound come from my dad. I know he's in pain, but I'm forced to leave before he sees me. Before I go, I press the button on his bed that calls the nurse, knowing this is the only help I can provide.

I stand outside the window, until I hear a nurse step into the room to know my dad is in safe hands. She fumbles with some of his wires and tubes, presses buttons, and removes and replaces a bagful of urine connected to the urethra. She leaves again after double-checking everything and gives him a fresh dose of medicine.

I step in one final time and watch as he slips back into unconsciousness. As I look out the window and see the sun going down, I know I have little time left today, or any day, with my dad. I've learned to think of each breath as if it were his last. I come see him every day and stand outside his window—his guardian angel.

"I love you," I whisper. I'm surprised when I see his hand move in response, and a smile crosses his face. I hold on to this memory as I run back to Phantom Lagoon, knowing it's impossible to know the future or predict its path.

Weeks pass and things get worse as my dad manages to cling to his small, thin lifeline that somehow keeps him alive. Whenever I see him in the hospital, I feel like I'm looking at the skeleton of my dad in both senses. Physically he is here, skin and bones, but mentally he's left in some hazed world from so much medication. The doctors want to try a new surgery, and my mom finally gives them the okay after much talk of the risks and benefits.

The procedure is painful, that much I can tell. Since my dad has been sick, he hasn't been talking much, but now he is almost unresponsive. He used to make sounds of pain and agony; now he's just quiet. My mom talks to him, and he stares back as if she isn't even there. This surgery turns out to be a huge mistake. His body responds in the worst way possible. His brain has started to swell and has shortened his lifetime dramatically, leaving us to count our moments.

It's been a long time since my dad has walked, and now his bones are so frail they can't support any weight. The nurses handle my dad with the utmost care as they attempt to bath him without hurting him. I try not to imagine the wails that escape his lips when they take off the bandages to clean his wounds, or put in more needles, or just move him. I have to remind myself that, if he can feel pain, he is alive. I tell myself that this is better than when he had kept quiet after the surgery that made his brain swell.

⁓

I hear my mom on the phone at our house talking to relatives. Some of them have come to see my dad to say their good-byes—it's clear now that his life is very limited in time. They come to see him, but he doesn't remember them. He doesn't remember anyone who isn't immediate family. He just stares blankly at them as they talk, sometimes mumbling a short response to something he sees. This afternoon my aunt is talking to my mom in the kitchen while I sit under the open window, hiding behind a bush.

"He didn't even remember me," my aunt mumbles.

I hear my mom looking through the cabinet for something while she cooks. "He doesn't remember anything now," she says.

"He seemed a lot better today than when I had seen him a few days ago..." my aunt trails off, shaking her head. "Today he seemed different, happy even. He looked at me like a stranger, but he was talking about Emma. He mumbled something about her coming to see him once, that she came through the window. He said that Emma came in after surgery and pushed a button when he couldn't breathe—she saved his life. Then after the nurse came and left, he said she came back in, but before she left, she whispered 'I love you.' I can't help but believe him, because I know she's looking out for him now. He knows who his guardian angel is."

"He said that?" my mom asks in disbelief.

"Every word. He was so sure when he said it too. He said he missed her visits but knows she can't always be with him. He kept saying, 'My little Emma...'"

There is silence after that, and I can tell my mom is absorbing every word that is coming out of my aunt's mouth.

He went into surgery again. The doctors keep trying, but nothing is working. Things have gotten worse, and they know that; something will slip soon.

I sit outside my dad's hospital window and listen to his heart monitor, counting each beat, making sure he is alive. I hear relatives tell my mom a miracle will happen, but it never comes.

My dad becomes more talkative, but his voice is hoarse—it took me days to even realize it was him speaking. He tells my mom the same thing he had told my aunt; I'm his guardian angel watching over him. I know I had made the right choice in coming back. My mom answers with a slight nod of the head and reassuring smile—nothing more. I feel abandoned by her now. In the beginning she had made sure that I didn't forget her. I knew that this time would come though. Someday she would leave me behind and convince herself it was all just a dream. And now it's happened.

I tell myself to forgive her. I can't get it out of my mind that she had never truly said good-bye. I remember clearly in my mind the last time I had talked to her. It was on the phone after my dad had just come to the hospital, and she found out he had brain cancer—she hung up after my dad made a loud cry. She forgot to say good-bye.

The last time I talked to her in person was the day I found out about my dad's illness. She told me everything she knew and walked into the house without saying good-bye or looking back at me. Even when she spoke to me, she looked through me, like I wasn't even there—like I was a ghost. I suppose this all happened when my dad became sick—maybe she's afraid to lose another loved one. I still wish she had said good-bye. I'm gone to her now. I exist more to my dad, and he needs me the most. My mom needed me once, and I needed her but not anymore.

Before I thought I was here to help her, but how can I do that when she is pushing me away? The only person I can help now is my dad. He'll be gone soon and then what? Will my mom need me again or will she continue to forget?

Two months later they give us the news. There is nothing more we can do. The treatments are making things more painful for him. We all know that but don't want to give up.

My mom is the one to make the final decision to stop the treatments. When I sit outside in the cold winter air behind my house, I can hear her inside, trying to figure out how she will let go of her husband. She must have fallen asleep, because soon the house falls silent. I stay until the final rays of sun fall across the sky.

When I return the next day, she is already gone. I sit in the backyard, leaning against the house until I hear a car pull up—two in fact. One is a van that holds my dad and his equipment that will keep him pain free but not alive. My mom is in the other car, and watches as nurses walk into our house and help my dad settle in. When I'm able to catch a glimpse of him, he looks much older than I had last seen him. Now it appears as if he's in his late seventies, not in his forties.

The nurses wheel him inside and put his IVs into place before saying good-bye. "Good luck," one nurse whispers to him, a final good-bye. My mom cries silently as they leave, closing the door behind them. The nurses that have helped my dad for so long drive away, leaving my dad behind.

I come to see him every day now. My mom is at his side each minute, trying to make sure he is comfortable.

I watch through the window as my mom cares for him. He is wrapped in a wool blanket my grandma had made for me when I was little. Its bright pink and blue, but my dad looks shocked when my mom takes it out of the closet.

"That's Emma's," he says in a rough voice.

My mom looks down at the blanket for a minute—maybe thinking back to when she had talked to me after I died, though she still thinks that was all just a dream now, I guess—but she walks over to my dad and places it across his body, until he is fully covered.

"She wants you to be safe," she says, and suddenly I think that she does remember; maybe I was the one who had left. But then when she sits down, I see her shake her head. I know that she's still trying to figure out if it had been real.

Later my dad sits in a wooden rocking chair while hooked up to his IV and other wires—there are few; only enough to keep the pain away. Every night that I have to return to the lagoon, I'm afraid he'll leave while I'm gone. There's no way I can stay by his side until he dies, and I know it's not my fault. If I had to choose a death for my dad, it would be in his sleep. That would be the least painful. I won't be there to hold his hand or watch as he slips away, but I can go through the rest of eternity knowing that he had been dreaming of how it had once been before I died—when we were a family and went on camping trips, and there was no pull trying to take me away.

My mom brings over a chair to sit next to him and holds his hand, his pointer finger encased in a device that measures blood pressure. She rubs his hands, scarred and bruised from IVs and needles, and keeps them warm while they talk. My mom does most of the talking—she tries to keep away from any subject that may pertain to his physical state. She reminds me what it means to truly love someone until the end. Here is my dad, unable to say I love you like he once had, but my mom is at his side, willing to be with him until the last moment.

My dad looks out the window, and I swear he sees me. I don't flinch away when he looks at me and neither does he. Instead he smiles and looks back toward my mom.

"I'll see her soon. My little Emma..." my dad whispers to himself in a quiet voice. I see a tear roll down my mom's face and fall to the ground, as her eyes squint shut. She takes a quick breath, and I try to see if she remembers me.

"I know..." she whispers back, as tears start to cover her face. She clutches his hands and looks at his scarred body. Countless surgeries have left him with red marks on every inch of his body. He looks so different.

"I love you..." he says in a clear voice. It reminds me of how he had once been—the head of the house, going to work, making me breakfast. I wish I could go back to that. But when I look at his aged face, I remember I can't change the past.

Sitting in his rocking chair, I see him draw an elongated breath and know it's his last. It's peaceful, his death; almost dreamlike. My mom, still holding his hand firmly, starts to cry as my dad goes into an unending sleep—she doesn't need to look at the monitor to know he's gone. He slips into the place we call Heaven, where all of his worries are gone....

To be said, in the long run, it was a short fight.

Chapter 24

Senility

Death, loss, and pain; something my family will always feel. It's like there's a curse on us. They say God does things for a reason; that there is a lesson to this. I'm not sure if this is true anymore.

Eternity folds in on itself. The days are obscured and events overlap. The timeline of my life jumps around and no longer makes sense. Year pass, days pass, months pass. Time is a question.

Months later I still find myself unable to let my mom go. I've found my permanent spot sitting under a window that looks in through the kitchen, giving me the simple gift of hearing everything within. Eventually my mom finds her strength again, getting up out of her chair with a fury. The table around her is filled with our family that has taken it upon themselves to take care of her after my dad's passing.

"Get out of my house," she says in a slow, angry voice. My aunt stares at her in disbelief.

"Honey, please sit down," my grandma says, motioning my mom to lower her voice.

"I can take care of myself." My family is shaken by her actions, but my grandparents—who have been staying with her—leave the table with a quiet good-bye. My aunt stands her ground, while my grandparents go around the house to pack their things. My mom sits at the table, falling apart in her own personal silence.

"We'll be back soon," my grandma says with a smile, as if my mom isn't uprooting them from the place they had lived for the past few weeks.

My grandparents let themselves out, leaving my mom and aunt alone. "Please, just leave me," my mom says, tears filling her eyes. They start to stream down the corner of her eyes, but she makes no attempt to conceal or hide them.

"But..."

"Please," my mom says again, cutting off my aunt before she can finish.

Some sort of understanding comes, and my aunt quietly gathers her things and departs.

My dad's funeral was not like mine in any sense. I was determined to stay the entire time, but once it started, I knew I would not last.

Everyone is quiet, silently crying to themselves. I find myself curled in a ball, in a bush near the church, trying not to burst out with an audible scream. I miss my dad and want to honor him today, but soon I find myself running back to the safety of my house, knowing everyone who might have been there before is now attending the funeral.

Rubbing my eyes, my chest is heaving by the time I reach my house. In my empty yard I don't know where to go but find myself climbing. Soon I'm in the trees above everything. I hug the branches, clinging to the bark with both fear and longing, looking over what is laid out in front of me. I want to scream, to yell to the world, "I'm alive." I stand, hands clenched on a limb above, feet unstable on the rounded branch of the thick tree. I inhale and am about to shout until I feel something inside me slip. My grip lessens, but I don't fall. Instead, I sit on the branch, my knees no longer strong. Leaning against the bark of the tree, I let myself release all the emotion I have been holding back since my dad got sick.

The funeral started in the early bitter winter morning—snow is expected. An hour or two passes, and it's like I'm frozen in place to the tree. I feel an odd sensation glide through my body and open my eyes to the first snowfall of the year. It's different from how rain feels. In Phantom Lagoon rain feels as if bugs are crawling on you. Snow is light—like a breeze.

With unstable legs I climb down from the tree and stand in the open expanse of my backyard. The sky is white, small puffs of snow floating down. Already the ground has a light layer blanketing the yard. Behind me there is the sound of footsteps and the rustle of tree branches. Turning around, I see Luna approach in her unmistakable ball gown. She wears a shawl to cover her shoulders in the cold.

"How do you do it?" I find myself asking.

She laughs and motions me to follow her to a picnic table near the back door of my house. I sit next to her and wait for an answer.

Luna fumbles with the lace on her dress, recalling some memory unknown to me. "I was born in 1326 on a full moon during a solar eclipse. My parents named me Adia de Luna, but they always called me Adia. I grew up in Marseille, France. We were just peasants, wondering if we would be lucky enough to eat that day. It took me centuries to learn death is hard to come by." She pauses, and I try to figure out what she means. Finally she looks down at her dress and rubs the floral pattern while speaking.

"While I was still human, I lived through the Black Death. I watched my family fall to the sickness, and one by one they all died. I tried to save them but could only save myself. I discovered the magic that's held on Earth, and now I live forever. It's a curse I've brought upon every soul in Phantom Lagoon, and a day hasn't gone by where I wish I hadn't tried to save myself in 1348. I was ignorant to my actions, and I never dreamed I would've succeeded. I spent the better part of two hundred years in Europe exploring. There was a gentleman...and soon I was risking everything for him. I loved him—the feeling was mutual." She pauses for the briefest moment, fumbling with her dress. "Horrible things happened, and I was forced to the New World. Even now I still wait for his return, thinking he will come for me. I know I can't let myself fall in love again—not when I will live forever. Phantom Lagoon was made to protect souls from the deadly stones, but some still wonder..." she trails off, closing her eyes.

She looks at me now. "Phantom Lagoon has different effects on people. Most become scared. Tyler is a unique soul. He was an orphan who worked in the mills before there were child labor laws. He was scared when he came but found his voice. He had no family to lose, so the lagoon became his playground. He became an annoyance to most, but we think of him as a part of our family. He's not perfect, but here in Phantom Lagoon, his life is far better than it had been working in the mills.

"Emma, you are just as Eliza. You two are so close to your families that it's hard to let go. You both go the full extent to save them and hold on to them. Eliza's father, David, is one who will be missed. When he came, he was not afraid. He took his soul and almost tossed it aside, when he saw the condition Eliza was in. He was willing to see her every day and tell her the secret, if he had to. He knew what could happen, and he tried his best to stop it. But Eliza did follow him one day, and now she's part of this family. David was thought of badly after that. I wanted to help him and to convince the others to overlook what happened, but he convinced himself that he had murdered his daughter. Although I know Eliza was happier here. Once David disappeared from Phantom Lagoon, Eliza went through a lot of changes and began experimenting like you. She got through it, and so will you."

"Luna, did the moon really cause this?" I ask in a timid voice.

"Yes, but there are things you wouldn't understand—still things I don't understand. The moon saved my life. I was born blind. During the eclipse of the sun, I looked up at it. I watched as the sun slowly came back into view. My grandfather grasped me immediately. He hadn't known I was born blind—but I had. For some reason, even at that early age, I knew something was wrong with me. But the sun—it gave me sight. While others looked away from the harmful rays of the sun during the eclipse, I was drawn to it. I could not see colors, but I had sight.

"My grandfather was superstitious—he blamed my loss of color on the day I was born. He said it was unnatural to birth life the same day the sky goes dark. I told him what happened, and he scoffed at me. 'To be born blind for only seconds is preposterous. The eclipse stole your sight!' He hated my parents for naming me after the moon. I don't know what would have happened if I had stayed blind—being handicapped was not an option during that era. I owed myself to the moon. When I became an Essence, I saw color and brilliancy for the first time in my life. That was when I realized my eyes were almost white. When I had looked to the moon, it had done something that can't be explained. It's not possible to be born with such eye pigmentation. It resembles the moon in ways that are uncanny. But to be able to live with sight...I would've given up more than just the color of my eyes.

"Phantom Lagoon is not just from the moon though, Emma—some things have so much to tell us. Those stones aren't for punishment. They're just here."

I put my hand to my neck and feel the stone around it—its visible flaws. I wish I could correct them—correct me.

"Emma, you have to realize people die. Some of us don't. Eternity is neither a gift nor a curse. We just need to know how to use it." She walks back to the forest without another word.

The snow falls to the ground, and I let it glide through my body, until I hear the sound of a car pulling up. Without thinking, I run toward Phantom Lagoon, knowing my mom no longer believes I'm here.

My mom is acting as if I'm dead; that there is no way on earth that I can exist. I do exist, but my mom ignores me. Once my dad became sick, I was forgotten—put on hold. Now she questions whether what happened between us is real and has come to the conclusion it isn't. She told me not to forget her, but she has forgotten me instead. I knew it would happen—but, again, things have come too soon.

I once stood in the middle of the room, determined to talk to her and get answers. But she walked by me without a second glance, acting like she had seen a ghost—which I suppose she had.

Two years pass, and I stop seeing my mom altogether. My mom lives alone and no longer wants to see her friends. At first they would come over to make sure she was okay, like my family had, but my mom didn't want anyone around her.

I don't abandon her though. I'm there, always watching, making sure she is okay. She doesn't know it, but I'm always close by.

My mom's life consists of staying in the house. She cries a lot; sometimes while holding my drawings, other times while she is holding something of my father's. She will just curl up on the bed and cry while holding our belongings. She didn't eat at first, and I began to worry about her—I knew I couldn't sit and watch her starve. I tried my best to help her, so I contacted her doctor once, telling him to come over immediately. He didn't question who I was or why I was calling.

When the medics arrive, they found my mom sulking on the floor. She refused to move, and they were forced to remove her from the house. It pains me to see her dragged from her home and placed in an ambulance to be rushed to a hospital, but I know they can take care of her for me.

They bring her to a "home" where she can stay and talk to others. It isn't for the mentally ill, but it does have nurses. There are apartments and privacy, but everyday a nurse comes by with medication. It's somewhere they can keep a close eye on her. Somewhere she can't get hurt. Somewhere she isn't alone. It's where she'll live from now on.

She doesn't like it. It takes her a month before she stops asking to go home. After that she realized there is no home to go to. With no one living there, family members decided to sell our house—a new family lives there now.

They have two daughters and a son—he is the youngest. His name is Justin, and he is no older than Kenzie. He's a handful and his two older sisters—one eight and the other eleven—enjoy helping him raid the house. I like watching them play in the backyard, but when they first moved in, it was hard to see my things taken away. All our furniture was put onto a moving truck and given to family members, since my mom has no use for it.

My room—which had been left undisturbed after I died— had all its contents taken out, which were either thrown away or given to Goodwill. I can't take anything with me or have a say in where they end up. The hardest thing to see go is a box that holds all my colored pencils and charcoal that I used for drawing. They are special to me, and it's difficult to see the movers carelessly throw them into a garbage bin, along with so many other things I wish I could've saved.

In a way I'm glad my mom isn't the one to make the decision of what she is going to keep from our house—I know, if she was the one to throw out that box, it would've hurt more.

More years pass and things get better. My mom no longer locks herself in her room, refusing to come out and socialize. She's made friends, and when family visits, she hugs and greets them. Sometimes she will ask when she gets to go home, but whoever is with her that day will just say that she already is home.

There are still those days where the pain of loss will overcome and almost take her alive. She will stop eating, and when people talk to her, it is like she isn't even there. Her eyes are so blank it is as if she's on another planet. I wonder sometimes if she remembers when I had visited her. If she still questions whether I'm real or not. I feel as if I've already had to give her up and let go.

Upon my mom's seventy-sixth birthday, she is moved into a nursing home which can treat people who need intensive care. I, on the other hand, am frozen at the age of fifteen.

Chapter 25

North Conway

I wander through town, watching as rain falls down from the sky and melts into the asphalt that lines the roads. Everything is quiet as people take refuge in restaurants and other buildings to get away from the dampness.

I don't know why I'm here. I've never visited town as an Essence, unless I was passing through to get somewhere else—which usually involved seeing my parents or family somewhere. But today I'm just walking through the forest, and eventually it opens up to a road. I forgot where it leads, and now here I am: North Conway. Shops line the street, and inside them people poke through the shelves, looking but not really buying.

The mountains line the perimeter, making the landscape background to this town a beautiful postcard picture. I wish the rain bothered me like it once had, but it doesn't anymore. Once upon a time it felt like bugs crawling across my skin, but now...nothing. I don't know if I got used to it, or if I just don't care enough anymore, but the rain continues to pass through me, nothing more than a tickle.

The air is cold but not enough to snow. The sky is dark, but it's only because of the rain clouds that block the sun. Out in the distance I can only see the base of the mountains, the misty air hiding the peaks. I still have a few more hours until Phantom Lagoon calls me back.

I step into a gift shop that sells T-shirts. They all say "New Hampshire" in bold, colorful letters and are overpriced for the simple design, but tourists still buy them. I look through the postcards, gazing at the photos of landscapes, bears, moose, and waterfalls.

"You aren't seriously going to buy that are you?"

I turn to the voice, and see a man grab a winter hat that has moose antlers and then places it on his head.

"What, I don't look good?" he says, turning and putting on a winning smile. The woman with him laughs and takes off the hat.

"Why do I go out in public with you?" she asks herself. When I see her face, I know her instantly. Sadie. After all these years she still has the same laugh. Her blond hair has light brown lowlights died for dimension and the length stops just shy of her shoulders. Everything about her is the same, yet amazingly different. On her left hand she wears a ring that is most likely a gift from the man she shops with now. They are both in their early forties.

"Don't you think Trish would love this?" the man says, holding out the moose hat again. He is about to model it, but Sadie takes it from his hands.

"Our daughter has higher standards than this."

"Willing to bet?" he says, a smile sprawling across his face. He gets money out of his pocket and holds it up to her face.

Sadie laughs and pushes away his money. "Your money is my money, remember?"

"All right." He puts away the cash. "If Trish doesn't like the hat—which she will because she's Daddy's girl and loves anything I give to her—then I'll bow to your every need and whim."

She smiles at the offer, already thinking of what she'll have him do. "And if she does like the hat?" she asks, crossing her arms, trying to find the catch.

"Then I get to bask in the wonderful words of 'I told you so!'"

"Fine, go ahead. Buy the hat." She ushers him to the register to pay, but she slinks behind. Sadie shakes her head, laughing to herself while her husband waits in line with the crazy hat with antlers for their daughter.

Her focus wanders my way for the briefest moment, and when our gazes lock, I smile at her. She freezes, looking me up and down. I see her eyebrows furrow, as she begins to turn to her husband.

"Honey?" I hear her voice say, as I rush out the door and back into the rain. The bell at the top of the door alerts her of my departure. In the rain I cross the street and stand under a canopy. Sadie walks from the store with her husband. They stand hand in hand, but she is searching the street for any sign of me. She isn't scared after seeing my ghostly form, like I thought she would be. Instead she just looks around, a small smile forming on her lips.

"What is it?" her husband asks.

She shrugs, never bothering to look across the street to where I stand. "I just thought I saw a friend that I haven't seen for a while," she says with a knowing grin. They walk away, but Sadie smiles as she does so, looking up into the rain clouds, as if expecting I would be there.

~

"Would you like to see a trick?" a man asks, as I walk through the rain, making my journey home to Phantom Lagoon. His clothes are brightly colored, and he wears a top hat with a green ribbon going across it. He's the type of street performer I'd see all over the streets in the summer, but now it's fall. The rain that pours down on us mutes the colors of his clothes and makes it cling to his skin.

I back away from him for a moment, afraid he may see I'm different. Unlike humans, the rain doesn't soak my clothing; it just glides through me. I'm not dripping wet or cold like this man; and if I stand in the rain long enough, he will notice. ·

A few more steps backward and I'm under a canopy again.

"Well, don't be scared, child!" He laughs, mostly to himself, an odd Irish accent in his speech. "I just want to show you something."

I don't speak a word, but I also don't move. He takes this as encouragement, and reaches into one of his many pockets and pulls out a long rubber balloon. He stretches it, pulling it, wrapping it around his finger to make a show of the simple gesture.

"Balloon animals?" I ask, speaking up. The man stands out in the rain still, unlike me, who has the cover of the canopy. He doesn't make a move to come underneath the shelter. He almost seems to enjoy the rain that continues its rhythmic pattern across his skin.

"No, no! I do so much more than just blow up balloons. You see, I'm more than just your average clown." He gestures down to his clothing and for the first time I see a plastic flower pinned to his shirt. I look him over in more detail, expecting to find abnormally large shoes, but his are just black and normal. "Why, I believe my balloons tell you things that may or may not happen."

"So a fortune teller?" I ask.

"If that's what you wanna call it." He smiles at me, handing over the deflated balloon. "Why don't you warm that up in your hands for me?"

The string of rubber hangs between us, and I take it carefully, knowing that, if I touch his skin, I will simply pass through.

"Go ahead, warm 'er up!"

I do as he says, rolling the balloon between my two hands. The rubber doesn't grow warm like it may if a human were doing this, but I decide to humor the man.

"All right, all right. You got enough of your DNA on there already. Hand it over," he says, as if disgusted with me.

I laugh as he cringes when the balloon falls into his hands again. "I'm going to have to sterilize everything after you leave," he mumbles loudly to himself.

With a shimmy of his shoulders and a clear of his throat, he blows into the balloon infected with my DNA. His eyes cross, and I can't help but laugh, as he puts on a show while just inflating the balloon. After a few deep breaths on his part, the balloon is filled with air, revealing its dark purple hue.

"Why...this looks like the color of the necklace you got there," he says, winking at me. I look down at my stone, and sure enough, they are a perfect match.

He observes the balloon, twisting and turning it to look at it from different angles. He brings it to his ear, listening to what the balloon tells him. "Hmm. Yep. Sure!" He speaks to it like it's a phone. He levels his head again and makes fast motions to shape the balloon. He stops suddenly, seeing I'm watching and makes a shocked face, as if I've just walked in on him.

"How rude!" he says, undoing all the work he's done to shape the balloon, turning it back into a straight line. He pivots, hiding what he is doing and begins his work again. I stand under the canopy, listening to the rain fall. The odd man makes a small grunt as he continues to work on the balloon.

"Aha!" He holds up the balloon and turns to me.

I try to hold in a laugh when he shows it to me. After all that work he seemed to put into his trick, the only thing I see is what looks like a lollipop-shaped balloon. I raise my eyebrows, suppressing a smile, when he puts up his finger to stop me.

"Do you see it?" he asks.

"I don't think so," I say, half giggling.

"It is a magnifying glass!"

He takes it by the handle and comes closer to me. He uses it, looking closely at my face, and I back away to make sure he doesn't touch me. He makes odd faces as he examines me. He steps aside, rummages again through his pockets and pulls out a needle. Without hesitation he pops the balloon, letting it drop to the ground and puts away the needle.

"Are you ready to hear what I have seen?" he asks, proper in his stance, hands behind him, chin up.

I nod, curious at what this man has to say.

"You will lose something soon. I would give you the magnifying glass, but..." He looks down at the rubber balloon in shreds on the ground. "It popped." He gives a disappointed face.

He observes my face again.

"Don't fret, my darling! Losing things is okay, because then it can be found!"

I try to smile to thank him for the entertainment, but in my heart, I hope his fortune is false.

I search my pockets to give the man money, but come up short. Instead I turn to the side-walk and pick a stray daisy, drowning in the rain, and hand it to the man. He smiles, bows in a curtsy manner, and takes the flower, tucking it behind his ear. I start to walk past him into the rain where Phantom Lagoon waits.

"Don't worry, child," he yells out to me. "Sometimes when you find something, it's better than you remembered it being when you lost it."

I turn around and eye the man, who is probably the strangest person I have ever met. Clad in his top hat, he sticks out like a sore thumb, but his face tells me that he wishes he could have given me a better fortune.

"Thank you," I say in a whisper.

I didn't think he heard me, but he takes off his top hat and bows to me again.

"Anything for you."

He stares at me for a moment too long and sees I'm different. His eyes register that the rain passes through my body and doesn't soak my skin. He opens his mouth, as if to say more, but stops himself. Instead, he smiles.

"You'll find it," he says.

Chapter 26

Runaway

Eliza and I plan to take Kenzie to see her family someday. We go without Kenzie to watch her family and make sure they are okay. The first visit is for Kenzie's fourth memorial birthday; her family holds a memorial at a park near their house. Eliza sits by herself on one of the swings, while she watches, and I want to sit with her too, but I'm afraid someone will recognize me, so I stay in the forest at the edge of the park.

Kenzie's relatives arrive with flowers, and they talk about going to the cemetery to put them on Mackenzie's grave. Her parents cry, but I can tell they are happy to have a family that cares for their lost little girl. There are smiles, and tears, but most of all, there is love.

At the end of the party Eliza comes to sit with me in the trees until everyone leaves.

"Did you notice?" Eliza whispers.

"What?"

"Look at Kenzie's mom, how she's acting."

She is talking to her husband while they hold hands, looking at the sun that is beginning to set in the sky. He kisses her head and wraps his arm around her waist. Finally she holds her hand to her stomach and leans into him.

"They're having another baby," Eliza smiles, eyes aglow in the setting sky. The two of us leave, giving silent wishes to Kenzie's parents as they start a family again.

Months later a baby girl named Jessica arrives into the world. She looks like Kenzie in so many ways, yet they still seem to be polar opposites at the same time. Jessica is born with black hair like her mother and seems quiet, unlike Kenzie who always has something to say.

Eliza visits Jessica during the afternoons to watch her play in the backyard. Her parents still remember Kenzie and sometimes I leave a pink ribbon in Jessica's room while she takes a nap. It's a message of love to Kenzie's parents, and it isn't long until they realize the ribbons don't come from Jessica. Her mom keeps every ribbon and puts them in a jar with Kenzie's name on it. I share the ribbons whenever Kenzie's family needs a lift in spirit, and it always does the trick.

Jessica marries her life partner on what would have been Mackenzie's twenty-fifth birthday. Jessica walks down the aisle, wearing a rose pink dress with Kenzie's pink ribbons incorporated into the bouquet of flowers.

Like the rest of us, Kenzie is frozen in age. She is still only three, the same as the day she arrived. Jessica is now twenty-seven and has a family of her own with twin sons only a few weeks old. Kenzie is an aunt, but she has no knowledge of it. She doesn't even know she has a sister or about the amazing things her family has done in her honor. Kenzie is still under the impression that she's an angel, waiting to earn her wings. Eliza and I have to remind ourselves that we lied to protect her, not to keep her away from her family. We've thought about telling her, but it always ends in a moot point, arguing over what would be best and whether Kenzie would even understand.

Since Kenzie has settled into her life at Phantom Lagoon, Luna stopped coming, unless someone needs her. She always seems to disappear into the forest and then shows up whenever there is tension, but no one ever calls for her. Things have settled down so much it has become quiet—nobody talks. When you have forever, there is nothing left to interest you.

Kenzie is hidden in the forest of trees somewhere, playing hide-and-seek. She is the best hider out of all of us, because she is so small. Sometimes, when we can't find her, we'll ask someone to tell us of her hiding place, so we can unveil her.

"Emma!" Kenzie screams out, jumping in front of me to reveal herself. She laughs, and Eliza comes to join us. "Eliza, your turn to hide!" Kenzie says, taking Eliza by the hand.

"How about you go play with someone else, Kenzie? I need to talk to Emma," she says, turning down Kenzie's game.

She's disappointed for a minute before running over to the many spirits that stay in Phantom Lagoon during the day. It isn't long before she's found herself a new playmate.

"What's wrong?" I ask, turning to Eliza.

"Kenzie is twenty-seven. She's smart. I think we should tell her."

I look over to Kenzie playing with a young woman who smiles brightly. Another older man—in his sixties maybe—watches her, laughing at what she has to say.

"I know."

Eliza pushes the subject. "She needs to know about her family."

"I know, Eliza, but I don't know how she will react," I say, watching the little girl I've known like a sister. Her human life was destroyed, but here in Phantom Lagoon, she seems so happy. I don't know if she still thinks about her family, but she never speaks of or asks about them.

"Tomorrow then." And Eliza walks away to join in Kenzie's game.

"Mackenzie, sit down," Eliza starts in a serious tone, letting Kenzie know right away it's important to listen carefully.

Kenzie sits on a tree stump, following directions. I settle to the ground, leaning against the tree, while Eliza kneels down beside Kenzie. We can hear the quiet murmur of talking coming a few feet away in Phantom Lagoon. From the short distance I can see the fence of trees that is supposed to safeguard the lagoon, but out here, we are away from its beauty and magic for a moment.

"Do you remember the day you met us?" I ask, picking a wild pansy, the same flower I saw the day my father died; it had shown me hope.

"Yeah," she says. "I was camping with Mommy and Daddy, and I saw you. When Mommy and Daddy were asleep, I went to look for you."

"Why?" I whisper, wishing I had just stayed away from Kenzie and her family.

"I heard you scream. I wanted to make sure you were okay."

Eliza glances at me. I take a long breath and close my eyes.

"Where were your parents?" Eliza steps in, holding Kenzie's hand.

"Asleep," she says, crossing her arms and taking her hand away from Eliza, as if to tell us not to question her actions. The rejection stings Eliza for a moment, but she smiles and turns quiet.

I grasp my stone as the memories surface of Kenzie's human death. There was a short moment—a fraction of infinity—when I thought she was going to be able to continue her human life. But she had found a stone. "Why did you leave, Kenzie?"

"I'm sorry, Emma," Kenzie tells me, putting her hand on my shoulder.

"No," I say, wiping my eyes out of habit. "It's not your fault."

"Kenzie," Eliza says, stroking her hair. "Do you know how old you are?"

Her eyes look around her for an answer. I can almost see her thinking, counting the years in her head, but I can tell her human memories are harder to put in order, making counting years difficult. She doesn't answer.

"Twenty-seven," Eliza states. "But you look three, because that's how old you were when you came to Phantom Lagoon."

"When I became an angel?" She perks up at the magical thought of having glorious wings that stem from her shoulder blades.

"You aren't an angel," Eliza says softly, running her hand through Kenzie's curls.

"Because I haven't earned them yet," Kenzie finishes, touching Eliza's arm. Eliza shakes her head, her lips growing flat.

"You aren't an angel, Kenzie. You're an Essence," I tell her. "When you picked up the stone in Phantom Lagoon, it trapped your soul. Your parents didn't give you to us. They think you're dead."

She sits there, processing everything, keeping quiet. Sometimes her eyes shift to some point in the forest; she memorizes it, and then looks down at her hands.

"I'm not an angel," she finally manages to whisper. It's a statement, not a question.

Eliza nods her head.

Kenzie's lips begin to tremble and soon she's taking small gasps of air. Eliza tries to put her arm around Kenzie.

"Mommy!" she cries, pushing Eliza away from her. "Daddy!"

"Kenzie, please, calm down."

I get to my feet to comfort her, but she pushes me away also, and runs from the lagoon and us. Her shove doesn't physically hurt but knowing why she did it torments me. We sit on the ground, knowing she may never trust us again, hoping one day she will come to forgive us.

"I'm sorry," I whisper to Kenzie as she keeps her back to us. Beside me Eliza stands, staring at the girl we both call our sister. A few seconds pass, and Eliza's knees buckle, and she comes to the ground next to me.

We both sit in silence, waiting for Kenzie to come back.

"What happened?" Luna bursts through the trees and comes over to where we sit on the ground.

"We told Kenzie the truth," Eliza says, wiping invisible tears from her face.

We all sit in the quiet of the forest for what seems like hours, but the sun has hardly moved its position in the sky. Eliza and I both wanted to search and find Kenzie, but there was a silent agreement between us that she just needed time.

"She ran away," I say quietly.

Luna nods, understanding Kenzie's motives. "Go find her. She doesn't know the difference between human life and an Essence. Make sure you're all back by nightfall." She takes a final worried glance around the forest where Kenzie has hidden before, leaving us to search.

We had forgotten. In all the talk of angels we had filled in Kenzie's head, we had never once mentioned she needed to be in Phantom Lagoon before nightfall. Eliza gives me a quick scared look, as she realizes what danger Kenzie is in. We both rise to our feet. It's a real-life game of hide-and-seek, and as always, Kenzie is the best at hiding.

Eliza and I are both quiet as we search, listening for some sort of sign from Kenzie.

"Do you think we shouldn't have told her?" I ask, moving branches out of my way to search paths of the forest and small hiding spots Kenzie has used in past games of hide-and-seek.

Eliza keeps walking, but I wait for her answer, frozen at the bush of berries that Kenzie used to win one game of hide-and-seek. When I move the bush slightly, red berries fall to the ground. Eliza sees I've stopped and looks back at me, taking a deep breath.

"I would want to know," she says, rubbing her arms for warmth out of a long-ago human habit. She looks at the berries on the ground. "I think we did wrong by lying in the first place." Our lie could only hold its place for so long, but like the berries on the bush, it fell.

She starts to walk again, but I stay in my place. "But if you could never see your parents again at the age of three, would you rather have the truth or the hope that you are something better in the world?"

Eliza shakes her head and continues to walk. "Better in the world," she mutters. "Emma, hope is an amazing thing, but it's not made to blind people. That's what we did to Kenzie, and if we don't find her soon, we'll never see her again." Eliza grows quiet and stops to finger her stone necklace before taking a deep, almost relieved breath.

"Do you think we will find her?" I ask.

Eliza looks at me, dumbfounded. "Only if she wants to be found," she finally says in a nervous voice, staring up at the setting sky.

We continue forward, never looking back, as we venture farther to find Kenzie in the small amount of time we were given. In front of me Eliza walks, always clutching her stone, as if it may disappear if it's not in her grip.

"There isn't much time before we have to turn back," Eliza says, her stare fixated on the sky, asking for more hours in the day.

I look around myself, seeing the forest grow orange with the sun's passing. "Kenzie, please come back," I whisper to myself.

Eliza turns to me, and I can see something is wrong. Her face is scared. All of a sudden everything about her demeanor has changed; the calm shell is gone, and she looks close to falling over. Taking her stone, she closes her eyes and kneels to the ground, breaths coming fast.

"I'm sorry." She whispers over and over. I can see her body shake as she says the words. She slumps closer to the soil of the ground.

I kneel beside her and take her hand. "It's going to be okay," I say with a shaky voice, even though I know it's not true.

"No, it's not." Eliza speaks louder and sits up to look me in the eyes. "It's not, Emma. How could we lie to her? How could we let her run away and not do anything? We let her leave." Her eyes plead with me, but then all at once, she gives up the fight.

"I know." I feel the fear of losing Kenzie build up inside me and try to push it away. "Once she feels the pain, she'll come back," I say, hating the words.

Anger flashes in Eliza's eyes, suddenly growing protective. "What if I don't want her to feel that pain? She doesn't even know her way back," Eliza says, rubbing her stone that lies across her neck. Her face has grown flush red, making her green eyes glow with the contrasting color. The emotion in her flops around, and I can tell she is torn; she wants to save Kenzie, but she's scared.

Eliza looks at the sky that grows darker by the second.

"I'm going back," Eliza says suddenly, as if something occurred to her. "There's nothing else we can do, and if we stay, we'll just hurt ourselves too."

Eliza gets up and brushes herself off, arms shaking slightly. Her eyes follow the sun's path in the sky, and I can see the fear in her face as she thinks about the amount of time she has to get back to Phantom Lagoon. Finally she looks at me. "I can't face the unknown, Emma. If staying meant being with Kenzie and my father, I would, but I'm afraid," she says, turning toward the direction of the lagoon. Her throat grows tight, making her speech slurred. "I will understand if you didn't come back."

She begins to walk away, always glancing up at the sky.

"Do you mean suicide?" I ask, still kneeling on the ground.

She looks over her shoulder, back to me, saying nothing. Turning forward again, she grabs something out of her pocket and tosses it in front of me. All at once she runs away and doesn't look back. An echo of a sob is heard, but it's so quiet, I can't be sure if the sound is actually there.

I reach out, across the enriched soil of the forest, for what Eliza gave to me. It's a piece of paper, folded five times, the edges worn from being read and refolded.

1993 – I'm sorry. I'm sorry I didn't listen to Mom. I'm sorry I didn't try to get better. But what I'm not sorry for is coming to Phantom Lagoon. You yelled at me and screamed, and I saw you cry for the first time; except there were no tears because of who we are. I'm sorry my fear brought me here.

2001 – Today you disappeared. Remember how you told me we always have to come back at night? You stayed with Mom after her car crashed and forgot me.

Mom died yesterday. Were you still there when it happened?

2004 – Is it wrong to think about killing myself? Is it even possible? How did you end your life?

2007 – I stayed out after dark today. I never knew your stone could fully disappear. I've seen it become translucent, but when it was gone, I knew something was wrong.

2008 – The pain from staying out in the dark is unbearable. I want to be with you, but it hurts. I'm so sorry.

I can't do this anymore. Will you save me?

2010 – There's a little girl named Kenzie who came to Phantom Lagoon. She followed Emma, so we've been taking care of her like we're all sisters—I guess we are family.

2034 – Kenzie left.

Chapter 27

Healing

"Kenzie!" As I shout, I can hear myself slowly growing quiet. I feel the lack of air in my throat threatening to stop sound completely. I keep searching after Eliza leaves, but there's no sign of Kenzie. "Please!" My voice cracks, and I lean on my knees for support as I cough.

"I'm sorry! You need to come back, Kenzie!"

I fall to my knees and listen to the leaves drift in the wind. The ghost sobs well up in my throat, before it finally releases itself. I break down and hold my ribs as a stabbing pain comes from within me. Above me the sky glows with a beautiful sunset.

When I look in front of me, I see a flickering coming from the ground. I clutch the stone at my neck, feeling it grow soft as it leaves me for Phantom Lagoon. I approach the glowing earth to find a pink stone.

She's left her soul.

"Kenzie," I mumble her name.

I take my stone from around my neck and place it next to hers. It's a bright pink, flickering as if calling her. Our stones fade together. My purple turns more translucent and even though I feel the stabbing pain, I don't react. Kenzie's pink stone radiates bright again—like a Christmas light before darkening—and then it disappears.

I feel her leave with it.

A piercing scream emerges somewhere in front of me. Instantly, I jump up and run in its direction, knowing exactly whose scream it is.

"Kenzie!"

Branches fly past my face; a bird scatters off its perch in a tree, as I come in a frantic whirl of motion. I freeze in the middle of the forest, using all my will to hear her voice in reply.

"Mackenzie!" My voice is raw.

"Emma." There is a quiet crying sound off in the distance. My feet carry me to her where she lies on the ground in a fetal position. "What's happening?" she mumbles, barely audible as her arms shake.

"We need to get back to Phantom Lagoon," I say, looking at the sky. The sun is going down as the sky turns from orange to purple—I can see half the sun, hidden by the horizon.

"I can't." She begins to cough.

I step forward, kneeling down to her, feeling every muscle in my body beg to just be still. I cradle her in my arms, watching the child grow pale. "It's going to be okay."

I try to walk as fast as I can, but after a few steps I fall to the ground with Kenzie in my arms. There's a scream, but I can't tell which one of us it is—maybe both. When I look over at Kenzie, I see tears in her eyes.

"How?" I ask, but Kenzie breaks into a cry and arches her back in severe pain. Her entire body is red and flushed, but when I look at my arms, I'm normal.

"Make it stop!" she screams, but I can't. I look at her eyes that were once brown but are now rimed in crimson. She makes another shrill scream, before the convulsions begin. Her body shakes, and I don't know what to do. I'm watching my dad have a seizure all over again; except this time, it's Kenzie's life on the line.

Her mouth is open, searching for breath but not able to find any.

"No," I whisper, feeling a stabbing pain down my spine. My arms threaten to drop Kenzie, but instead, I hold her closer, promising myself I won't let her disappear. "I'm supposed to save you," I whisper, but it's no more than a faint sound in the wind. And even though I can feel every muscle burn as I carry Kenzie, I continue forward.

In my arms Kenzie takes a gasping breath of air, and even though I want to stop and see if she's okay, I start into a run. As I do, I can feel tears run down my face like they had for Kenzie. I run faster, knowing that the tears mean more pain is coming.

When we come to a more familiar forest, a flash of pain comes to the surface. It feels as if a knife is going straight down my spine, only stopping if I let out the familiar scream of death. I fall to the ground on my knees but manage to keep Kenzie in my arms. We are so close to safety, yet it's far beyond our reach.

Get up! If you fall, we all fall!

I hear it out loud, my voice. I didn't speak it.

Now! Once you hit that ground, you will never get back up!

I've heard this voice before; even as a human, in my dreams. My soul—my other half that's always been protecting me.

I find my strength and hang onto Kenzie in my arms. She's quiet, and I don't have time to look at her, so I tell myself that she's okay, even if it's a lie, and move forward.

The sky turns from purple to a dark blue. I wonder how I'm alive until I see it—Phantom Lagoon. As I break through the trees, I realize I had been holding my breath since I first saw the fence of trees. I kneel down and release Kenzie, letting her body roll out from my hands. When I try to stand again, any last remains of energy leave, and I fall to my side instead.

There's a small silence, and then a brush of air as everyone from Phantom Lagoon circles around us. I close my eyes and feel a tear roll down my cheek.

"She's crying," someone whispers. Such a simple fact for a human; but for an Essence, it's so much more.

I break into a sob at the words and feel more tears well up at my eyes.

"Something's wrong with them, Luna," another person whispers. I can almost picture the scene like a movie. Here are these people, standing around me like a rat that has just been tested on. The experiment didn't go as planned, but the scientist—the people of Phantom Lagoon—poke and prod at me to see if I'm still alive. *Can we resurrect her?*

I feel Luna put her hand to my face and open my eyes. No images form, and I'm blind. I convince myself this is it—this is what it must be like to disappear. She examines my arms and pushes away anyone who comes too close, giving me room to breathe.

"Bring them both closer to the lagoon," she says, her voice growing farther away from me.

For the next few minutes there is a lot of movement, and I think I'm being lifted. Talking surrounds me, but I can't understand anything. Why are they even trying to save me? I can feel myself fade away into oblivion. The next thing I know, I'm being dropped into freezing water—the feeling of needles piercing my skin remind me of when I had jumped into the water when I was camping with my mom and dad. Soon all memory disappears quickly, as my mind is numbed, but it doesn't make sense because it just...hurts.

Everything halts as I cry out in pain, left for dead.

If you look up the meaning of healing *you can find many different definitions. There's the adjective, noun, and verb (with and*

without objects). For argument's sake we will use the verb. Still there are many definitions. The one that fits here is to free from evil; cleanse; purify; to heal the soul.

Free from evil, *even if you didn't know it was there.*

Chapter 28

Void

I thought I couldn't breathe—that's why I was holding my breath. With a harsh thud, I awaken and air violates my lungs. It's unwelcome at first, until I feel the cool tendrils of oxygen filtrate through my breath.

"Emma." At the sound I open my mouth to the oxygen that fills my lungs—air.

Black, there's nothing to see. I move my feet and kick something—no sound.

"Emma."

My name, that's right. My parents call me Emma, but I was born with another name. If only I could remember. I can feel it inside me—that's not my real name; it's something else. The name itches at the back of consciousness, letting me know there is more, but I come out empty and unable to find my real name.

I can still hear someone repeat my name, over and over, but I ignore it, trying to think of my real name.

"Emma. Emma."

I become annoyed with the pestering and kick again—still no sound. I know I hit something. Why doesn't it make a sound? I kick again.

"Emma," the voice says firmly.

"Stop," I try to say, but I can't hear my voice. "Stop!" My lips form the words but they don't come. "Stop."

Maybe I can't speak. Was I born like this? A mute? Or did something happen?

I try to draw the memories; a cold or sickness, an accident maybe. Nothing. What startles me the most is just that—nothing. There's nothing to remember but my name; my fake name. Emma. Who am I?

"Emma."

"Who am I?" I ask the voice that speaks to me. I say it slow, taking my time with each syllable, not even sure if I am making the words. There is no voice to back up my thoughts. No way to know what I am really saying. "I'm not Emma." The name comes easily to me, and I feel myself sicken because I'm not Emma; I'm someone else. "Who am I?"

A short pause before I hear the words again. "Emma."

"No!" I say, trying to yell, feeling my throat sting with the action. Still there is nothing. "I'm not Emma," I say, feeling as if my voice cracked, being tortured by the curse of not being able to hear my words. I want to cry. I feel myself gasping for help, and I scream my useless sobs.

Time passes and my throat burns. I become what I am: mute. The voice is still there, calling me by my false name. "Emma," it says. I'm not Emma. I don't know who I am, who I was, or what I'm going to be.

I want to scream—I've tried to scream. I can't; something is wrong with me. I can't remember.

"Who am I?" I ask again. My throat scratches, but I can hear it. I said something. It's a quiet, painful whisper, but I've spoken. Now the voice calling me Emma has disappeared. I listen for some sort of reply, but there isn't any. I kick my legs again to see if I will be able to hear the sound, but I feel as if I'm in midair. I thrash around, but my body doesn't touch anything.

"Help," I whimper. I become more hopeless as the seconds pass. I gain my voice, as I scream for my life. "Help!"

How long has it been? Minutes, hours, days?

There's only black in front of me; I can't tell if my eyes are open or closed. I can hear my breathing. Shallow, hollow. I don't sleep.

Sometimes I sing a song. I just started; it came to me from nowhere. *Hush, little baby.* That's the only part I know. Once I sung the entire song, it was incredible, the feeling of saying the words. It felt like I was complete. It wasn't until that moment that I knew I was missing something. Then after I sang the song, I knew there was more out there for me. But when I tried to sing again, nothing came to me. I couldn't remember anything. As hard as I tried, I couldn't get one verse of the song. It aggravated me, so I kept trying until I got *Hush, little baby.* There's more; I know there is, but I can't find it.

Insane. That's what I am. A simple word, a simple meaning—crazy. I don't talk to myself; never. I feel as if I should though. Talking and thinking are the same, right? If there is no one to hear you, are you really talking? *If a tree falls in a forest and no one is around to hear it, does it make a sound?* I don't really know where the question came from, it just seemed to come, like *Hush, little baby.* This time I made sure to remember it.

Maybe I'm wrong; maybe someone is right next to me at this moment, but I can't see them. I guess I'm blind, and they're mute.

Blind or mute? Which would you pick?

Mute. I would choose mute. It's killing me right now; the fact that I can't see. My guard is down. What if someone sneaks up on me? I don't know what's there.

"Are you afraid of the dark?" I ask the person that may in fact be right next to me. There's no response. No touch on the shoulder, no other sound to tell me that I'm not alone in this abyss. I'll be quiet now.

Blind. What if there isn't anything to see? I'm probably not blind; maybe the world just isn't there. I don't remember ever seeing anything. I felt something once. When I first got here, I kicked something with my feet. Wait...was there ever a first? Is this a forever?

I wish this moment could last forever.

I always wonder where these thoughts come from, because they aren't mine. I still remember all of them. *Hush, little baby.* The song—I still think there is more that I can't remember. *If a tree falls in a forest and no one is around to hear it, does it make a sound?* I've spent a long time thinking about this question, and I always come up with the same answer—what tree?

I wish this moment could last forever.

I don't.

Have you ever asked yourself if you are sad? I have. And I've thought about it, and I don't know what sad really is. Is it when you cry or when you aren't happy? Because I've never cried, but I've never been happy. I don't know what I am.

Sad.

Three letters for a short word that holds a lot of emotion, but what is it really?

What's happy? I would think that when you do have this emotion you wouldn't think to yourself, "I'm happy." You would just be. So does that mean I'm happy? Maybe I'm okay.

Are you okay?

Another unknown thought that isn't mine.

Am I okay?

I don't know. I thought about it for a long time. I'm not happy, because I've never known another thing other than this—black, dark, forever. I don't know anything. I don't know if I'm okay or why these thoughts come into my head. All I know is that my name is not Emma.

Then I begin to question myself. Maybe I am Emma. It could be my name—Emma. Where does Emma come from?

Florida.

That's it; Florida. I know it. Emma is from Florida. Where is that?

Amelia.

That's my name—Amelia. Emma is short for Amelia. Amelia Clarice Barton.

Then something crazy begins to happen; I can remember. Suddenly everything comes back to me in an overwhelming rush.

Keep my soul safe. Phantom Lagoon is my home; my safe harbor. I no longer belong to a family; I am a loner. I feel no pain here, because it does not exist; nor will I let it exist. My soul is concealed in this stone; it is my life. I must let go, forget, and never look back. The blame shall be none but my own, for I was born of only half, to be reunited later in life. I am an Essence.

What was once an unknown thought is one no longer—my soul is protecting me. And it always will.

The Return

Sometimes it all becomes too much. Your body and mind will just give way. Part of you may want to blissfully fade into nothing, but you never do. After a while all the memories and emotions make you shut down but never fully disappear—it's safer for you this way, to be excluded. It's a time to be alone, to heal, and to find yourself. It doesn't mean you've given up or stopped trying; it just means you know what's best for you.

Breathing is medicine. I forgot how to breathe, but I'm learning all over again.

I'm coughing up what seems like gallons of water when I wake up. There is gravel underneath me, and it feels familiar. When I look above me, I see the crystal walls of the cave of Phantom Lagoon.

There is no light except a small lamp a few feet away from me; there is also a blanket. I crawl over, shaking from the cold, and wrap it around me. When I feel the fleece, I realize I'm dripping wet. My brown hair is slicked back, close to my head. I draw it forward, squeezing out the excess water. I continue to cough and wrap the blanket tighter around me. I hear something in the cave and don't bother to hide. After a few soft footsteps, Luna comes into view.

"Emma," she says in a relieved voice; almost like a mother after finally seeing her child after an accident. "Does anything hurt?" She comes to my side and another shiver convulses through me.

"Hurt?" I say with a hoarse voice. I cough again, feeling a faint burn in my throat.

She takes her old green shawl that matches her dress and wraps it around me for warmth. "So much has changed." Her French accent lingers as she speaks. "You've been gone for a long time."

It takes me moment to process the words.

"Where did I go?" My voice hurts to speak at normal volume, so I fade with each word, finally into a whisper.

Luna sits next to me, her gown flares out around us, and she places her arm around me. "I don't know." The words hover between us, and the only thing I hear is the faint trickle of water from the pool within the cave. "What's the last thing you remember?"

The question bothers me. What's the answer? It must be so simple, but I can't think. Luna stares at me, intrigued and scared for me at the same time. "I was stuck."

That's all I can remember—the nagging thought that I couldn't escape; the knowing of something more being out there, but the inability of ever being able to reach it.

"And before that?"

I let myself think for a long time. Before that. It seemed like there had always been a black, dark abyss. But there was an Emma whose real name was Amelia—that is me. I'm the Emma that was being called. I couldn't answer the voice; then when I did, it was gone.

"Do you remember Eliza?"

The face flickers in my mind: olive skin, red hair—she didn't want to remember what her dad looked like.

"Yes, her father disappeared from Phantom Lagoon."

Luna is quiet before her next question. "What about Kenzie?"

Her face bombards my memory—blond curls, big smile. It fills me with both good and bad memories. The last thing I remember about her is that she ran away. Eliza and I tried to find her, but when our time ran out, Eliza gave me a note before leaving—a note that was originally meant for her father.

2034 - Kenzie left.

"Is she okay?" I can barely whisper, and I'm unsure of my words. I remember I found her, and we ran. I remember drowning.

"Are you okay?" she asks in a soft voice.

I don't look at her and concentrate on my hands instead. They are withered because of soaking in the water and feel like ice. I see in front of me the pool of water that Eliza had showed me once. The liquid crystal.

"You didn't disappear like the other souls do," Luna tells me, following my gaze. "Even after your stone disappeared, you stayed. You didn't disappear, but we could see you growing pale. I tried something that I always do when someone arrives back at Phantom Lagoon late by just a moment."

"You tried to drown me." My voice is lost in the whispers of the cave.

She stares at me in shock. "Your soul—I was trying to drown your soul. There are myths in our world, just as there are for a human's. There are theories that water acts as a force field—that's why some people think the mirror stones have to be kept in the lagoon. We thought, if we could drown your soul while it was still inside you, it would be trapped there." She shakes her head in disbelief. "No one ever dreamed it would work."

"What happened to me?" I ask, feeling more vulnerable with each second.

"After we drowned your soul, you didn't wake up. I could tell you were still with us, but not for long. We tried talking to you.

"Nothing worked for days. Someone always watched over you and said your name. Sometimes we were able to get a response from you—you would kick, move, but you would never talk. I saw your lips moving once, but there was no sound. I could tell when you were in pain. It was sketched so plainly on your face. It scared Eliza, and after a while, she said she couldn't watch you anymore. Complete strangers stepped in to take her place. In an odd way it united us. We thought there might be a way to help someone who stays out after dark too long. People began to have hopes again."

She smiles, but the emotion is gone in the next second.

"Sadly our hope died fast. A month passed, and you still didn't wake up. No one wanted to take their shifts anymore, because they were sure you would never wake up. We moved you into the cave because people began to think of you as dead. As discouraged as I was at their decision to give up on you, I could understand their feelings, and on the days you never moved or showed signs of life..." she trails off, lost in a memory. "I felt the same—I thought you were gone. Other days we could hear you screaming from within the cave."

I feel Luna's gaze on me, but I don't look at her. I can only see the liquid crystal I had been placed in, after everyone gave up on me. I feel my throat burn, trying to hold back questions and cries. Finally I release a world's amount of tension, and I lean into Luna as my body heaves the emotions I couldn't express while I was lost in my void. I cry. No tears, but my lungs seek oxygen all too much, and my chest expands and releases, until I am calm enough to breathe again.

Luna wraps her other arm around my shoulder. "Amelia, ça va bien se passer. Shh, it's going to be all right." It was the first time I had heard her speak in her native tongue. It passed through my core, as if I could feel it healing me. "Rien ne va vous faire du mal. Nothing is going to harm you, Emma."

She is quiet except for her soft whispers, calming me to a safe sleep, where there is no void.

"I feel like I've never made the right choices," I tell Luna as we sit in the cave, talking about everything I need to hear before I go out into the real world again.

She lets out a long breath. "Sometimes, if you let your thoughts build up inside you, evil will grow. It's important to let go of things that make you upset, because it will only drag you deeper into your own hell."

I let her words repeat themselves inside my head. *It will only drag you deeper into your own hell.*

"Why did this happen to me? I mean, what about Kenzie? Is she all right?"

"Kenzie got back in time. She was upset for being lied to, but we've explained everything to her, and she understands now. No forgiveness, but understands. As for you, Emma, I think you brought yourself into that trance."

"What do you mean?" I pull my knees to my chin, feeling safer but not trusting what Luna might say.

"Amelia," her French accent makes my name beautiful as she rubs my back. "You had already built your hell around you. I could see you, everyday getting worse. You were blaming everything on yourself. You never forgave yourself for leaving your family behind. Even from the first day you came here, I saw immediately how you condemned yourself for things that happened by fate. Your death was no one's fault, and it's a part of life. I know you don't want to be an Essence—nobody does."

I stare forward into the cave, hearing Luna's calming voice next to me. "But why did I go into the trance, Luna? What does this have to do with anything?" I go instinctively to wipe a tear, still none. I thought after years of being an Essence I would learn, but there will always be that moment when Kenzie and I both cried real tears again, each of us dying as an Essence.

"You needed time for yourself," she says. "You didn't know it, but your soul did. Everyone needs time to forget and relax."

"But I didn't feel safe. I knew there was more out there, even though I couldn't think of it. It ate away at me," I tell Luna, feeling myself getting worked up again.

"Remember how you lost part of your soul after you were born?" she asks me, turning to face me, trying her best to keep me calm.

"Yes," I say.

"You grew separately. When it joined with you in Phantom Lagoon, it knew things you didn't from just being here longer. When Mackenzie left, it must have known you needed time to heal yourself, so there has always been part of you keeping yourself safe."

"I know. I've heard it before. Especially when I was human—right before I became an Essence—it was like it was warning me what was about to happen, letting me brace myself for when I left my human life. Especially the first few nights in Phantom Lagoon, I could feel it helping me."

"Have you ever felt better by just holding your stone?"

"Yes," I say.

Out of the corner of my eye, I see Luna adjust herself and take out a necklace. She hands me a pale purple stone secured on a leather string.

"Is that mine?" I stare at it, not believing the change in color. It had once been a deep purple, but now it was a soft lilac. The only way I recognize it is by the brown dent that has always been there, a scar left from leaving my family.

"Yes." She places the cord around my neck, and I instantly feel warmth radiating from the stone. "It's changed in the time you have been away. Some scars have healed, but there are some that never will or just need more time."

"Why is the color different?" I ask, fingering the stone and seeing that some of the small cracks on the surface have been erased, smoothed over, and even though I can still see the brown dent on the side, I rub it as if it were a sore muscle.

"Because you're different." She smiles. "These stones are truly a part of us. They provide strength for everyone. It's what makes us immortal."

"Do you have one?" I release the stone from my grasp and let it fall to my neck where it belongs.

"It had once been a dark almost-red pink." She takes a chain off her neck and holds out the stone. It looks like it was larger once, but was cut in half. It's a light almost-white pink now, and except for the jagged edges that make it seem to be only half of a stone, that's the only scar; the rest is smooth, making it appear as a river stone.

"What happened to it?" I ask, running my thumb over the rough edge.

She drags her pointer finger across the surface with slow, gentle care. "Things worked differently back then. Magic scared everyone, and you could die if someone thought you could control it. I don't know if Phantom Lagoon works with magic, but there was a time when you didn't need it to stay alive. When I lived in Europe, we just needed the stones and natural water. I'd always stay near a stream at night, fingering the stone and hoping someone wouldn't find me." She stops for a moment and smiles. "But I guess being found by your soul mate isn't bad."

"That's how you met him?" When she thinks of him, I can feel her stone radiate with happiness, and I have no doubt that this man was truly meant for her soul.

"He was human, and I wasn't. I didn't tell him, but I know he understood I was different. We fell in love quickly, and soon I trusted him with my secret. I didn't know what to call our in-between state, but after I tried to describe everything, the first thing he said was, 'You're a beautiful essence of everything that is good in my life.' That's what I decided to call our kind. An Essence."

She's quiet for a while again and smiles, as if she's in her own world. I can tell she is remembering him; maybe even hearing his voice. The grin leaves her face, growing more serious; and she looks at me again.

"I had to leave for my own safety, but he couldn't come with me. It was like I left half myself behind with him." She fingers the spot on the stone where a large part of it appears to be missing. "I waited for him to find me for years, until I knew he must have died from old age...or something." She mumbles the words, and I can feel the pain in her unfinished love story. "I've been looking for a way out of here ever since."

Chapter 30

Homecoming

"Are you ready?" Luna steps up and offers me her hand. I take it but don't follow her when she starts walking.

"Luna, how long was I away?"

I stare around me, seeing the cave with open eyes. It hasn't changed at all. The crystal walls still glimmer when light passes over; the liquid in the small pool appears as a false solid that runs through my fingers.

Luna stops but doesn't turn to face me. "Mackenzie was able to leave the cave at the beginning of October, so it's been four months."

"Months?" I try the words on for size, but they don't fit. "So, it's January now?"

"Almost February," she says, looking back at me over her shoulder, waiting for me to follow. "There's still snow on the ground."

She continues to walk, so I hurry to catch up to her. I try my best to not look at the bodies while we pass through the crystal cave, but I can't help but notice a few that weren't here the last time.

Luna notices my wandering gaze. "Hikers—an entire family. They came right before winter struck and each of them picked up a stone. A mother, father, daughter, and son. Sherri, their daughter, gets along with Mackenzie very well since she is only a few years older. Their son Drew is ten, like Tyler, so it's double trouble," she says, smiling to herself. "But they are happy."

I stare at the face of Sherri, long brown hair to her elbows; I can almost picture her playing with Kenzie. "What about the parents?"

Luna is quiet. "Still adjusting."

When we round a corner and light from the opening begins to stream into the cave, the sun reflects off the crystals making the entire place glow. When I look outside, I'm blinded temporarily, but as my eyes adjust, I see a sheet of fresh white snow covering the ground. Icicles cling to the rock wall that surrounds the lagoon's water. The moss that used to coat the trees and rocks is gone. In its wake are snowflakes pure in color and untouched. The water of the lagoon is partially frozen as the ice slabs lean into the water. Trees are weighed down by wet snow and hang low. The sun is high in the sky, shining down in a blinding manner. The white reflects the light, as the snow begins to melt, preparing for spring.

"Here we are." Luna stops just shy of the opening and gestures for me to go first. "Everyone will be thrilled to see you." She smiles at me for encouragement. Her face is serene, relaxed, telling me to do the same.

I squint my eyes past the bright snow and start to recognize faces. When they look back at me, they freeze, stunned, seeing a ghost. I don't know what to do. I look around for Eliza or Kenzie, but I don't see them. The air is still, as everyone tries to figure out how I'm standing here. No one moves toward or away from me, but they stand, astonished and amazed at the sight of me.

"Emma?" The voice comes from my left side, and when I turn, I see Eliza. Her red hair hangs limp around her face, curling toward her cheeks. Her eyes are tired when they look at me, and I can see, by the way she holds herself, it is as if she hasn't slept in weeks. But now her face has a glow to it. Maybe she doesn't believe I'm here, because she doesn't dare look away from me.

"You're...okay?" Her voice cracks the smallest bit on the word "okay."

She steps toward me like a dream, thinking I will disappear with a sudden movement, just dust in the wind.

"Oh, my God." She covers her mouth, but I can still see a smile.

I smile back at her, but I don't know what to say.

"Oh, my God," she says again, taking her hands down, stepping toward me. "Are you okay?"

I look around me and see everyone staring at us intently. Suddenly I feel overwhelmed by all the faces, and part of me wants to take cover in the cave again, but I breathe and muster an answer for Eliza.

"I think so."

Eliza rushes to me for a hug. Her arms lock around me, and I can hear a quiet sob coming from her. Soon I'm doing the same thing. She releases me to get a better look, as if to make sure it is me and not a figment of her imagination. "I can't believe...you're here."

"Emma?" Luna's voice calls me to her, and when I turn around, I see Kenzie at her feet. Luna ushers her forward, and Kenzie stares at me in awe.

"You're back now?" she asks in her high voice. Her large eyes stare into me, holding the undying attention they always possess. Her lips move as if she wants to say more, but she stays quiet.

I half laugh, half cry, finally relieved to see her safe, as I kneel down to give her a hug. "I guess so."

Kenzie smiles and jumps into my arms, holding me tight in her small grasp.

"I'm so sorry," I tell her. "We didn't want to lie to you."

She buries her face in my hair. "I know," she says, giving me a kiss on the cheek.

I release her, and she takes my hand and guides me to the family that came here on their hike.

"This is my new best friend, Sherri," Kenzie introduces me, and Sherri smiles with a wave. The little girl's hair falls in long cascades down her back, in front of her face if she leans forward. "And that's her big brother, Drew." I follow her finger to a ten-year-old boy with brown hair like his sister. He waves quickly before returning to the game he is playing with Tyler that includes gun sounds and running around.

"Excuse me." I turn around to see Sherri and Drew's mother. Her husband, a broad, tall man, has his arm around her waist. Both of their faces look unsure of everything around them. The woman looks exactly like Sherri but has a short pixie cut that frames her small face. She steps forward with a shy smile. "I don't know what happened to you, but I don't think anyone does." She half laughs in an awkward silence.

I wait for her to continue.

"We've only been here for a few months now, but we were here when you were kept outside—when people took shifts to wake you. I've never seen such a bond before."

"What do you mean?"

She smiles at me and looks to her husband. After he nods, she begins to talk. "We were scared when we came here. Luna explained things to us, but we didn't trust people. The two of us didn't want our children hurt." She looks past me at Sherri and Drew. "Seeing everyone work together to keep you safe is what made us finally able to see the brighter side of things."

I smile, knowing exactly what it is like to come to Phantom Lagoon, but I didn't help this family. I want to correct them, to say that it is everyone here in the lagoon she should thank, because they are the ones who took care of me when I was lost in an abyss—they are the ones that instilled trust. I'm about to speak the words, but the woman comes over to hug me in thanks.

She steps away and smiles. "This is my husband, Henry, and I'm Elli." Henry offers me his hand, and I shake it, grateful to already be welcomed back.

"I'm Emma," I tell them both.

"Oh we know you, Emma. Your family too—I used to work for your dad," Henry tells me.

"Really?"

"I was his intern on my first job. Makes you work hard, but he knows what he's doing. What's he up to these days?" Henry asks with a casual smile.

I feel my breath catch in my throat. "He...he had a seizure." I look past these two strangers, trying to talk about my dad for the first time in years, seeing the sun outline the trees in the background. "They diagnosed him with brain cancer, and he died a few months later."

"Oh, honey," Elli murmurs, and I see her clutch for her husband again. "We're so sorry."

"It's okay." I look at them again, still watching the sun glow its perfect rays in the corner of my eye—they couldn't have known. "It was a relief really. He was sick for a long time."

Henry clears his throat, and when I glance at him, I see his gaze is fixated on the lagoon. "It was amazing..." Elli stares up at him and hugs his body, burying her face in his broad chest. "We just went out for a hike as a family one day. It was a spontaneous sort of thing—we didn't even remember to pack a lunch." He laughs to himself. "Sherri had run ahead of us, and I guess she found this place. Just a second before she ran through the trees, she was laughing, but as soon as she stepped in, everything went quiet. Drew followed behind her...still nothing."

Elli sniffs in his arms, and he holds her closer.

"What did you do?" I ask.

"Elli and I went in after them. We both assumed that if they had gotten hurt, we would have heard a scream. It was so beautiful, once you got through the trees, but the only thing we saw was our children, lifeless in the pool of water. We had no idea what had happened, but that's when I felt it. Even with the horror of believing both my children were dead, I couldn't be distracted by this...need to get closer. It was like the water was calling to me, and when I stepped into the water, I didn't even have to think about what I was doing. It was instinct. The last thing I remember is standing in knee-deep water, Drew and Sherri lying half on shore, and looking into the stone and seeing my reflection. It was...amazing. It felt like I was going in on myself."

In his arms Elli whimpers and wipes her face with the back of her hand, confused by the lack of tears.

"We can't cry," I tell her. "The emotions are there, of course, but not the tears. You don't really get used to it."

There's silence between us, and I want to lift the mood. "There is a good thing about Phantom Lagoon though." They look at me waiting. "Your family is here, and you're frozen in time. If you're going to be stuck with someone for all eternity, it might as well be your soul mate."

They both smile, looking at each other, and Elli speaks up. "We know." Henry kisses her forehead.

"Plus there's no rent to pay," he adds, and we all laugh.

Chapter 31

Dwelling

I follow Kenzie's path through the forest to a spot we both know. She stops at the campground—the last place she saw her parents. I don't know if she's aware I'm behind her, so I remain quiet while she takes a seat at her old campsite. Her blond curls blow in the wind, and she sits still in the cold. I stay behind a tree, when she gets up and looks into the circle of rocks that once made up a campfire.

She almost drops to the ground, as she puts her face into her hands. I can see her body heave, and I can feel myself ache as I watch her. A long time passes, and she leans to the side, until she is lying on the ground in surrender.

"Kenzie?" I finally step through the trees.

She stirs but doesn't get up from her spot.

I try again. "Are you okay?"

"No," she says.

I stand a few feet from her, but I can tell she doesn't like my following her. I sit down, letting her know I'm willing to wait and stay quiet with her. A few more minutes pass, and I can hear a sob coming from her again.

"Sometimes I wish we could cry," I tell her. "It feels like I'm not really here, because I can't express emotions fully—whether it is tears of joy or sorrow."

She ignores me and curls into a tight ball.

"Maybe it's just me."

A light wind comes through the trees' branches, covering Kenzie's face with her hair. She doesn't move.

"I miss my family too."

No response.

"I even wish that I didn't remember them sometimes. I guess, if you don't remember, you don't feel that ache in your chest anymore."

I can hear a sniffle coming from Kenzie, and she moves into a more comfortable position, keeping her back to me.

"When I was in that void for the last few months, I didn't remember anything. And even though I couldn't remember, I knew there was something else. And as much as I hate the feeling of being truly alone, the worse part of the void was that I knew there was more. All I could do was think, trying to remember, even though I couldn't find anything."

I bring my knees to my chest, the sun radiating on my back as the last of the winter season fades away, spring just a blossom away. "I couldn't remember my family. That ache from their absence that's here in Phantom Lagoon, it was gone. I know you might think that's a good thing, but I never truly forgot. I don't think you can ever forget your family."

"Are you saying it will always hurt to think about them?" Kenzie asks.

I smile, hearing her voice, but it disappears as soon as I listen to what she is saying.

"Maybe," I start. "But not always. For a while it will, but soon..." I pause trying to find the right words. "I guess you become numb." I sigh, hating myself for saying that, but knowing I'm giving her nothing but the truth.

Kenzie gets up, and I'm startled when she breaks the distance between us and collapses into my arms. "I miss them," she cries while I cradle her.

"I know," I whisper, rubbing her back. She's a dead weight in my arms. Her body is tired and limp; the only thing that tells me she's alive is her shaky breathing. Every now and then she shudders and falls deeper into my arms like she wishes to disappear.

"Do you still miss your dad?" She lifts her head and her eyes bore into me. Her eyes are red and irritated, and the brown irises look almost black as she stifles her cries.

I watch her as she breathes in slow and deep breaths. "Yeah, but I know he's safe now."

Kenzie smiles and points to the sky. "In Heaven?" The sun reflects off her eyes and creates the glow of joy that she once possessed when she was with her family, just a human.

I nod again, losing my voice. I feel a smile form across my face.

"Do you think he's an angel?" she asks.

I think for a moment about what he might be doing right now in his piece of eternity. Surely he hasn't left my mom when she needs him. "No, not yet anyway."

Kenzie looks at me, confused.

"When my dad died, he had to leave my mom behind. But I don't think he would ever truly leave her. Especially now, when she needs him most. So I think he is going to wait for my mom, before he passes on and becomes an angel."

"Will he wait for you?"

I'm put back by the question. Would he wait for me? I don't even know if it's possible for an Essence to pass on. It takes me a moment to come up with an answer.

"I don't think so. I don't need any help here. I've got my family right here at Phantom Lagoon. My mom is alone at a nursing home. That's why she needs my dad."

"Your mom has you. Can't you visit her?"

Her question makes me remember the last time I saw her. I was peeking in through a window of her new room she had just been moved into with another woman who lived in the nursing room. They were talking about grandchildren, and when my mom was asked about hers, she just said her daughter died very young. When the other women asked what happened, my mom couldn't remember.

"You know how I used to visit my mom every day?" I ask and Kenzie nods in reply. "Well, that's because she knew what had happened to me. I was an Essence, but I still talked to her."

"Really?" Kenzie's eyes suddenly turn bright. "Can I visit my mom?"

"I broke a rule by doing that, Kenzie. It's something you're not supposed to do. Eliza's father did that, and she followed him to Phantom Lagoon. That's how she became an Essence. I didn't know that when I told my mom."

Kenzie's face falls, so I try to get back on subject.

"Kenzie, I can't visit my mom in her nursing home, because she forgot about me. I don't know when it happened, but she doesn't remember a lot of things now."

Kenzie frowns, and I try to lighten the mood. "I visit her. I just can't talk to her."

"Can I do that?" Her face brightens slightly, but I can tell she's preparing herself for rejection.

"Can humans see you?"

She frowns. "No, Eliza tried to see if I could be seen, but I don't have any superpowers like you guys."

I smile at the thought of them being superpowers, but I guess, in Kenzie's eyes, they are.

"Then that makes this much easier for us." And when I tell her that, one of her best smiles crosses her face, and she hugs me with the most strength she can muster.

Chapter 32

Enshrine

"Where are they?" Kenzie jumps around, hidden within the trees. Just a few feet out is a park—the same one Kenzie's family goes to on her birthday to celebrate her life. "Emma, where are they?" She grabs my hand and tries to pull me out to the break in the trees.

"They're having a family reunion," I tell her, stopping in my tracks, so Kenzie doesn't go any farther to where her unsuspecting family enjoys each other's company.

"Come on!" She tugs on my arm again.

I grab her by the shoulders, so she looks me in the eyes. "Kenzie, I want you to see your family again, but you have to remember that they can see and hear me. I can't interact with you. Understand?"

She nods her head. "Can we go now?" she asks in an excited voice.

I smile, and take her small hand in mine. I can feel her radiate with excitement as we begin to approach the park. A field begins to open in front of us as the trees disappear. The grass stretches across the circular park, picnic tables scattered every few feet. There are a few metal grills anchored to the ground for public use, and several people have already begun to barbecue, filling the air with the smell of summer. Kenzie stops when she sees her family through the last of the trees. They stand at a table, arranging food and treats, talking among themselves. At first I see a flash of disappointment on her face, but she manages a smile.

"What's wrong?" I ask, bending down to be at her eye level.

She rocks back on her feet for a moment, looking ahead at her family before answering. "Mommy and Daddy look different."

I follow her gaze to her mom and dad. Her mom once had long dark hair, but now it's cut short with streaks of gray shining out. Her father wears glasses while he reads to his grandchildren, who are only a few months old—they look so much like Kenzie and her sister, Jessica.

"It's been years, Kenzie. Time does different things to humans."

She just nods in reply.

Eventually she sits on the ground against a tree, watching as her family talk about what has changed since they had last seen each other. I try to read the expression on Kenzie's face, but she just concentrates on them with intense care, showing no outward emotion. I sit against another tree next to her, allowing her space but wanting to be there for her.

"Is that my sister?" I follow her finger to a young woman holding hands with her husband.

"Yes, have you seen her before?"

She shakes her head no. "She looks like me and Mommy. Who's she holding hands with?"

"Her husband. They have twin boys," I tell her, pointing out her nephews. "They're the little babies your dad is reading to."

With all her questions answered, she sits quietly, as if she had never spoken a word. I look to the sky and notice the sun start to fall—only a handful of daylight hours are given to us in this world. I look over to Kenzie to see if she has noticed, but her stare follows her baby nephews.

"What should I do?" It had been a long silence, and I had almost forgotten Kenzie was next to me.

She sits perfectly, legs crossed and back straight. Her gaze lingers on her family even as she speaks.

"What?" I ask, not understanding.

"Is there something I can do to let them know I'm here?"

When she asks I don't see a small three-year-old, but a child mature beyond her years. I could feel the intensity in her voice as she talked about her family, and I knew exactly how I could help.

I get up and reach into my pocket for a pink ribbon. "Here."
I place it in her small palm and close her fingers around it. "Give it
to them. Eliza and I have been putting pink ribbons in your home to
let your family know you were okay—they will know what it means."

Kenzie smiles and begins a slow walk to the table her family
sits at. Halfway there she looks back at me for guidance. I smile to
her with encouragement before she turns back to them. She stops in
the middle of the crowd of people, looking around, probably thinking
of the person who should receive the ribbon.

Someone approaches her from behind, and I can see the fear
stricken on Kenzie's face like a billboard as they walk through her
body. She holds still for a while, not knowing what really happened,
and looks at me with a million questions. I usher her forward to
continue.

Kenzie walks over to the table where her mom and dad are.
She sits next to them, and they stop talking. Her parents look at each
other, knowing something has changed in the atmosphere. Then
something amazing happens. Kenzie reaches over and hugs her mom,
and when she does, there is no line between human and Essence—
she does not pass through her mother's body like an Essence is
expected to. At Kenzie's touch, a tear falls down the mother's face,
and her husband gets up from his seat across from her and hugs her
also. The three of them enjoy their unknown hug that is a miracle in
itself. When Kenzie finally releases her mom, she drops the ribbon
into her lap. With a few hesitant steps backward, she watches them.

"I could feel her—Kenzie, just like she had never left," her
mother says, another tear forming and falling down her face.

"I know," her father replies, wiping the tear and giving her a kiss on the forehead.

The moment comes when both parents look down and see the single pink ribbon laid out in front of them. Kenzie's mother takes it gingerly in her hands and gets up from her seat to hug her husband again. They both cry in each other's arms, as they remember their first daughter who died at the young age of three.

Chapter 33

Savior

The trails that run through the White Mountain National Forest are winding and seem endless. As soon as I think I've found the end of one path, I look up and find a turn in the trail that uncovers more. It seems like hikers are contently on the trail rain or shine. Nothing is more magnificent in this area than the waterfalls. When it does rain, the added water just makes the falls so much grander.

Eliza leads in front of me. We don't normally travel along these paths, because we might run into and be seen by hikers. It isn't that they may recognize us from when we were alive, it's fear that they'll see we're different. Although we can both physically be here, water passes through us. The hard stone and soft bark of trees may be solid to our skin, but water moves through us like it isn't even there.

The roll of thunder sounds above us. This is why we are here. The beauty of the waterfalls may be precious enough to call hikers out during a shower, but it isn't enough to bring people in during a storm. Hiking on a path is dangerous enough during a rainy day because of the rocks and roots that stick out, never mind adding in lightning.

A flash lights the sky. In front of me, Eliza has stopped walking.

"One one-thousand, two one-thousand, three one-thousand."

Crash.

The sound is loud enough to be felt. It's a dramatic long rumble in the sky. Eliza turns around to face me, a look of awe and wonder on her face. "And with the thunder in the air, nothing can stop me," she whispers as the crash fizzles away in the distance.

"Three?" I ask. Years ago my dad had told me to watch the lightning in the sky and count. For every five seconds that passes, it means the lightning is a mile away.

Eliza nods, smiling for a moment as she watches the sky. "It's close."

The wind picks up and brings a shower of rain with it. Like always, it passes right through us, giving the feeling of bugs crawling across our skin. Eliza hugs herself, bracing against the wind, but continues to walk forward. With the wind and rain increasing in strength, it feels like needles being jabbed into my skin, passing through my soul in a slow breath and coming out the other side. I try not to let it slow me down, but Eliza has noticeably lessened her pace.

"Are you okay?" I ask, just as the rain picks up again. The sounds of the drops hitting the ground fill the forest, and it's almost as loud as the waterfalls that surround us.

Eliza shivers, composing herself, ducking her head down without looking at me. She makes a quiet cough and huddles in on herself. I can see the pain she's going through as the rain passes through her. Every time the wind grows stronger, she cringes, trying to shield herself from the effects, even though it's a useless effort.

"Eliza?"

She looks up at me then, her body shaking. She isn't cold—an Essence can't physically feel cold—but something is wrong.

"I'm fine," she says, pulling her chin up. Another roll of thunder orchestrates through the air. Her body stills as the sound passes through, and it's like the thunder has given her strength. I remember what she had said just seconds ago.

And with the thunder in the air, nothing can stop me. I can see her mouthing the words now, convincing herself the words are true.

Eliza smiles at me as if to say she's fine and then just continues on.

I follow without a word, seeing her pace steadier than ever.

Just out of the corner of my eye, I see a sharp white line flash across the sky. It's thin and smooth as it spirals downward toward the Earth. Like a dagger, the lightning aims for something on the ground. Not even a second later, a sound very similar to a whip snaps in the air.

It seems like the world stops. Eliza is frozen in her tracks, afraid to move. The only thing I can hear is my breathing, loud and nervous. It was as if I could feel the sound waves of the lightning pass through me, but now the entire forest is silent. I close my eyes, listening for something to tell me that whatever the lightning hit, it wasn't near us. It's a useless hope, because I saw it. The strike was so frighteningly close, and the snap it made as it crossed the sky was deaf defying.

"Emma?" Eliza's voice reaches me, and I can hear her slow footsteps as she comes closer to me. When I open my eyes again, she's standing just a foot away, hugging her body again like she's a small pup. "Did you see that?"

I swallow, my eyes flickering to the corner of the sky where I had witnessed the lightning.

"We have to leave." Eliza begins to pull my arm back to where we had come from, away from the lightning.

"But..." I say, not quite sure why I feel like we have to stay; something keeps me in place.

Eliza looks at me like I've gone insane. "Come on." She tugs on my arm again, clearly frightened.

"Help!" The muffled sound is farther away in the distance. Neither of us spoke the words, so we stare at each other in disbelief.

I turn my body to the source of the sound, away from the path that would lead us back to Phantom Lagoon.

"What are you doing, Emma?"

"Finding whoever that was." I pull away from Eliza's grasp and toward the sound. It came from one of the waterfalls. The voice sounded close, but with the loud rush of water coming from the falls, it also felt impossibly far.

"You'll get yourself killed!" Eliza shouts back at me. Even though she may not believe in my struggles to save whoever is out there, she follows anyway. She's just a frightened shadow behind me. Eliza doesn't follow because she wants to help; she follows because she doesn't want to be alone.

"I can't be killed, remember? But whoever is out there can," I say.

Eliza just stares at me, the falling rain passing through her body. None of it soaks her skin or drips through her hair.

"Do you remember what you told me, when I first came to Phantom Lagoon?" I ask, but her face is scared.

She doesn't want to stick around here much longer, let alone have a lengthy discussion about right and wrong.

"You told me that you thought saving a life is a ticket out of here. That's how you pass on. It's why you tried to save me." She looks away from me. "Eliza, you couldn't save me then, but maybe you can do it now."

"I can't." When she says it, it's almost a cry. There are only a few feet of distance between us, but she begins to back away from me.

"Why?" My voice is a whisper. She doesn't understand how frail one human life is. I've seen my father die in front of my eyes; Eliza's parents have died, but she's never seen death. I watched my dad draw his last breath.

"I can't fail again, Emma," she whispers. "I failed to save you and failed to save Kenzie when she ran away." Another step away from me.

A quiet, muffled yelp comes from the waterfall again. Eliza hears the sound too and perks up a bit. For a moment I can visibly see strength in her, but she doesn't step forward.

"If whoever that is dies...I don't know what I'd do." A final crash of thunder rolls over the mountains, and Eliza turns away from me.

I don't stop her, because I know it's useless. She knows her limits, and she doesn't dare cross them like I do. It's kept her safe here in Phantom Lagoon, but that's the problem. No one knows how to leave. What if there's more out there? What if we can pass on?

Between the rolls of thunder, I hear the whimpers again. The rain beats down the ground in a rhythm of percussion. The forest is filled with so much noise and life in this one simple frame of time; yet within all that, I can still hear the struggles of the human.

It doesn't take long to find the helpless man.

Following the sound, I see a man with graying brown hair. He's held prisoner in a stream of rushing water, holding on only by a slippery rock near the edge. The water is deep enough that the man can't find any footing to get out and other rocks within reach are smooth to the touch with no way of gaining traction. Shrubs and loose tree limbs crowd around the stream, having accumulated from the winter storms. There's very little room for the man to move. Every time he finds purchase on a branch, it just falls loose and makes him slip deeper into the water.

He doesn't even see me as I approach. Although his arms are rigid, trying to hold on to the rock that keeps him out of the water, his face displays nothing about the situation at hand. His lips move, forming words that he whispers to himself. There's only a short distance between us, and I can see his entire frame shaking from the cold.

Kneeling just inches from his hand, which has a vise grip on the rock, I lean forward to grasp his shoulders. It was stupid of me really, because I forgot what I was. Just like that, I lost touch with reality and forgot the simple fact that an Essence can't make contact with another human. Instead of grabbing the man's shoulders like I thought, I pass through his body and fall onto the rock he holds.

We share the same space—he holds the rock, and my ghost form lies across it. I stumble for a moment, and the man notices. His face lifts just long enough to see my face, as I back away. I focus my energy as quickly as I can so I can haunt the man—the beat of a heart, the rush of blood pumping through my system, but most of all the rise and fall of my chest as air passes through. With as much concentration as I can muster, I slip into his body and take control.

A jolt of freezing cold tingles my skin. The water of the stream rushes against his body and forces me up against the rock. His grip is holding, and I can feel the muscles strain against the push of the stream. Something weighs down on me, and I realize it's the man's clothing, drenched and heavy, clinging to his body.

Everything happens so quickly that I don't even hear his thoughts—or maybe he was too scared to process anything—but I use my will to urge him out of the stream.

"Out!" I shout to him. His arms pull him up, but it's useless; he doesn't have enough energy.

"Pull yourself up! Use your feet to kick yourself up!" I scream this time, fear instilling in myself. I haven't felt this vulnerable in so long. I feel so close to death, and it hurts. The cold wind pushes down on us, trying to stop us, but I urge him forward.

"Go!" I yell, and this time it works. He uses all his might to fight his way out, but then I feel him give up. He lets me take control, as if he knows I'm there to catch him if he falls. In full command I pull his body the rest of the way out of the stream and onto land. He's reticent in his own body.

"Wake up," I whisper.

I'm not even sure if that will keep him alive, or if it's a useless effort, but I try anyway. There's a stir, as his mind begins to take control again, so I slip out of his body and into the real world. I lose some of the senses that accompany a human, but this time I welcome it. I no longer feel scared or frantic like I had. I'm not cold or hot, because there is no feeling, and for the first time I'm thankful for that, as the rain continues to beat down.

Everything is a blur for moment. I can't find my place, and whenever I try to move, it feels like my limbs are weighted. A few feet away, the stranger lies on the forest floor, coughing up water, but besides that, he seems fine.

I try to bring my feet forward to walk away before the man notices me, but I stumble and land on the ground. The man hears me and looks up. A roll of thunder sounds, and it calls his attention for a moment, but it fades away quickly.

"What the hell was that?" He laughs to himself, picking himself off the ground in a nonchalant manner. Leaning against a tree for support, he gives me a full appraisal. Nothing about me says that I've been standing in the rain. My long brown hair looks perfectly dry; my clothes have mud on them, but no water. He looks down upon himself, clearly confused because he is drenched. He sees the stark difference between us but chooses not to voice it out loud. On the ground, I lie on my side slightly, propping myself up with my elbow. Then it hits me. I know this man.

"Why, I do believe I've told your fortune before!" Just like that, he forgets what happened only seconds ago. Even though his clothes are soaked and heavy on his frame, he pays it no mind. Instead, all his focus is on me. I didn't recognize him at first, because he's no longer in his colorful street clothes, but this is the man I ran into in North Conway. "Did it come true?"

"Yes," I say. "It came true."

"That must have been unfortunate," he says, coming to sit next to me. Around us the rain continues to pour, but the thunder is passing. With each flash of lightning, the crash is staggered, farther away.

I sit up and scoot away from the man, so he doesn't accidently touch me. It's a useless effort really, to try to hide that I'm different. When I walked away from him in North Conway, I saw the look on his face, as he registered I wasn't human. Now it's only a moment of time before he voices his thoughts or tries something to prove any theories he's thinking.

"What are you doing out here?" I ask, trying to turn the attention back toward him. Now he shivers and wraps his jacket around him. Today he is wearing dress pants and black shoes with a navy blue button-down. The formal wear is the reason I wasn't able to recognize him in the first place. His jacket is soaked, but he wraps it closer to himself anyway.

"I was searching. You must be too, I can imagine." He smiles at me.

I don't understand this man. Everything about him is so...different. Any other human would rush at the moment to be able to run away from this forest in the middle of a storm, yet here he sits with me on the ground. His pants are covered with mud, his face drips with falling water, but he still finds reason to smile.

"What were you searching for?" The waterfalls around us muffle my voice, and I'm not sure if he even heard me, because he stays quiet.

"Well...I don't know," he says. "I was waiting for something to find me. You found me all right!"

His laugh is like a drunk man's, slurred and unending, but for whatever reason, I find comfort in it for this moment.

"Tell me, though, did you find it?" he asks me.

"What?"

"You lost something. Did you find it? Because surely it wasn't me!" He laughs again and reaches out his arm toward me. It would have brushed against my knee, but instead, it passes through my body. As quick as I can, I draw up my knees; an attempt to make it seem like his finger didn't come into contact with me.

As soon as my arms are wrapped around my knees, he stops laughing. His face is serious as he examines me. It's clear to both of us now. I'm not human, and he knows it.

There's a hard silence between us. Neither I nor he moves to speak, but then he nods his head as if to encourage me to talk. "Did you find it?" he asks after another few seconds.

"Umm..." I struggle for words. "Yes. Yes, I found what I had lost."

He smiles and nods his head. "Good. That's good to hear." There's an uncomfortable space between us, and I look around the forest for a way out.

"Did it come back better?"

"Excuse me?" I ask, calling my attention back toward him.

"The thing you lost. When you found it, was it in better condition than when it had disappeared?"

I think back to Kenzie. Before she ran away, she had been living a happy bliss, thinking she would be an angel someday, but then she found out the truth. Sure, she's forgiven me and Eliza, but in no way, shape, or form is she better than how she started.

"No, not at all," I tell the man.

He looks shocked. "Then maybe that's not what you lost."

I give him a questioning gaze so he continues.

"It always comes back better." He smiles at me.

"I don't get it," I tell him.

"I do."

He smiles at me again, clearly amused. Part of me wants to walk away and just forget about this odd man, but something about him keeps me grounded.

"It's you, milady. You lost yourself, but I can tell now, you've changed—found yourself. It's a truly gorgeous feeling, isn't it? To discover yourself! To be lost, then found..." His speech fades away, until it seems like he's just mumbling to himself.

But I can't help myself from smiling. "How do you know these things?" I ask.

"How did you save my life?" He smiles at my silence. "Aha, just what I thought! I can't tell you my secret, if you have a secret of your own."

"But..." I start to say, then give up easily once he raises his eyebrows, challenging me to try to change his mind.

"You can't tell me," he says matter-of-factly.

"What?"

"Well I suppose you could..." he muses to himself. "But that wouldn't be right, now would it? If you told me how you saved my life—because I know, for a fact, that a young girl like you doesn't wander in the forest during a storm like this old hag—but if you told me...it wouldn't be right. Disrupt the natural way of things maybe?"

"Yeah, I guess so."

Around us the world has quieted. Thunder can still be heard in the distance, but it's no longer a threat. The rain still falls in the heavy and steady passing, but the wind has died down enough so the rain doesn't feel like needles going through my body.

"My name's Harvi by the way," the man says.

When I look at him again, I see he's shivering. Everything in me wants to escort him out of the woods to somewhere I know he'll be warm, but I'm afraid to spend too much time with him. The longer I stay, the more opportunities I give him to question what I am.

"Emma," I tell him, bringing myself to my feet to leave. Harvi gets up also, taking off his jacket to wring it out. What must have been a gallon of water comes from the cloth, and I cringe looking over his attire; although formal—like he was planning on going to dinner at a nice restaurant—it is now ruined.

"Thanks for saving my life, Emma."

He puts his hand out to shake, and I step away. He stares for a moment, observing my behavior like I'm an otherworldly creature that should be adored.

"Oh, I get it. I get it..." His voice is free-spirited, as if lifting any worry from my shoulders. "Germaphobe."

I laugh at the thought.

"See ya later, kid!" Harvi says, turning away onto a path in the forest. He doesn't look back to make sure I'm okay, and I welcome the easy parting. I watch as he steps into the rainy forest, oblivious to the weather, as he hums to himself.

I'm amazed by the man. Whatever is in him that he possesses, it allows him to live. He doesn't question the strange; he just observes.

So the theories were wrong. Saving a life doesn't help you move on. I wanted to crumble to the ground, feeling defeated, thinking I might have had a chance to no longer be an Essence; I'm still here. The rain still crawls across my skin, and there's still no heartbeat in my body. I'm just as lifeless as ever, but seeing Harvi walk away happy and alive expels the defeat. He's okay, so I'm okay.

Chapter 34

False Security

Everything seemed...perfect. I can't describe how at peace I am. Kenzie visits her family, and they know she is safe. Sometimes I will watch her as she goes up to her parents and gives them a hug. I told Luna about it, and she said it must be Kenzie's power.

Eliza and I spend our days together watching Kenzie and Sherri play different games. Sometimes we worry about Elli and Henry because they keep to themselves so much. Eliza is worried because Elli stopped talking to Sherri and Drew, but Henry came to me one day, saying Elli just misses her other family members. Just yesterday Elli and Henry went to watch their family at a birthday party. I know they will adjust to things here; we all do.

"Can we play hide-and-seek?" Sherri tugs on my sleeve, catching my attention.

I smile at her and look over at Eliza, running her fingers through Phantom Lagoon's pool of water.

"Let me see if Eliza wants to play," I tell Sherri. She smiles and runs over to Kenzie, letting her know about the game.

"You all right?" I ask, crouching down next to Eliza, hearing the crunch and churn of the gravel under my feet. She stays quiet while she takes her hand from the water, watching the liquid drip from her fingers. She dries her fingers on her jeans.

"Did you read the letter?" she asks in a plain voice, scared to hear my reply but not wanting to show it.

"Yes," I respond, knowing she means the one she gave me the night Kenzie disappeared.

She takes a deep breath. "Okay." I can feel the tension radiating off her body while she tries to think of what to say. "I'm sorry. I'm sorry you had to read that, and that I'm a coward for not staying with you. I...I just can't do that." As she says it, she glares into the water, and I can tell she's doing everything in her power not to make another ripple in the water—or better yet, a splash with a rock, making a tidal wave, ruining the calm surface like the lagoon had done to her life.

"Do what, Eliza? Kill yourself? I didn't want to die that night. I wanted to save Kenzie. You know that," I tell her.

"I know." She shakes her head. "I want to die. I've always wanted to die, but I can't. I don't think there's an afterlife for us."

She runs her stone over and over in her hand before letting it fall to her neck again, always held in place because of her necklace.

I'm quiet for a moment, thinking through what I'm about to say. "Eliza, this is our afterlife. I honestly don't think there's something else out there for us."

I can see her lips tremble, and she tries to hide it. "I know, but I don't care about me. I don't care if I'm here forever, Emma." Her voice lowers into a whisper. "I just want to know what happened to my dad." She curls her legs up to her chest and wraps her arms around her knees so tight it almost looks painful. "He's out there somewhere, right? Someone can't just disappear."

"I wish I could tell you but..." Eliza stops me before I can finish.

"But you don't know. Luna told me the same thing." She's quiet, staring into the water that looks almost like a mirror. "Why did you come over here?" she asks.

"Sherri wants to play hide-and-seek. I came over to see if you wanted to play," I tell her, adjusting my body into a comfortable position.

"No, not that."

I stare at her, not understanding what she's asking.

"Why did you come to Phantom Lagoon?"

"I was born with half of my soul." Even now, after all I've been through, the words don't seem right, like it's not possible for someone to be with only half their soul.

"Yes, that means you didn't have a choice to come here, Emma. That's what I'm trying to tell you. Don't waste your time worrying about me, please. I came here under my free will. Whatever happens is my fault. If I'm meant to spend eternity on Earth, then so be it, but I don't think all of us here are meant for that."

"What do you mean?"

"Emma, I don't think you're meant to be in Phantom Lagoon—at least not for eternity. And I think your soul was trying to find a way out, when you went into that void. This place isn't your destiny."

"I don't get it. How can you know this?"

"I don't. I just have a feeling. Whatever happens, I'm sure it will be the right thing for you."

I look at her, confused.

"Never mind. Let's go play with Kenzie and Sherri."

She gets up, wearing a mask over the feeling she had just revealed seconds ago, and I follow her. Before I have the chance to join the three of them in hide-and-seek, Luna grabs my arm, taking me to the side.

"Your mother needs you now," she says all too fast for me to understand. I want to ask more; but before I can, she walks away, disappearing into the trees of Phantom Lagoon, her gown just a hallucination of the past.

When I arrive in the parking lot of the nursing home, everything seems fine. I enter, hoping to find my mom—nobody recognizes me now, so I can walk around in broad daylight.

Going down the long hallway, I find my mom's room, trying not to panic. As I come closer, I hear voices of doctors through the thin walls of the building. They are talking about my mom.

My hand unconsciously goes to my stone. Its new glow warms me, telling me to calm down—just be with my mom until her last breath; everything will be okay in the end. The stone seems to have its own energy. I look at it, thinking it might actually be glowing, but it's the same shade of lavender it had been when Luna gave it back to me.

The energy that pulsates from the stone to my hand brings me home, reminding me of my mom's hugs. She had always been there to comfort me. I want to get closer, to be able to see her, but I don't want anyone to see me or ask questions. Out in the hall, I shy away from others and keep a distance from my mom. The linoleum lines the floor, and the entire building smells of old and overdue adult diapers. For a second I wonder how the nurses put up with the smell, then one walks out of my mom's room and into a freshly cleaned bathroom. It occurs to me what to do.

Pushing open the door, I see four stalls, all of which are empty, and the nurse is washing her hands. I wait until her attention is back on the sink, before I come in next to her and begin to haunt. I let myself be absorbed by her thoughts, taking her skin and becoming part of her for the time being. As I step into her body, I long to be able to feel the presence of my mom, not just see her.

Flashes of my mom sick in bed bombard my mind. The nurse sees everything my mom has been through; therefore, in turn, so do I. Her hair a mess, her clothes in need of being washed. Most of all the face that my mom possesses: a bored, withdrawn visage that displays joyful emotions when the time is right. Behind all the memories and recollections, there is something else too. One I can't miss; something that is obvious to an Essence but overlooked by every human.

To be able to feel again... I remember all the different textures from when I was still alive. Soft clothing, cold steel, the warm touch of another human. Everything I have lived so long without comes back to me in one quick rush.

I make the nurse run her hand across the scrubs she is wearing—they feel so soft. I command her to go to the sink—the false granite counter is hard and cold. She puts her hands together and the warmth coming from them is almost unfair. How they take for granted such things....

The window in the bathroom reveals it is raining outside. I urge her to open it and stick out her hand. The first thing I notice is the cold breeze—sharp, biting, and awakening—then comes the rain. Those drops of water that feel like crawling bugs for an Essence feels like nothing more than a slight rhythmic pattern to a human.

"Go check on the patient again," I tell her. The nurse walks forward, out of the bathroom, across the hall, and into my mom's room.

When the nurse comes through the door frame, I'm finally able to see my mom's face for the first time in months. She is so fragile looking. Her head rests against a pillow, not able to keep her head up on her own. All her skin is covered with age and wrinkles. Even her eyes are closed in an expression I can't decipher. She isn't relaxed—in fact she emulates the state of anger or irritation than anything else—but then she coughs, and all emotion is wiped clean from her face.

The room has two beds. My mom occupies one, and the other is left empty. The empty bed has photos and birthday cards on the side table from various family members who have visited. When I look to my mom's side of the room, there isn't anything decorating her walls or table. The only thing is a calendar that gives the schedule for the patients at the nursing home. A doctor stands at the foot of my mom's bed, looking at her charts on a clipboard. He flips through the pages and looks up to my mom.

The nurse I occupy steps into the room, and the doctor looks in our direction. "Can you check her vital signs again?" As the nurse comes forward, I veer toward the doctor, careful as the woman's hand brushes against his arm.

I focus my mind on the point of contact and the heat that rushes through the doctor's pulsing skin. I picture myself flying through the veins of this woman's body, jumping toward the doctor. Charts and vital signs float in my mind, code words that are used as a doctor's own personal language attack me and countless images of patients—dead or alive—settle in my mind. I'm inside the doctor, and his world overwhelms me, until his current thoughts are the only thing I make out.

Vital signs still aren't looking good. Just keeps getting worse. Hope she can make it through the night again....

No, she can't die. Not now...

Guess we'll just have to pray she can make it.

The doctor and nurse start to walk out of the room, and I panic. What are they doing? Leaving her to die? She doesn't have any family to stay with her, only me.

"Stop!" I command in a fevered voice, before the doctor can walk out the door.

"Why isn't she at the hospital?" I ask the doctor in a firm voice that turns quiet with fear.

Refuses to go, can't force her. If she wants to die, we can't stop her....

My mom wants to die. And there's nothing stopping her. What is left for her? Her memory is gone; she doesn't know her family. Of course she wouldn't want to stay here. At the hospital she'd be surrounded by machines, poking at her, keeping her alive, but for what? To wake up alone again?

My decision is made. The only solution is to stay with my mom until the end.

I have the doctor go to my mom and take her temperature. She is burning up, but that doesn't matter. I ignore the pain that courses through me as I leave the doctor and follow down his hand to my mom where she lies. I enter her body, withered and fragile. Everything feels so different. The world is hot, closing in on me. The lungs I use now—my mom's—can only take in enough oxygen to keep alive, but not enough to be comfortable. My throat—her throat—is dry like sandpaper. Sweat covers the skin I occupy, but it doesn't do anything to relieve the heat.

I didn't know how painful it would be to haunt a dying body.

Chapter 35

Death

Soon I will see them.... I get to join them....

My mom keeps mumbling this to herself repeatedly. Her thoughts are not expected. She is happy; excited almost. Like my dad, she acts as if she looks forward to death. Maybe when you go through so much, it's not wrong to see death as a good thing.

Hearing my mom's thoughts makes me realize the truth. She has forgotten everything. She'll see my dad after she dies but not me. She forgot the vital point that keeps me away from her: I'm an Essence. When she dies, she'll go wherever it is a soul has as an afterlife—she'll join my dad—I'll be here.

Even though I want to tell her that she won't see me, I keep silent in the back of her mind, and the thoughts continue in her blissful world. I hear her heartbeat fall to a slower pace, and the pain around us eases—either it is disappearing, or I'm growing used to it—until it is just a background to my mom's thoughts.

Soon...very soon...

I stay with her for hours. I listen to her thoughts and realize just how long she has truly been gone. The day she learned of my dad's sickness is when she left me. After my dad died, she thought I was a dream, a ghost. On the days I wandered around the house, waiting for her to make contact with me, she was sure she was seeing the ghost of her deceased daughter. There was never anything wrong with her. In reality, it was my fault for pushing her to believe in me.

Hours pass, and I refuse to leave her. Through the window I see the sun put on a show, lighting the sky to different colors. First orange, pink, yellow, and then purple, until finally blue. I begin to feel something, not the ache of being away from Phantom Lagoon but something else. A heart beating, not mine but my mom's. In time we have become one. I'm no longer haunting her; instead we share the same body, the same pain. Outside the sun is setting, leaving only a sky that turns black with the coming night.

I choose to bear her pain, leaving my mom able to die in peace. An agony passes throughout my entire body, as my mom slips into a dreamless sleep. It hurts to move and breathe. There is a protest when I try to rotate my hand to see if there is an injury—which there isn't, only the brittle hand of my mom. All at once, what had been only a background of pain grows acute. I can feel the full force of my mom's affliction and wonder how she has been able to keep quiet for so long; why her thoughts don't center on the torment.

It becomes so agonizing and I want to scream. Then, out of nowhere, it ceases. It just stops. As one, we become light-headed and numb.

We are dying, not just my mom, but the both of us. I can feel it—we are slipping away.

So this is what it feels like to really die. It's something I have never experienced in my life—something I never thought I would. Even though I have never felt much pain while living, I knew bearing my mom's pain would not last—only as long as she was alive. Now it has completely disappeared—the feeling after the pain being gone is overwhelming. Initially it feels as if you have the entire world on your shoulders, then somebody who cares for you lifts it. In doing that, the person is not only saving you from the pain and suffering but also welcoming you into a world so perfect you can't imagine it being real.

Only now did I know who is saving me. I only wish I had believed from the beginning. God has a plan for all of us. For some reason I wasn't ready to die before. I was meant to stay at Phantom Lagoon and now, through my mom, I can go to Heaven. I know that, throughout this afterlife, I have learned more than I ever could living.

Life is not something to tamper with. Every moment is meant to be savored, because one day it will be over. Only now I know how fast forever can leave your grasp. But I can let it slip through my fingers, without hesitation—I know where I am meant to go.

For some, forever is a gift, others a curse. I always thought it was a curse, something that fell upon only the unfortunate. I thought I was one of them. Forever will end someday for every soul. That day will not be known as a time of darkness but of relief; for there are others who suffer with each breath.

When I gain my bearings, I notice we are no longer in my mom's room. It's like we are up in the sky, slowly ascending into the great beyond. I feel no need to go faster to where my journey will end, because that's where it begins. I'm not scared as I float away from reality and into a dreamland. I know wherever I'm going is meant to be cherished—I've learned that now.

Emma? my mom asks, suddenly aware of my presence. She doesn't sound surprised—it's like she expected me to be there with her.

"Yes?" I answer. My voice is hesitant after such a long time without contact. Energy radiates off my mom's essence, and it's lifting and extraordinary.

Emma, we're going to Heaven!

Just like that, my mom is back. After decades of abandon, I've found her. I promised her something once: that I would never forget her, and I didn't.

"I know!" And I can't help but laugh more. As I do, I slip out of my mom's body and into the open air.

My mom catches my hand before I can fall.

We are both there, side by side in our blissful state, waiting for the last moments of our life to end on Earth. We hold our hands together, as the air around us begins to glow; then it seems like we are floating in the sky.

Everything is light and free. There are no bounds, no ropes to tie me back. Just this: the open air passing over my skin, the moist droplets of the clouds clinging to me. It's a moment of smiles. The type of moment where you feel like you should hide your happiness but come to terms with it and realize you deserve this moment. Smile.

When I look down, the string about my neck breaks and my stone descends back to Phantom Lagoon. On its fall, it turns back to its original silver mirrored state—no longer part of me or my soul. Finally it drops into the lagoon where it belongs.

On top of the cave in Phantom Lagoon stands Luna. She waves up to me with the biggest smile on her face—she must have known. We don't disappear; we pass on with our family. I try to imagine why she hasn't left herself. I realize, even though she doesn't have any family, that's not why she has chosen to stay. She stays because she wants to. As much as she's lived through, she knows her place. Luna is there to protect others from Phantom Lagoon and watch those who live there now.

I will miss Eliza and Kenzie. They are like family, but I guess there's an end to everything. They are a different type of family that will never die or fade away. Even when there is a barrier between us, I know they will remember me. I will be remembered as another soul that disappeared. There will be tearless sobs today. Eliza and Kenzie will both lose a sister.

A bright light illuminates the sky. It should've been blinding, but it is beautiful and impossible to look away from. It holds me like a trance, and I welcome the glow as it comes closer—or maybe I'm the one moving.

Soon shapes come into view. It's hazy and hard to make out, but then the clouds clear, and all that's left is a fine pink mist.

My dad is the first one I see, and he no longer looks old or beaten down by chemotherapy. Beside me I can feel my mom's radiant glow as she sets eyes on her husband, happy and healthy. Her face glimmers with happiness, already in her own personal Heaven.

Other shapes come; a face I don't know but looks so familiar. As it comes into focus, I know it must be Eliza's dad, and next to him is Eliza's mom, both holding hands—he died with his wife after her car accident, just like I died with my mom. I know Eliza misses them, and I'm going to make sure I tell them of their daughter.

Then comes other family members like my grandma and grandpa. They are standing next to my dad, eagerly waiting for us. Everyone is here.

When I least expect it, a bright flash of color comes in front of me. It appears as a movie, answering all the questions I have ever had. Some things I had only been mildly curious about, while others are things I struggled with my entire life. With those answers come a peace of mind so blissful and complete, it almost feels as if it isn't true. The feeling of fear, pain, and loss is finally gone.

Suddenly everything I have gone through doesn't matter. I don't care that I've missed most of my life. It doesn't matter that my dad has been forced to die at a young age. Suddenly everything from the excruciating to the numbing doesn't compare. For this, it is worth it. The only thing that matters is that I'm here with my family, and it's over.

Then, when I thought it couldn't get any better, I see it. And I knew, only then, that I'm truly in Heaven.

About the Author

Mandi Lynn is the young adult author of her debut novel, *Essence.* Beginning to write the story when she was only thirteen years old, after three and a half years of hard work, *Essence* was published and in print. To graduate in 2014, meanwhile Mandi goes to a vocational high school where she takes cosmetology alongside writing novels and doing regular schoolwork. Mandi can now be found on YouTube hosting YA Ink—a series of videos about writing and publishing—and sharing her journey as a writer.

mandilynn.com

youtube.com /mandilynnVLOGS

twitter.com/Mandi_Lynn_

facebook.com/MandiLynnAuthor

Acknowledgments

Essence has been a novel that's been in the works since the beginning of 2010. The year 2011 greeted me with the first of many rejections when I entered *Essence* in a publishing contest, and since then it has been through ten drafts. I still can't believe I can finally say I'm a published author, but of course, there are so many people I have to thank!

Among those are the only people who read the first draft of Chapter 6: my best friends Carolyn Trottier and Kaitlyn Panagiotou, and Mrs. Cavanagh (my junior high English teacher). Kaitlyn, or KT, especially, who read the entire first draft and somehow liked it.

My parents, to whom this book is dedicated. Thank you for putting up with my tears and erratic behavior whenever I came across a problem while trying to publish this novel. Most of all, thank you for *not* allowing me to go to the New York City Pitch Conference. If I had gone, this book wouldn't be in print right now. Thank you for taking me to Sabbaday Falls so I could stand in a dress in freezing weather, just a few feet from snow, to get a breathtaking photo for the book cover. And of course, thank you for allowing me to spend the money I saved to buy a car on publishing instead. I promise you won't regret it.

To all my friends at school who unknowingly read the first chapter of my book for my science project to see if people could tell the difference between an adult's writing and a teenager's writing

(P.S. People couldn't tell a difference). Though I can't name everyone who gave me my first five-star ratings, it meant a lot to know I could actually write something people enjoyed.

All my teachers, from middle school to high school, who have helped me form the high standards in everything I do. It doesn't matter if you taught me history, pre-calculus, English, chemistry, or cosmetology, you have all shaped me to be the person I am today.

My editors at BubbleCow. Gary Smailes, for helping me direct my inner monologue. And Denise Barker, you're the best copy editor I could ever ask for. You both gave me hope I never had before.

Wendy Burt-Thomas, for replying to every e-mail and always believing in me when I didn't believe in myself.

Auntie Donna, my unofficial editor, who made me think about my book in the most incredible ways and allowing new chapters to form.

Huge thanks to anyone on YouTube, Facebook, or Twitter who have followed me on my publication journey. You guys believed in me, even before I had a book to hand you. Words cannot describe how happy I am every time I see a new comment on one of my videos.

Most of all I have to thank all thirty-nine literary agents who have rejected me. You've forced me to rewrite my novel and make it better. Without all of you, my book would never be what it is today. Maybe you'll hear from me again someday.

Made in the USA
Charleston, SC
16 July 2013